WILLIAM W. JOHNSTONE

HUNTED

PINNACLE BOOKS
KENSINGTON PUBLISHING CORP.

This novel is a work of fiction. Names, characters, places, and incidents are either the product of the author's imagination, or are used fictitiously, and any resemblance to actual persons, living or dead, events, or locales is entirely coincidental.

PINNACLE BOOKS are published by

Kensington Publishing Corp.
850 Third Avenue
New York, NY 10022

First Pinnacle Books Printing: December, 1995

Printed in the United States of America

WHO ARE YOU, DARRY RANSOM?

"You ever see that young fellow who built the cabin up in the big lonesome, Rick?"

The ranger shook his head. "Not very often, Tom. Sometimes he hikes down to get supplies and then hikes back up at night."

"You mean he hikes back up in there in the *dark?*"

"He's pretty surefooted."

"He must have eyes like a wolf, too. What's his name, again?"

"Darry," Rick said. "Darry Ransom."

"He doesn't do any poaching, does he?"

"No. And no trapping, either. Funny thing you should mention that, though."

"Oh, why?"

"Well, since he got here, there haven't been any reports of any poaching at all—by anybody. And we've started getting a lot of sightings of wolf packs in the area."

"Funny thing. . . ."

Book One

And God standing winding His lonely horn, And time and the world are ever in flight.

—Yeats

PROLOGUE

They prowled the silent edges of the darkened village, never getting too close to the man-smell. They would pause occasionally to listen, wise eyes shining, their ears erect for the first sign of what they had traveled far to witness. They ventured as close to the narrow streets as they dared. They communicated with head movement, body language, subdued sounds, and with their eyes and their tails and their teeth and their tongues.

They waited for the first sight or sound of new life to wail out from the small house.

Outside the house, standing in the snow and the bitter cold, an old priest and a young priest argued quietly but heatedly. They were not yet aware of the packs of wolves that sat or lay or crouched in silence, completely encircling the small village in Romania's Transylvanian Alps.

"I will tell the father to kill the child," the old priest said.

"And if he listens to you, I will stop him," the young priest replied.

"You are a fool, Doru! This child is not heaven-sent. This child comes from the bowels of hell!"

"Viorel, you are imagining things. You had a nightmare, not a message from God. We are religious men. We don't do harm to children."

The old priest caught a shadowy movement in the timber, only a few dozen yards away. He stared for a moment, his eyes picking out other shapes. Icy fingers of fear clutched at his heart. He could clearly make out the shapes of large wolves. He looked up the street. There in the snow he could see other wolves. He stepped away from the house and looked between the house and the hut located off to one side. Wolves. There had to be dozens of them; maybe hundreds.

The old priest stumbled back to the side of his younger friend. "Go see for yourself, Doru. The devil has sent his emissaries to stand guard on this night of the birth of his spawn!"

Doru laughed softly, his breath steaming in the cold air. "It's very cold, Viorel. The wolves are hungry, looking for scraps of food. Nothing more than that."

"Bah!" the old priest said, just as a thin cry of newborn pain wafted from the cottage.

And with the infant's first thin cry of life, the wolves began howling in one voice, until no other sound could be heard. Inside their homes, the residents of the small village huddled together in fear, for this was the time of werewolves, and the people were highly superstitious. But strangely, when the infant heard the primitive calls, he ceased his crying and listened, his eyes bright and alert.

"He's dead!" the father cried as the child fell silent.

The mother smiled as the child began to feed at her breast. "No, he's very much alive."

"But the others, they cried and cried at birth."

"This one is different," she replied.

She would soon find out just how different he really was.

It was Christmas day, A.D. 1300.

I

Spring, 1995. Idaho. USA.

"You ever see that young fellow who built the cabin up in the big lonesome, Rick?"

The ranger shook his head. "Not very often. He doesn't get out much. He hikes down to the ranger station where I let him park his old pickup and drives into town about every couple of months for supplies. It's usually dark when he returns, and I'm in bed."

"He hikes back up in there in the *dark?*"

"He's pretty surefooted."

"He must have eyes like a cat."

"More like a wolf," the ranger muttered.

"What's that, Rick?"

Rick Battle shook his head. "Nothing, Tom. Nothing at all. Just talking to myself."

"This job will do that to you," said Tom, the ranger in charge of the district. "What's that young fellow's name?"

"Darry. Darry Ransom."

"He doesn't do any poaching, does he?"

"Oh, no. No trapping either. He hunts in season and fishes a lot. But no poaching. It's funny you should mention that."

"Oh?"

"Ever since he got here, there hasn't been *any* poaching that I'm aware of."

"None? No reports at all?"

Rick shook his head. "None."

"That is odd. Rick, I'm getting reports of wolf packs in this area."

"Oh, yes. They're certainly here. I lay in bed at night and listen to them. I've caught sight of them a few times. Timber wolves."

"Well, that should make some groups very happy and others very unhappy." The environmentalists, and the ranchers and farmers, in that order.

"I'm glad to see them return."

"In this part of the country, you're in the minority, Rick."

"I am well aware of that, Tom."

The two men stood in silence for a moment, surrounded by the majesty of the Idaho wilderness. Tom smiled and said, "You ready for the influx of summer tourists, Rick?"

Rick grunted. "As ready as I'll ever be, I suppose."

His boss laughed and punched him on the arm. "See you later, boy."

"Yes, sir."

Rick stood for a long time after his boss had left the lonely one-man ranger station located on the edge of the Great Primitive Area. "Who the hell are you, Darry Ransom?"

He was named Vlad Dumitru Radu, and his mother sensed early on that this child was no ordinary baby. He seldom cried, and after six months, he never cried at all. Vlad was a handsome baby, with a shock of dark brown hair and strong features. But it was his eyes that held and captivated her. They were a very pale gray, almost spit-colored, with a slight slant . . . much like a wolf.

Since the birth on that snowy night, the old priest in the village had never set foot in the cottage. The word had gotten to Vlad's mother that the old priest thought the boy to be evil. She would not learn why until years later.

Vlad made it very clear at a young age that he preferred to be left to his own devices, and that he much preferred the company of most animals to humans. Dogs flocked to him; cats gave him a wide berth. The night of Vlad's birth, the family cat disappeared from the cottage and never returned, taking up residence at a neighbor's house.

Vlad was not an unfriendly child; but he was aloof and standoffish, and that did not endear him to others his age. Still, if the opinion of others mattered at all to him, Vlad never let it show.

Darry stepped out onto the porch of his cabin, which he had built himself, and sat down in a chair that he had also built, breathing deeply of the clean, fresh and cool air. His two dogs, which he had named Pete and Repeat, came around the side of the house and lay down on the porch. The animals were hybrids, a very foolish mixture of husky and wolf. Sometimes the breeding of wolves and domesticated dogs worked out well, but not often. It was unfair to both wolf and dog, for no one could be certain which genes would be dominant, the animal didn't know whether it was a wolf or a dog, and it was virtually impossible to domesticate a wolf. Wolves were fun to watch (from a distance; if you could get that close). With each other they were social and playful and the bond between them was strong. But wolves were wild animals—period.

Sadly, in many cases, the hybrid animal proved to be too much for the owner, and it attacked some child and had to be destroyed or was abandoned in the timber. A hybrid wolf was not a plaything. The wolf side was highly complex, and there were things one simply did not do with a wolf. Most humans never took the time to learn the do's and don'ts and ended up getting hurt, or getting someone else hurt. Sadder still, the hybrid was the one that suffered the most. People who wanted to make cute with wolves often forgot that wolves were predators.

Darry had found the two abandoned hybrids, or rather, they found him, shortly after he arrived in the area; and a bond was quickly formed.

Pete and Repeat were large animals, each weighing just over a hundred pounds. They were fiercely protective of Darry, and he with them. The hybrids had sensed immediately that while Darry stood upright and was human in appearance, there was much more to the man-shape than met the eye.

Pete and Repeat were correct in that assumption.

''Maybe we can live in peace here, boys,'' Darry spoke aloud. ''Maybe we have found a home after all.''

Pete and Repeat cut their very expressive eyes to him as if saying, ''You have to be kidding!''

''Don't be such pessimists, boys,'' Darry said, picking up on their feelings. ''I've made it work many times in the past.''

Indeed he had. For over six hundred years.

Vlad soon began spending time on the edges of the dark forest that surrounded the village of his birth. As he grew older, he began to venture deeper into the foreboding woods. At first his mother was frightened half out of her wits when her son would disappear into the timber for hours at a time, but as the months passed, she began to relax when no harm came to her son.

It was in the hushed quiet of the woods that Vlad felt most at peace. He was well aware of the dark shapes that flitted silently about him, and knew what they were. But he also knew, while not knowing how he knew, the big wolves would not harm him.

After a time, Vlad realized that the wolves were pacing

him to protect him from other predators. And that brought a smile to his lips.

By the time Vlad slipped into his early teens, he knew all the wolves in the timber around his village. He had been accepted into the pack society and had named them all. He could walk freely among the wolves, lie down beside them during their rest periods, and play with the newly born without fear of being harmed.

Vlad had attained nearly all of his adult growth. He was a couple of inches below six feet tall, and had turned into a very strong young man. He could move as silently as his four-footed friends and often warned the various packs when the men of his village were about to set out on a wolf hunt, for the wolf was as much misunderstood by the majority of humans then as it would be hundreds of years later.

Because Vlad would take no part in any wolf hunting, he became someone not to be trusted. He was shunned by most in the village.

Which suited the young man just fine, for he knew with a certainty that anyone who feared a wolf was just ignorant.

Darry enjoyed sitting on the high bluffs above the river and watching the tourists traverse the white water. The area nearest to his cabin was actually a smooth-flowing stretch of the river, and many times the boaters would pull over to the shore to rest for a time or camp for the night along this tranquil stretch. When that happened, Darry and his hybrids would vanish, for Darry sought no human contact.

Darry would occasionally run into someone who lived year-round in the wilderness, and they would pause for a moment to exchange a few pleasantries. But for the most part, the people who chose to live in the wilderness were loners, and tended to mind their own business. Live and let live, so to speak. Darry was aware that the media referred to these people by several names: survivalists, separatists, segregationists, racists, and other often insulting and very ill-chosen names. Darry had found that most were just people who had said to hell with modern society and gone off to live closer to nature. Some did not like the direction their government was taking. Others were sure a race war was imminent. Still others were certain the government was on the verge of collapse. Some wanted to teach their children values they were not receiving in public schools.

There was a small commune of what used to be called hippies living not too many miles from Darry's cabin, and he found them to be open and honest and friendly. It was with them he socialized the most . . . which was not much according to society's interpretation of the word. The hippies raised sheep and goats and chickens, tended their gardens, and were good neighbors. Darry would occasionally come up on a tiny patch of cannabis growing in the woods, and left it alone, knowing it was not for sale and distribution on the streets but for someone's personal use. The nation's furor over marijuana amused Darry, for in his opinion the smoking of the weed was far less dangerous than the consumption of alcohol or the smoking of cigarettes, although he personally imbibed only occasionally but had not smoked in years.

But Darry also knew that some miles away from his small but snug home, there were the cabins of a group of men and women who subscribed to a very dangerous and violent philosophy. They loathed anyone not of the Aryan race and worshipped the memory of a man who they felt would have been the savior of the world: Hitler.

Shortly after his fourteenth birthday, just as the weather was beginning to warm, announcing the nearness of spring, Vlad's world underwent a drastic change. Since entering his teen years, Vlad's senses had sharpened and increased. He could see and hear and smell far beyond the capacity of a "normal" human being. He could sense danger before it happened. He could smell fear in another human. He could see things clearly that lay far beyond the eyesight of humans.

Vlad told no one in the village of his finely tuned senses. He knew the villagers did not like or trust him. His brothers and sisters did not associate with him. Even his own father had little to do with his youngest son. Only his mother showed warmth and love and affection for Vlad.

Vlad was returning from spending the day in the timber when he came up on three boys his age tormenting a small puppy. The frightened puppy was whimpering in pain and fear. Furious, Vlad felt a strange force take his mind as he hurled himself toward the trio. He opened his mouth to yell at the boys to get away, to leave the animal alone. But it was not words that sprang from his mouth. It was a hideous snarl. Unable to control what was taking place in his mind and body, Vlad dropped to all fours as he ran toward the boys. He felt his skin change, his face change, his legs change, his hands and feet becoming clawed and pawed. When he was fifteen feet away from the now panicked and terror-stricken boys, Vlad leaped and struck the trio with all his weight, knocking them rolling. He stood protectively over the puppy, huge fangs bared, snarling at the boys.

The trio leaped to their feet and ran away, screaming in sheer horror. "Wolf, wolf!" one screamed hysterically. "Wolf in the village!"

Suddenly, Vlad was standing upright. He lifted his hands to his face and gingerly felt his skin. "I must have imagined it," he murmured.

But in his mind, he knew he had not.

He knew what he had become.

He picked up the puppy and comforted it until it had stopped its whimpering. Then Vlad walked slowly to his cottage. There was dread in his heart, but it was mixed with a curious sort of relief as he knew his days in the village were over. If his parents were to be spared their lives from the superstitious wrath of the villagers, he would have to leave, and do it quickly.

He dropped off the puppy at the home of the priest who had been his friend since birth and entered his own cottage through the back door.

His mother met him. ''You must go,'' she said. ''The men of the village have already been here and taken your father away for questioning. If you stay here, we all will die.'' She looked deeply into her son's strange-colored eyes. ''What are you, Vlad? What are you?''

The boy answered as truthfully as he knew how. ''I don't know, Mother. I just don't know.''

The wind shifted, and Darry heard the faint sounds of gunfire. The group of racist malcontents had returned to the area and were blasting away at paper targets. When they had pulled out for the winter months, Darry had gone over to the site and inspected it. Not knowing what to expect, he had been surprised to find a very neat camp, military in appearance. The cabins were well-built and maintained, the latrines covered. The group had left no litter scattered about, and Darry had found only two brass casings. A 9mm and a .223. The windows of the cabins were covered with heavy shutters, locked in place, and it would take a man using a sledge hammer to smash in the doors, and then only after a considerable amount of work.

Darry was uncomfortable in the camp, for he could sense the hate that hung like an invisible shroud around the area. Pete and Repeat stayed close to him as he walked the camp, the wolf-dogs as uneasy as Darry.

On this warm spring day, Darry looked at the hybrids and said, ''Stay. Guard.''

Pete and Repeat hopped up onto the small porch and

lay down. They would obey him only because Darry was the dominant male, and he was as them. He had shown them once.

Darry hiked toward the camp of the hate group. He carried only a sheath knife on his belt. He seldom needed any other weapon. Over the long and seemingly countless years, Darry had wandered the world, learning self-defense tactics from the masters. But there was still another reason Darry seldom carried a weapon: how do you kill an immortal?

The hunt was on, and Vlad knew the men of the village planned to kill him. Unknowingly at first, Vlad shape-shifted and quickly outdistanced his pursuers. Then he loped straight into a pack of wolves. They were at first hostile, but that lasted for only a few seconds until they realized that this interloper was really no stranger to them. Then came the happy, ritualistic greetings: muzzle biting, face touching, and body gestures. The younger and subordinate members of the pack stood with legs bent, ears back, tails low, signaling to the big stranger that they recognized his superiority. Then they came forward, one at a time, and pressed their noses against the bigger wolf's face, after that, sprawling on their backs, legs in the air. Total submission.

Vlad signaled danger, and the wolves headed out, quickly pulling away from the humans in pursuit, the alpha male and alpha female leading the way. They ran with ease and without harm through thick bramble and brush that would rip and tear a human's flesh. They ran for miles, deeper and deeper into the darkening forest, until they reached an area so foreboding the pack knew no human would dare enter. There, they fell to the ground and rested, safe.

The pack watched as Vlad shape-shifted; then they again went through the welcoming ritual. When the pack had rested, they went on a hunt, leaving Vlad alone by the tiny spring. Vlad ate bread and cheese from the packet of food his mother had given him, and then slept. The pack returned to find him asleep on the ground. The alpha male and female snuggled up close to him, to provide him warmth while in his human form, and all was well.

Darry lay in thick brush on a hill overlooking the camp and watched for an hour. He had circled the area before approaching and had spotted the guards. They were in good positions, but Darry bypassed them easily. The wolf in him knew by instinct to become one with his surroundings. Back in the old country, so many, many years ago, Darry had played with the younger wolves at their fun but still serious games of survival, sometimes abruptly shape-shifting in front of them and literally scaring the shit out of the pups. The pups would then scamper yelping and yipping back to the adults, pouring out their tales of fright, while Darry rolled on the ground, laughing at their antics. Then the adults would all rush to Darry and jump on him, play-biting and tussling, for a wolf is almost always ready to play . . . with his or her own kind.

Darry counted forty men and women in the camp, and they were not here for fun and games. Darry could sense their seriousness: they were training, and they were very, very good at practicing for war.

But war against whom? People not of their race? The government? Darry didn't know, and wasn't really sure he should attempt to find out. These people had not made any attempt to harm him or his hybrids. Darry had a hunch the people below him would not be very friendly toward him; but so far they had made no hostile moves against him, and until they did, what they were doing was none of his business.

Darry had learned the hard way not to get involved in other peoples' affairs . . . although he still did on occasion. He'd almost lost his head when he fought against Vlad Tepes, known as Vlad the Impaler, escaping his native country only by the barest of margins. On the hill overlooking the camp, Darry recalled that night he swam the river Dimbovita and eventually left his home country for good. The year was 1460, he thought.

Darry had so much history it was sometimes difficult to separate the jumble of events in his mind.

He backed away from the hill, skirted the guards, and began the hike back to his cabin. If those paramilitary types left him alone, he would leave them alone. But if they chose trouble, he was more than willing and able to give back ten times what he received.

For the man who now called himself Darry Ransom was the world's consummate and eternal warrior.

And had been for almost seven centuries.

2

"How far down the river are we going to go?" the boy asked his father.

"To here, Paul," Dr. Ray Collier told his son, pointing to a spot on the map. "We'll camp on up these bluffs, and then we'll spend a week exploring."

"All right!" Paul said.

"Radical!" Terri Collier said, two years younger than her older brother's seventeen years.

Both kids loved camping; their parents had seen to that. They had started taking their kids camping when Paul was three and Terri was one, and had been doing so at least three times a year ever since.

That was not to say the kids weren't normal, healthy teenagers, with a love for junk food and music loud enough to raise the dead. But they also loved camping and could do without pizza, ice cream, and rock and roll for extended periods of time.

"Will there be any other people, Dad?" Terri asked.

Doctor Collier shook his head. "I don't think so, honey. That's pretty much a wilderness area."

"Good," the girl said. "Peace and quiet."

The parents smiled at each other. Paul and Terri had turned out well. Both were straight-A students in school, Paul was an above average basketball player, and Terri had a flare for the dramatics and was the youngest member of her school's drama club. Both kids were well-liked.

Karen Collier, who was a partner in a very prestigious L.A. law firm, took her husband's hand in hers and gently squeezed. She was looking forward to getting out of the city for a few weeks and spending some quality time with her family.

Vlad lived in the forests with the wolves for several years. A year after he left the village he learned both his parents had been killed by angry villagers, accused of being werewolves. The charge was brought by Vlad's older brother, Octavian, whose life was spared because he had cooperated with the village elders.

Now Vlad truly was cut off from any human contact in the world outside the forest.

He occasionally stole articles of clothing from clotheslines to cover his nakedness, and at night, when he could, he slipped into henhouses for eggs and chickens, which he cooked. The wolves Vlad lived with never understood why he insisted upon cooking his food; to them the meat had no flavor when cooked. Sometimes he would watch a house until he was certain all the family members were gone, and he would go inside and take bread and cheese to add to his rather meager diet. Mostly he fished and trapped for his food.

And he would occasionally be sighted by some hunter, running with wolves. The legends grew about this strange young man who lived with wild animals. Bounties were placed on Vlad's head, but not even the king's soldiers cared to venture very deep into the dark woods in pursuit of him.

The average life of a wolf is between seven and nine years, although some live to be fourteen or fifteen years old. As the years rolled by, the older wolves in the pack that had adopted Vlad began to die. Vlad noticed that if death came naturally and there was time for such rituals, the old dying wolf would be left food by others in the pack, in a comfortable place in the woods, and when the dying was complete, they mourned for a time, just like humans.

When Vlad realized that he was no longer aging, he sensed it was time for him to leave the pack and once more venture out into the human world. He thought he was about twenty-five years old, but he was not certain of that. He joined the pack in a howl, then rolled in play for a time, and touched faces and muzzles; then without another gesture, he walked away, leaving one world behind him, and began his return into the world that had rejected him. He did so with the tears of sadness in his eyes.

Darry knocked on the door of the ranger station just after dawn. He had been watching for the first signs of smoke from the lodge to signal that Rick was up and making breakfast.

"Come on in, Darry," the ranger said with a smile, for he liked this strange young man. Rick thought he was a few years older than Darry and had mentioned that to him once. To this day he could not understand why Darry had found that comment so amusing. "I thought it was about time for you to come in and get your truck. You running out of supplies?"

"Yes. The winter was especially hard. And I need to pick up some dry dog food for Pete and Repeat."

"Some breakfast?"

"Yes. Thank you. That would be nice."

Rick broke the eggs on the edge of the cast-iron skillet and said, "Those dogs of yours are hybrids, Darry."

"Yes. I know. Probably abandoned by some fool who didn't know what he was getting when he got them and didn't have the patience to learn."

"They stay in your cabin, Darry?"

"They sleep on the floor right beside my bed." Darry sugared his coffee and took a sip. Just right.

"A wolf in the house," Rick muttered, laying out strips of bacon on a paper towel. "Aren't you afraid they'll turn on you someday?"

Darry smiled. "No." His thoughts were flung back centuries to a huge female wolf he had named Shasta, who used to snuggle up close to him during the winter months to help keep her adopted human warm. "I am not afraid of wolves, Rick. No human has to be afraid of wolves, if only he will take the time to understand them."

Rick grunted. "You'll never convince most ranchers and farmers of that."

"Many of them have legitimate gripes about repopulating the wolf. The wolf is a predator. But the answer to that is simple. And you know what it is."

Rick chuckled. "Keep the hunters out of selected areas and let the wolves maintain the balance of nature."

"As God intended it to be."

"Something tells me you are not a member of the NRA, Darry." Rick slid the eggs on a plate, added strips of bacon and fried potatoes and set the plate before Darry.

"I'm not a member of anything, Rick. But I am a hunter. Genuine hunters have nothing to fear from men like me."

Rick sat down with his own plate of food and said, "How many trophy heads do you have on the walls of your cabin, Darry."

Darry smiled, shook his head, and Rick laughed. "Yeah. That's what I mean," the ranger said. "You hunt for food and survival, not for sport."

"There is no sport in killing, Rick. I use every part of the deer I take; every part that is possible to use, that is. It's an argument that will probably never be really settled." He started to say "in our lifetime," but cut that off short, thinking: Not in *your* lifetime, Rick.

"You mind picking up a few things for me in town, Darry?"

"Not at all. You have a list?"

Rick fished in his pocket and handed Darry a short list and some money. He wondered how this young man earned a living; where he got his money. Darry could certainly keep an engine running. He wondered where he'd learned to do that.

Rick would have been amazed to learn that Darry had helped build the first assembly runs of Henry Ford's famous Model-T. Any color you want, as long as it's black.

"It's bullshit, Stormy," the man said, tossing the weekly newspaper to the desk. "And you know it. The people who write for that . . . rag"—he pointed to the newspaper—"wouldn't know the truth if it bit them on the butt." He laughed. "The Man Who Could Not Die," he read the glaring headlines. "Sounds like an old movie title." He frowned. "As a matter of fact, I think it *is* an old movie title." He paused, looking at the woman who stood before his desk. Stormy was one of his top reporters. Blond and beautiful and sometimes arrogant, the viewing public loved her. She didn't have the temperament to become an anchor—not yet anyway; maybe in a few years—but she did have a very large following. He sighed. "All right, Stormy. All right. I guess you want Ki to go with you?"

"That's right. She's the best there is, and we work well together."

"Two women, alone in the wilds of Idaho," the department head muttered.

"You're a sexist pig, Bobby," Stormy said with a laugh.

"Yeah, right. What are you going to do if you stumble upon Big Foot?"

"Interview it," Stormy said with a toss of her blond mane. "See you, Bobby."

"What did the President want?" the deputy director of Central Intelligence asked the director of Central Intelligence. Also present in the room were the deputy director for Operations and the deputy director for Intelligence.

The DCI blinked a couple of times, as if confused, which was a normal condition for the DCI, since he was a political appointee and seldom actually knew what was really going on. He looked around him at each man. "What the hell is a man who could not die?"

"Johnny McBroon," the DDO muttered under his breath. Nobody heard him.

"I beg your pardon, sir?" the DDCI asked.

"That was the President. He wants to know what we know about the man who could not die."

"Who is the man who could not die?" the DDI asked.

"That's what I just asked *you*."

"What are you talking about?" the DDCI asked.

The DDO held up a hand. "Wait a minute. Hold on here. I'm getting confused."

"I *am* confused!" the DDCI admitted.

The DDO looked at the DCI. "The President wants to know something about a man who could not die—correct?"

"That is correct."

"But no one here, in this room, knows anything about a man who could not die—correct?"

"That is correct."

"Good," the DDO said, picking up a phone.

"Who are you calling?" the DCI asked.

"DDST."

The DCI furtively slid out a panel on his desk to look at a sheet of paper he himself had typed, to see what part of the CIA that was. He had a hell of a time keeping up with all the departments. Deputy Director of Science and Technology.

"Say what?" the DDST said, after hearing the question.

"Forget it," the DDO replied, and hung up.

"Before we call anyone else, and make idiots out of ourselves, I have an idea," the DDI said. "Let's ask a secretary."

"It's an article in this week's edition of the *National Loudmouth,*" she told the men. "It's about a man living somewhere in Idaho who is rumored to be hundreds of years old."

"What does he do?" the DCI asked.

The secretary shrugged her shoulders. "Just gets older, I guess."

"Thank you, Miss Lawrence," the DCI said.

When the door had closed behind her, the DCI looked at the men seated around his desk. "The President wants us to investigate this person."

"You have got to be kidding!" the DDO blurted.

"Do I look like I'm kidding?"

The DDO sighed. Then he smiled. "I have just the man for the job."

"Who?" the DDCI asked.

"Johnny McBroon."

"You're not serious! The man's an alcoholic and a lunatic. Besides, we haven't used him in several years. Officially, we don't know him."

"Then he's perfect," the DDO said. "If he screws up, we can't be blamed." Then he shook his head. "The President of the United States actually reads the *National Loudmouth?*"

"Of course not. Don't be absurd," the DCI replied quickly and a bit stiffly in defending his boss and his friend. "I'm sure it was one of his junior staff members who brought it to his attention."

"I would certainly hope so," the DDO replied.

* * *

Darry drove into the small Idaho town and pulled into the parking area by the side of the town's only grocery store. He sat for a time behind the wheel, wondering if his cover was about to be blown—again. Darry had developed a sixth sense about that.

"But why would I think that now?" he muttered to himself.

Nothing untoward had happened. But something had triggered the thought.

Don Shepherd, the county deputy assigned to the area, and who lived in the small town, drove by and waved at Darry. Darry returned the friendly wave from the young man and watched the sheriff's car until it was out of sight.

No warning bells went off in Darry's head, and with a sigh he relaxed and walked across the street to the tiny post office. The only mail in his box were three checks from a bank in San Francisco. He walked over to the small branch office of a bank and deposited the checks, keeping enough cash to buy his groceries and other supplies.

When gold had been discovered in Colorado, Darry had struck a nice vein and had carefully invested his money, his attorney setting up companies and corporations for him. Darry never touched the principal, and over the decades his investments had grown. He was by no stretch of the imagination a wealthy man, but he was comfortable. The law firm that handled his money was one of the first to open up in San Francisco, and descendants of the original partners still ran the office.

Darry also had small amounts of money in banks and investment houses all over Europe. He often thought, with typical dark humor, that if a man couldn't set aside a nest egg over a span of nearly seven hundred years, he must be doing something wrong.

Darry bought his supplies and the articles for Rick, and

loaded his purchases in the back of his pickup, covering them with a tarp and securing it tight. He walked over to a cafe and ordered a cup of coffee and a piece of pie. The cafe was a favorite gathering place and, at mid-morning, filled with men and women taking a coffee break and gossiping.

Darry knew a few of the men and women gathered there and spoke to them as he walked to a table in the corner. Over pie and coffee he listened to the people talk.

''I hated to see those damn nuts come back in again this spring,'' a rancher said. ''I thought maybe we were rid of them.''

''Maybe we're the ones who are nuts,'' a man in a business suit countered. ''At least they're getting ready to cope with what we all know is bound to happen sooner or later.''

''Oh, come on, Ned!'' a woman said. ''Sam Parish and those with him are a bunch of dangerous kooks. Sheriff Paige told me they probably have a million rounds of ammunition buried in bunkers up there. They've got emergency food and radios and God only knows what else cached in the wilderness.''

''That's their right,'' another man spoke up. ''And the goddamn government has no business interfering with them. What happened to Randy Weaver should have been a lesson to us all.''

''I'll damn sure go along with that,'' a man said. ''This is one sorry-assed government we have ruling us. And I mean, they rule us. This is no longer a democracy. We're borderlining on a dictatorship.''

Darry knew all about the Randy Weaver incident, which had occurred up in North Idaho back in 1991, and personally felt it was a total travesty of justice. Because he had lived under tyrants and harsh government rules and regulations, Darry could read all the signs, and he felt that America was moving very quickly toward socialism and eventual total government control over the lives of its citizens.

And he knew, from personal experience, that the first step was the disarming of a country's citizens. All gun bans did was prevent heretofore law-abiding citizens from protecting themselves with guns. And in many cases, the laws turned decent people into criminals, because law-abiding citizens wanted to be able to protect themselves and would illegally purchase weapons to do so.

America, once the most powerful and free country on the face of the earth, was rapidly turning into a socialistic state, whose citizens were now facing the very real threat of having to live in fear of the police and federal agents . . . who were supposed to be in place to protect citizens, not harass them.

What it boiled down to, in Darry's opinion, was that government had no obligation to defend the individual citizen, and with gun-control laws becoming more firmly entrenched and harshly enforced, the individual had no means by which to defend himself.

Sad, Darry thought, listening to the men and women in the cafe talk. It's all so sad.

Darry paid for his coffee and pie and left, thinking that Big Brother was everywhere . . . even in the pristine wilderness of Idaho.

3

Stormy and Ki landed at Boise and picked up their four-wheel drive Bronco. Ki studied the map while Stormy asked directions to the nearest sporting goods store. At the sporting goods store, the two women made the clerk's eyes shine as they picked out the items they were familiar with, and then asked his advice on other camping equipment.

He didn't load them up with unnecessary gear, but he did outfit them well.

"Now show me your shotguns," Ki said.

Stormy looked at her in surprise. "What do you know about guns?"

"I was raised on a farm in Missouri, Stormy. I've been around guns all my life. We're going into country that has attracted some pretty strange people over the years. I want some protection."

The clerk's eyes widened as he put a name to the face. "Say now, you're Stormy—"

"That's right," she cut him off. "Pleased to meet you." She turned back to Ki. "I don't like guns, Ki."

"I know. But I'm still taking a couple of guns with us."

"A couple?" Stormy questioned.

"Yes. Watch."

Ki picked out a twelve gauge pump shotgun that was

chambered for three-inch magnum rounds—with a shortened but just legal barrel—and several boxes of shells.
She looked at Stormy. ''I'm ready. Let's get on the
road.''

''I thought you were buying two?''

''I brought my pistol with me,'' Ki said with a smile.
''In my luggage. It's all legal and declared. I have a per-
mit for it.'' She paused, then turned back to the clerk.
''And give me two boxes of .38 rounds, hollow-nose.''

Stormy rolled her eyes and muttered under her breath.

The two women packed the rear of the Bronco and
were getting ready to pull out when the clerk walked up to
the vehicle. ''Exactly where are you two going?'' he inquired.

Stormy told him their destination, but not why they
were going.

The clerk shook his head. ''That's survivalist country,
ladies. More importantly, that's where Sam Parish's
group is headquartered.''

That name nudged Stormy's memory. ''The Citizen's
Defense League.''

''That's the one. They're dangerous, ladies. And they
don't like the press.''

''We'll try to keep a low profile,'' Stormy assured the
man.

''You go into that country, ladies, and they'll know
you're there. Bet on that.''

Darry sat on his front porch, Pete and Repeat on either
side of his chair. He enjoyed this time of day, just as the
sun was sinking into the western horizon and the land
was, for a short time, hued with purple shadows. He
would have enjoyed it more if the faint sounds of gunfire,
coming from the survivalists' camp, were not punctuating
the quiet. What disturbed him most was the knowledge
that they were now using fully automatic weapons . . . and

he doubted that group was using legal and registered arms.

Darry suddenly experienced a sensation of dark and lurking danger. It made him very uneasy, and the hybrids quickly picked up on his feelings and stirred restlessly. Over the long and often danger-filled and bloody years that stretched out endlessly behind him, Darry had honed his senses to a razor-sharp edge. He had taken part in so many conflicts around the world, he had difficulty recalling them all. And Darry was certain, from listening to the news on his portable radio, and by reading the newspapers and the few news magazines he bought every couple of months or so, that his adopted country, America, was in deep trouble . . . heading straight for armed conflict. Not against some foreign power, but against its own citizens. It never failed to happen when a government got too big, too powerful, too arrogant, and attempted to interfere in the lives of all its citizens . . . and especially in the lives of those citizens who voiced a strong opposition to the political party currently in power.

And Darry felt certain he was going to be caught up smack in the middle of it.

"Damn!" he said.

"We don't even know where this person is, Stormy," Ki said. "Do we?"

"It was a free-lancer who did that story for the *Loudmouth*. I called around and found out she lives just outside a town called Grangeville. She's quite an outdoors person. Really into camping and hiking and so forth . . ."

"Just like us," Ki said drily.

Stormy laughed. "Yeah. Right."

"That still doesn't tell us where this guy is."

"Somewhere along the River Of No Return."

"That has a real ominous sound to it, Stormy."

Stormy smiled at that. "We'll spend the night in

Grangeville and start looking first thing in the morning.''

Ki consulted a map. ''It's about thirty-six hundred population. I'm sure the accommodations will be luxurious.''

Stormy laughed and said, ''Nobody said life would be easy.''

''Wherever we stay will beat the hell out of Somalia,'' Ki replied.

''You want me to do *what?*'' Johnny McBroon asked the voice on the other end of the line.

The statement was repeated.

''That is the nuttiest goddamn thing I ever heard of,'' Johnny said. ''That is even dumber than trying to set Castro's beard on fire.''

''This might be a way for you to redeem yourself, Johnny.''

''And come back in? Screw coming back in. Who needs it? In case you don't know, and you probably don't, I'm now making a respectable living doing wildlife articles. I shoot things with a camera and then put words on paper. If you'd ever learn to read, you'd know that.''

''May we dispense with the personal insults, Johnny? Thank you. We think you're just the man for this job, Johnny. I really mean that. You have a fine record with us, and—''

''You can cut the bullshit,'' Johnny interrupted. ''Officially, I don't exist with you people, and all my records have been destroyed. So if I took this job and screwed up, you people don't know me and are standing in the clear. That's the bottom line.''

''You must have stopped drinking, Johnny. You're actually lucid and making sense.''

''I've always made sense, and I have never been an alcoholic. I just don't like to kiss ass. Especially your ass. A thousand dollars a day and all expenses.''

''Done.''

"You're kidding! I was sure you'd say no."

"I never kid, Johnny."

"Yeah, that's right. I should have remembered you have about as much sense of humor as a warthog."

"When can you leave?"

"In the morning."

"You know who to report to. Good luck." The connection was broken.

"Asshole!" Johnny said, looking at the buzzing receiver.

Some two thousand miles away to the east, the vocal sentiment was exactly the same.

"He is somewhere in this area," the men were told, their eyes on the map, on the spot touched with a pointer.

"He really exists, then?"

"Yes. For years I've thought it was nothing more than rumor and myth. I couldn't get people into Romania to dig around until the Ceausescu regime was overthrown and the country opened up. But he is real. He is alive and well and has been so for nearly seven centuries. He was christened Vlad Dumitru Radu, but he hasn't used that name in a dozen or more decades. He's about five-ten, well built, muscular, with dark brown hair and very pale gray eyes. He speaks a dozen or more languages, and he is a very dangerous man. The ultimate, consummate, eternal warrior—always bear that in mind. The man has fought in every major war since the thirteenth century. He's been a teacher, a priest, a writer, a singer, an actor. He was a gunfighter in the Wild West here in America. He's worked as a mechanic, a bookkeeper, a salesman. He can do practically anything. I've recently discovered that while working in Colorado during the gold rush, he found a very nice vein, staked it out, dug it up and, with the help of a San Francisco law firm, invested the money. That investment has grown over the years. He does not have to work. He's changed his name, again, and got a new social security number. Then he dropped out of sight. Questions?''

"He has to be taken alive?"

The man who was paying the bounty hunters' salaries gave the questioner a pitying look. "I just told you, he *can't* die. He *cannot* be killed. At least not by any method that I am aware of. If Vlad has an Achilles heel, it has never been found. I want him for study. The man holds the key to eternal life. I want to be the one who unlocks that secret."

Robert Roche looked at each of the twelve men standing around him. "You gentlemen come highly recommended. You are supposed to be the finest mercenaries in all the world. You're being paid well, certainly more than you have ever received for any job. Now prove your worth."

A dark-complexioned man with hard obsidian eyes spoke up. "What have you not told us about this man?"

"What do you mean?" Roche questioned.

"There is more that you do not tell us. Why?"

Roche hesitated for a second, then said, "Because it is unsubstantiated rumor, that's why."

"What is the rumor?" the hard-eyed man pressed.

Roche sighed. "The man you are searching for is rumored to have the ability to change into animal form. Of course, that is pure bunk."

"Shape-shifter," the questioner whispered. He had been raised in the white world until he was ten, when his Indian mother divorced the man she'd married and took him to the reservation. Now the Indian in him surfaced. "He is doubly dangerous. What animal is he akin to?"

Again, Roche hesitated. With a sigh, he said, "Vlad is rumored to have the ability to change into a wolf."

The Indian's eyes narrowed. "You will never have this man. He is a brother to the wolf. The most intelligent, dangerous and cunning predator to walk the face of the earth. I tell you now, you are wasting your money."

''Then you refuse to take the job?'' Roche snapped out the question.

George Eagle Dancer smiled. ''I did not say that. I will take your money, and I will do the best I can. And I alone will survive the hunt . . . along with the shape-shifter. The rest will fail.''

''George, you're a bleedin' harbinger of doom,'' the Englishman standing next to him said.

The Indian merely grunted a noncommittal reply.

''If there are no more questions? You know your assignment. Find Vlad Radu and bring him to me,'' Robert Roche said. ''Everything you asked for in the way of equipment has been purchased and is at your disposal. I don't expect to see you again until this is over. Good day.''

''What the hell is the Pickle Factory up to now?'' the director of the FBI asked, using their nickname for the CIA. The CIA referred to the FBI as the Cabbage Patch Kids.

''Leaks out of the White House say the President ordered them to find this man.'' He laid a copy of the *National Loudmouth* on the director's desk.

The director quickly scanned the article about the man who could not die. He looked up. ''You have got to be kidding!''

''No, sir. I've contacted our office in that area and have two agents standing by.''

''To do *what?*''

''Ah . . . go look for this man, maybe?''

''Are you serious?''

His secretary buzzed him. ''Justice on the horn,'' she said.

''What line?''

''The one that's blinking,'' she said matter-of-factly.

The director gritted his teeth and offered no retort. That

might bring some sort of lawsuit down on him. He sighed and stuck the phone to his ear and listened for a moment. He finally said, with a very weary note to his voice, "Yes, ma'am," and hung up. He looked at his assistant. "She wants an investigation into the man who could not die. Who do we have out in that area?"

"Jack Speed and Kathy Owens."

"Recent graduates?"

"Right."

"Have they done anything major yet?"

"Not really."

"They can get their feet wet—probably literally, and their asses, too—on this . . . assignment." He said the latter mockingly. "Better tell them to get some camping gear together."

"Yes, sir. You all packed and ready to go on your trip, sir?"

"Yes. Hopefully, when I return, this—" he tapped the article—"nonsense will be concluded."

"I'm sure it will be."

The director sat for a time after his assistant had left, staring at the story in the *National Loudmouth*. "Shit!" he finally said.

4

Darry was surprised to see Rick show up on his doorstep, for it was a good five-mile hike from the ranger station to his cabin—and it was not an easy hike. The ranger was carrying several newspapers and magazines.

"Thought you might like something to read, Darry," Rick said, sitting down on the porch. Pete and Repeat looked at him, inspecting him carefully before moving over to him and sniffing. Rick sat very still while the big hybrids gave him the once-over. Satisfied they had met the man before and he posed no danger, the hybrids allowed Rick to pet them for a moment. Then they moved back to their positions by the side of Darry's chair.

"Thank you," Darry said. "Would you like something to drink?"

"Glass of water would be fine."

Darry pumped them glasses of water and returned to the porch. Sitting down in his chair, Darry said, "You didn't hike all the way up here just to bring me a few magazines, Rick."

"No. I've received reports of heavy gunfire over that way." He jerked his thumb in the direction of the survivalist camp.

"I've heard it. Is that Sam Parish's bunch?"

Rick cut his eyes. "What do you know about Sam Parish?"

"I heard people in town talking. Some seem to support him, others don't."

"And you?"

Darry shrugged. "I guess I'm neutral. I don't really know what it's all about."

"He's a racist, Darry. Believes in the violent overthrow of the government."

"A lot of people are unhappy with the government, Rick. Millions of people are unhappy with the government. A lot of them with very good reason."

"You including yourself in that bunch?"

Again, Darry shrugged. "As long as the government leaves me alone, I'll remain neutral."

"Is there any reason why the government should bother you, Darry?"

"The government doesn't need a valid reason to harass its citizens, Rick. And you know it."

"We've had several dozen chats over the past months, Darry. I wasn't aware of this side of you."

"I see what is taking place around me. I listen to the news on radio and read newspapers and magazines. It doesn't take a genius to reach the conclusion that the government wants more and more control over the lives of its citizens."

Being an active government employee, Rick wasn't about to admit agreeing with Darry, but he certainly did agree with him—silently.

"I'm going to hike over to the survivalist camp, Darry. You want to come along?"

"Sure. I believe I can fit you into my busy schedule this morning." He smiled and Rick laughed. "Are we going into the camp, Rick?"

"Maybe. Like your acreage here, their camp is privately owned. Most of the land around here, as you know, is owned by either the government or logging interests. But I can legally get very close to their camp, and also, legally, enter their camp if I feel game violations have occurred.''

Darry had noticed the side arm Rick was wearing, and the lever action rifle he had carefully leaned up against a porch support post. ''You ready to go?''

''Anytime you are. You going to carry a weapon?''

''I don't need one, Rick.''

''You are a supremely confident man, Darry,'' Rick said with a smile.

''Just a man who knows his capabilities and limitations,'' Darry replied.

''That's a good thing to know.'' Rick rose to his boots and picked up his rifle. A .30-30, Darry thought, but he wasn't sure. ''How long did it take you to master that art?''

''A lifetime,'' Darry said, with a very small grin.

''You'll be going into some rough country, girls,'' the woman told Stormy and Ki. ''For the most part, the men you'll encounter are good decent people who'll help you if you need it. But there are a few bad apples in there. Either of you armed?''

''I am,'' Ki said.

''Can you use the weapon?''

''Oh, yes.''

The free-lance writer smiled. ''But *will* you use it is the big question.''

''I'll use it if I have to,'' Ki said.

The woman studied Ki's face for a few seconds, then chuckled. ''Yes. I think you would. All right, girls, let me show you something.'' She spread a map out on the coffee table, after shooing the cat away. ''Here we are.'' She pointed to their location. ''You go over to this junction and cut south—that means you turn right . . .''

''I can read a compass,'' Ki said, just slightly annoyed at the woman's condescending attitude.

"I'm sorry," the writer said. "But over the years I have been involved in dozens of search and rescue missions . . . most of them looking for city folks who got lost. Before you leave, I'm going to give you very detailed maps of that area. Maps that I helped draw up. They feature landmarks and creeks and so forth. Now listen up, I want to tell you a few things that just might save your lives . . ."

The twelve mercenaries hired by Robert Roche to capture Darry Ransom took different routes and methods of transportation getting to Coeur d'Alene. There, they picked up four four-wheel drive vehicles to be driven in and stored—two Ford Broncos in that small city, two Broncos over in Spokane. The vehicles had been prepacked with supplies and all the equipment the mercs had requested . . . which was considerable. Since this mission would not involve killing, the men would carry only side arms. Each carried the side arm that he was most comfortable and familiar with. The pistols ranged from .44 mags to 9mm.

The mercs pulled over at the first rest area and gathered for a chat. The Englishman, Nick Sharp, said, "First time in my life I ever went on an op with only a pistol."

"Guns are no good against this man," Billy Antrim said, opening a soft drink.

"If he exists at all," Tom Doolin spoke the words that lay in the back of the minds of all but one of the mercs.

"He is real," George Eagle Dancer said. "Believe it. He is the man my people have been singing and telling stories about for centuries. And this man is dangerous. Probably the most dangerous man on earth."

"We all have tranquilizer rifles," Mike Tuttle said. Mike was the leader of the bunch. "The drugs will neutralize this dangerous person. Then we put him in a cage, call in for a chopper, and our job is over. We collect the balance of our money and then go our separate ways.''

George Eagle Dancer smiled at how easy Mike made it all seem. George sensed—no, he *knew*—this job would be anything but easy. And he did not believe they would succeed in capturing this legendary shape-shifter. Besides, George wasn't at all sure he wanted to capture the man.

Mike said, ''We'll stop at the first decent-looking motel we find and spend the night. Shove off at first light and get in the general area and set up camp.'' He looked up at the sky. ''Tomorrow promises to be a fine day.''

A good day to die, the Indian in George Eagle Dancer sprang to the surface.

Sam Parish faced the ranger and Darry. Darry sensed very quickly that there was no back-down in the man. The federal badge on Rick's chest did not intimidate him at all.

''I've got a ninety-nine-year lease on this property,'' Sam told the ranger. ''And you've got no business snoopin' around here. We're not breaking any laws, so why don't you and your pissy friend here''—he jerked a thumb at Darry—''just haul your asses on away from here.''

Darry immediately thought of a dandy place to stick Sam's weapon, a semiautomatic, legal version of the famed Russian AK-47. But Sam probably wouldn't like that very much—it would be awkward moving about.

Darry learned something about Rick, too. The ranger said, ''I can go anywhere I damn well please to go, Mr. Parish. If I suspect you've been poaching, I can enter your cabin and search it from top to bottom. So don't get too damn lippy with me.''

Sam Parish relaxed, and a grin wiped the scowl from his face. ''Okay, Ranger. Okay. We've both blustered at each other and found that neither one of us is afraid of the other. You want to come into our camp and have something to drink?''

''Some water would be nice,'' Rick said.

''Come on. I can't offer you anything stronger. I don't allow liquor in the area.''

Smart move on his part, Darry thought—if he's telling the truth. Guns and liquor are a bad combination.

Darry's experienced eye noticed that every man and woman in the camp looked very fit and very healthy. The men and women smiled as they were introduced and shook hands, but the smile did not reach their eyes.

''No poached game here, Ranger,'' Sam told Rick. ''We send someone into town once a week for fresh vegetables and milk and meat. Most of the time we eat field rations.''

''There are no minorities in your group,'' Rick pointed out.

''Is that against the law?'' Sam asked with a faint smile.

''No. Not at all. I was just curious about it.''

''We're separatists, Ranger. All of us here are. That's the reason for our being here. We believe in the purity of the white race. We don't want to see it contaminated with the blood and genes of inferiors. We've never denied our beliefs and never will. Is that against the law?''

''Not that I am aware of, Mr. Parish. Not unless you're planning to wage war against those not of your race.''

''We plan no such thing. We wish no harm to come to anyone. We believe the government of the United States is on the verge of total collapse. We're training to survive after the collapse. That's all.''

Darry noticed that the weapons being shown were all legal ones. They were military look-alikes, but all semiautomatic and legal. The ones the press and the liberals liked to call ''assault rifles,'' a term that always amused Darry. When George Washington's troops assaulted a British position with weapons, the muskets they carried were assault rifles.

As he stood by Rick, listening to the exchange, Darry quickly picked up on the close scrutiny he was being given by the members of the camp. For several mornings running he had found boot tracks at the edge of the clearing near his cabin and knew someone had been circling his cabin and checking him out. Of course he knew it in other ways, as well. During those nights when someone had prowled around the edges of the clearing, he had awakened at the same time his hybrids had, alert and listening.

"This a new ranger?" Sam asked, his eyes flicking over to Darry.

"No," Rick said. "Just a friend. I imagine you know where he lives." He introduced Darry.

"For a fact, I do. For a fact. You live out here year-round, don't you?"

"That's right," Darry replied.

Sam Parish stared into Darry's pale eyes for a moment and felt a slight chill run up and down his spine. Something about those eyes was very disturbing to the man. After a few seconds, Sam dropped his gaze and concluded that this young man—Darry looked to be somewhere between twenty-five and thirty; hard to tell—was a man who knew how to take care of himself.

Sam was sure right about that.

A man who had been introduced as Willis Reader said, "Those dogs of yours are hybrids, aren't they, Ransom?"

"That's right, Reader," Darry said.

"You ought to keep them things penned. I don't like dogs. They wander over here, they're gonna be dead dogs."

Rick tensed as Darry shifted his feet, facing the man. "My dogs almost never leave the clearing unless they're with me. Sometimes they will chase a rabbit a few hundred yards into the timber. But they don't go far. I have a ninety-nine-year lease on all that acreage around *my* cabin. And the acreage is considerable. Don't you ever let me find you on my land. And you can consider that a warning. And I'll tell you why: I don't have much use for people who don't like dogs. I think it's a severe character flaw. Now, as to my dogs, I wouldn't like it if someone harmed my dogs. I would probably become very irritable and hostile. And you wouldn't like me should I become hostile.''

Willis Reader was taller and heavier than Darry. A man in his late thirties who looked to be in excellent physical condition. Indeed, he was a man who had done hard physical labor all his life. He was also a bully, and had been a bully all his life. Willis poked Darry in the center of his chest with a thick, blunt-ended finger. ''Don't threaten me, sonny-boy. And you don't insult me. You got all that?'' He poked Darry again. Bad mistake on his part.

Darry hit him, the blow coming with rattlesnake speed. Darry struck just below the V of Willis' rib cage with stiffened fingers, nearly paralyzing the man. Before the sickening thud of the first blow had faded, and just as Willis was bending over, making horrible retching sounds on his way to the ground, Darry struck again, this time with his open left hand. The palm impacted over Willis' ear and sounded like the crack of a rifle. Willis Reader screamed in pain and hit the ground, the hearing gone on one side of his head and his stomach feeling as if it were on fire.

The whole thing had taken one second.

Then Darry growled, and Rick and those standing close by were shocked to hear the menacing animal sound coming from a human throat. Sam Parish didn't realize he was doing it, but he took a step back from Darry. Rick had never heard a human make such an authentic animal sound.

''Easy now!'' Sam found his voice as the members of

his bunch moved toward Darry, menace in their eyes. "Just stand easy."

"You really don't want to assault a federal officer." Rick quickly defused the situation. "Willis Reader initiated the first physical move against Darry, and I am a witness to that. So don't do anything stupid."

Sam pointed at two men. "You two pick Willis up and carry him over to the cabin. The rest of you back off and go on about your business. It's over." He turned to Rick and Darry. "You boys better leave." His eyes shifted to Darry. "Don't come back here, Ransom. You made a bad enemy with Willis. But I give you my personal word that nothing will happen to your dogs. He had no right to say what he did."

Darry nodded his head and turned around, walking out of the camp. Rick hesitated for a second, then nodded at Sam and caught up with Darry.

"Darry, Parish was right back there. You did make a very bad enemy."

"Willis Reader doesn't worry me. None of that bunch really worries me. But if they harm my dogs, there will be trouble."

"I think Parish will keep his word, Darry."

"He better."

"Where did you learn to fight like that, Darry?"

Darry smiled. Where? How about Korea in the fifteenth century? How about in France learning savate in the 1600s? How about Japan before any other white man ever set foot on their island?

"I've knocked around a bit," Darry said, smiling that strange smile.

"I believe you have, Darry," Rick said slowly. "And I also think you're a lot better educated than you would like people to think."

Darry did not reply. But he did recall the time in Paris when Nostradamus told him the same thing.

5

Jack Speed read the fax and handed it to Kathy Owens. "You're not going to believe this one," he told her.

She read the order and looked over at her partner. "The Man Who Could Not Die?"

"That's what it says." The fax machine clanged. "That would be a copy of the article. This should be real interesting reading."

The small field office, located on the western side of Idaho, near the Washington state border, had not been open long. The agent-in-charge was due to retire in just over a year. He came out of his office, read the latest fax, and smiled at the two agents.

"You young people enjoy camping?"

"Oh, I just love communing with nature," Kathy said.

"Me, too," Jack said, very unenthusiastically.

"Wonderful!" the older man said. "How I envy you both this assignment." That was said very drily. "You're going into rough country, so get outfitted." He handed them a map. "The area is circled. Good luck." He went back to his office and closed the door. Then he started laughing.

"I'm glad he thinks it's so damn funny," Jack said. He looked at Kathy. "Do you like camping?"

"I hate camping!"

"Me, too," he said glumly, then stood up. "You ready to go exploring?"

Kathy said a very ugly word.

The mercenaries left their vehicles miles north and east of the ranger station and, shouldering heavy packs, began marching into the designated area just about the same time Stormy and Ki arrived at the ranger station. Since the *National Loudmouth* was one of the newspapers he'd taken up to Darry's place, Rick had a pretty good idea why the reporters were in the area. Rick didn't believe a word printed in the *Loudmouth,* and he certainly didn't believe that Darry was almost seven hundred years old; but somebody obviously thought the story worth investigating.

Still, Rick wasn't about to give the reporter Darry's location—not without Darry's permission. Rick shook his head. "This story sounds pretty far-fetched to me, miss. I don't know of anybody living in this area who is, ah, seven hundred years old." He chuckled. "Although there are some mighty crotchety old characters living back in the wilderness."

Stormy shook her head. "This man would look about thirty years old."

Rick smiled. "All I can do is wish you good luck and give you the names of some local guides. There is a man who can helicopter you in, or you can rent horses and go in that way."

"Horses sound good," Ki said. "I used to ride every day back on the farm."

Stormy was city born and reared. She gave Ki a very dark look. Then she sighed and nodded her head. "All right. We'll do it that way."

Rick wrote out the man's name and gave the women directions to his place. They thanked him and left.

Rick immediately closed up the ranger station and set

out for Darry's cabin. This time he saddled up and rode. Much faster that way.

"You're just in time for lunch," Darry told him, holding up a string of fresh-caught trout.

"Sounds good to me. Let me loosen this cinch and I'll help you clean them."

When the fish were battered and sizzling in the pan, Rick said, "There is a well-known reporter and cameraman—camera-person, I guess—in the area. They're here about that article in the *Loudmouth*. The Man Who Could Not Die."

"A major network is wasting its money on stuff like that?" Darry questioned.

"Darry? If there is anything in your past you don't want uncovered, I'd suggest you head for the wilderness and lay low for a time."

Darry turned the fish. "I'm not a criminal, Rick. I have a bank account, a social security number, a valid driver's license, and a current hunting and fishing permit. You know all that. Why should I run?"

"Because there are things about you that don't add up, Darry. And if I can sense that, you know damn well a skilled reporter can, too."

Darry smiled. "What is it about me that doesn't add up, Rick?"

"Even though you've tried to hide it, you're a very well educated man. I've seen your library, remember? Everything from Voltaire to William Buckley. You're somewhere between twenty-five and thirty years old, a young and handsome man, yet you live like a hermit, with very little outside contact. Old Buckskin Jennings saw you playing with a wolf pack last year, Darry. He watched you for the better part of an hour. When you finished playing, you lay down with them and went to sleep. I'm the only one he told about it. You want me to go on?"

Darry pointed to the skillet and then to a plate. "Eat your lunch."

They ate in silence for a time. Darry said, "So I have a way with wolves, so what?"

"A *way* with wolves? You lay down in the middle of a pack of wolves and went to *sleep,* for Christ sake! Darry, I've watched you from time to time . . . through binoculars. You move through the woods like a ghost. I've lost sight of you a dozen times when you were out in the open not a hundred yards away from me. Darry, I don't think for one moment that you're a criminal, or that you're wanted for anything. But there is a hell of a lot more to you than you've admitted thus far—at least to me. And this Stormy person is going to zero in on you like radar. And if you can't account for every minute of your back trail, she's going to cut you to pieces. So you'd better get ready for it."

Darry said nothing. He speared another piece of fish and spooned more fried potatoes onto his plate. Pete and Repeat lay on the porch, snoozing in the shade. "Maybe it's time for me to move on," Darry finally spoke.

"Run again?"

Darry shrugged.

"Darry, where were you born?"

"My birth certificate says I was born in Illinois."

"Would it stand up to a thorough check?"

Darry smiled.

"That's what I thought. Darry, have you ever leveled with anyone about . . . whatever it is you're hiding?"

"A few people, over the years."

"How many years?"

"Oh, as near as I can figure it, pretty close to seven centuries."

Rick's plate suddenly fell out of numb fingers and clattered to the ground. He sat and stared at Darry.

"There has to be something to it," the air force general said. "The CIA is on it and so is the FBI. By God, we're not going to be left out in the cold. Isn't Pete Cooper winding up an investigation in that area?''

''Yes, sir. He's close. Out at Mountain Home.''

''Tell him to get on it ASAP.''

''Yes, sir.''

''Do you suppose there is any truth to it at all?''

''I don't know. But if there is, do you realize what kind of a weapon this man would make?''

''Of course.''

''Find him!''

''Yes, sir.''

''What in the hell is going on out in Idaho?'' the general asked. ''And why in the hell weren't we informed of it?''

Fort Meade, Maryland, home of the National Security Agency. A civilian agency, but always headed by a ranking military officer.

''I have no idea,'' the deputy director admitted. ''I just returned from vacation.''

''How was Bermuda?'' the DIRNSA asked.

''Very pleasant. Relaxing. What's this about Idaho?''

''The CIA has sent a man in . . . at the President's orders. Then the Bureau got their drawers in a wad about it, and they've ordered people in . . . at the request of Justice. Now the air force is sending a man in. We seem to be sucking hind tit on whatever is going on. I don't like that.''

''No,'' the D/DIRNSA agreed. ''We certainly can't have that.''

''Where is Al Reaux?''

The D/DIRNSA lifted an eyebrow at that. ''You want to send in the first team?''

''Might as well. This has to be big.''

''It must be. Do you have any idea what it's all about?''

"Not a clue. But whatever it is, I don't want to be left out of it. Hell, we *can't* be left out."

"I agree. We should have been the first to be notified."

The general buzzed his secretary. "Find Al Reaux and get him in here."

Rick Battle finally found his voice. "You're putting me on!"

Darry shook his head. "No."

"But that is impossible!" Rick insisted.

"No. I'm told there are others like me, but they've managed to avoid detection over the long years. I have no idea where they might be. I met one during this country's civil war, but lost track of him at Gettysburg."

"Are you sitting there and telling me straight-faced that you fought in the goddamn Civil War?"

"I fought in this country's revolutionary war."

"Jesus Christ!" With a very shaky hand, Rick poured himself a fresh cup of coffee.

"I knew you suspected something after you brought me that copy of the *National Loudmouth.*"

"I can't believe this, Darry. My mind just won't accept it."

"I don't blame you."

"Have you . . . ah . . . ever been married, Darry?"

"No. That would be very unfair to the woman. She would age and I would not. I have had many close relationships—many. But I always have to leave. Joan knew who I was, and finally sent me away."

"Joan?"

"Jeanne d'Arc."

"You had an affair with Joan of Arc?"

"Not a physical affair. But one of the heart."

"Joan of Arc!"

"Yes. She was a saint. Truly. The Church finally realized that in 1920, under the rule of Pope Benedict the XV.

One does not engage in pleasures of the flesh with a saint. It would be . . . unseemly.''

''Unseemly!'' Rick shook his head, his coffee cooling and forgotten. ''Were you . . . ah, there, ah . . .''

''When she was burned? Yes. That was . . . 1431. It was not pleasant to look upon. Our eyes met several times before her soul left her body.''

''You loved her?''

''Yes.''

''My God, my God!''

''Her final words.''

''This really pisses me off,'' the general said, waving a sheet of paper at Army Intelligence Agency headquarters. ''Everybody and their brother is racing toward Idaho, and we sit here with our thumb up our ass.''

''What's going on in Idaho?''

''Hell, I don't know. But it's big. Has to be. I want somebody on this and I want them on it right now.''

''Major Waters is wrapping up out at Fort Lewis.''

''Get him on this immediately. I want to know what the hell is going on.''

''Yes, sir.''

The vehicle unloaded, rafts inflated, supplies safely stowed and lashed down, Dr. Ray Collier smiled at his family. ''Is everybody ready to go?''

''Yeah!'' Paul and Terri shouted.

Karen smiled at her husband. Ray and Terri would be in the lead rubber raft, she and Paul in the second raft. They had all done this before, but never on a river this wild. They had talked about hiring a guide, but all had reached the conclusion that would take some of the fun out of the trip. They decided to go it alone.

''All right!'' Ray shouted. ''Man your boats!''

"Person your boats," his young daughter corrected.

Ray laughed. "She'll be president of NOW before she's out of her teens."

The Collier family shoved off and were soon lost from view around a bend in the river.

"If keelhauling was still in practice, I'd order it done," the admiral said, obviously highly irritated. Headquarters, Office of Naval Intelligence. "How come we dropped the ball on this one?" He lifted a manila folder and tossed out the question to the men seated around the long table.

"Sir, I can't even get a fix on what is going on. Everything is screwed down tight."

"Well, somebody had damn well better *un*screw it and do it fast. It looks like we're the last ones to know."

"Know what?" a ranking officer said.

The admiral slid the folder down the table. The officer opened it and stared at the single sheet of paper. "This doesn't tell me anything. What the hell is operation Mountain Goat?"

"That's what we're calling this," the admiral said. "Where is Jay Gilmore?"

"Washington state."

"I want him moving by twelve hundred hours."

"Yes, sir."

"You're leveling with me, right? You're not pulling my leg, are you, Darry?"

"No. I'm telling you the truth."

"But . . . how . . . ?"

"I don't know. For years I thought I was placed here by God for some reason. I rejected that theory centuries ago. I was a priest at one time; but I soon realized that was not my vocation and left the priesthood." He smiled. "I like the ladies too much for that."

"Wait until you see Stormy. She'll knock your socks off."

"Stormy what?"

Rick told him.

Darry blinked. "You're kidding!"

"Nope. Catchy name, huh?"

Darry sat down on the ground and laughed until tears were running out of his eyes.

"I hate horses," Stormy said. She hadn't been in the saddle an hour and her butt felt like it was on fire. Back at the outfitter's, Ki had told her to put on a pair of longhandles to help prevent chafing on her inner thighs. Stormy had refused. Up until now. "Let's stop," she said. "I want to put on those longhandles."

"According to the map, we'll be in camp in about thirty minutes. Can you wait?"

"Only if you brought along a well-stocked first aid kit. I think I'm dying."

Ki laughed at her. "Tomorrow will be even worse; then you'll begin to toughen up. I promise."

"This nag only has one gait," Stormy bitched. "Uncomfortable."

"You'll live," Ki assured her friend.

"If I go to hell, I know now what my punishment will be. Riding around the pits on a horse."

"You'll hurt your horse's feelings."

"Not nearly as much as he's hurting me."

"These are mares we're riding."

"Nightmares, you mean."

Ki started laughing and it was infectious. Soon Stormy was laughing at herself—despite the pain in her ass.

6

Rick Battle had left Darry's cabin with just enough daylight remaining to see him safely back to the station. He had talked with Darry for hours, and was convinced that Darry was who he claimed to be. It boggled his mind. He still could not entirely grasp the enormity of all that Darry had said . . . he doubted he ever would.

Rick had a telephone at the ranger station—the government had seen to that—and there was a message on his answering machine to call Tom Sessions at the district office.

"Tom? Rick. What's up?"

"Rick, I spoke with Munson up at the springs this afternoon. He told me an even dozen hard-looking men parked their vehicles up there and off-loaded equipment, then headed south, toward your area. He said if they weren't military types, he'd kiss a beaver's butt."

"Military? That's odd. We've had no word that the military would hold any survival training in this area, and they always tell us."

"Munson said if they were still in the military, they had to be senior sergeants, at least. He said some of them were pretty beat up looking, like in time-worn."

"What are you saying, Tom?"

"Munson said it. Mercenaries."

"Were they armed?"

"Pistols only, as far as Munson could tell. He said they all wore them in shoulder holsters or those military type rigs that fit on the chest."

"Mercenaries?" Then Darry popped into his mind. "Could they be bounty hunters, Tom?"

"Now . . . that's an interesting thought, Rick. That hadn't entered my mind. But who would they be after?"

"I don't know," Rick lied. "They may have received information about some fugitive hiding out in this area. It has happened before."

"Or they may be marching in to join up with Sam Parish and his bunch."

"That's an idea, for sure. I'll check them out, Tom."

"When you do, boy, you go in armed. Not much spooks Munson, but this bunch did."

"I'll keep that in mind."

After Tom hung up, Rick sat for a few moments, mentally digesting the latest news. There was no doubt in his mind—none at all—about who those dozen or so men were after.

He recalled Darry's words: "If blood samples were ever taken from me and put under a microscope, it would be all over for me. With the new equipment science has, the DNA testing and all that, I'd be placed in a cell and kept there for the rest of my life. If the doctors hadn't been in such a rush for warm, breathing bodies during World War Two, they would have spotted the difference. By the time Korea came around, I had changed my name, again, and was living in Canada, up in the Yukon."

"Have you leveled with me about everything, Darry?" Rick asked.

Darry smiled. "Not quite. But you're not ready for the rest of it. All in time, Rick."

Sitting in his small living room, Rick thought: But you just may be running out of time, Darry. And after all you convinced me of today, what else could there be? What else could you possibly tell me?

* * *

The faint call of a wolf echoed from the wilderness.

"What the hell was that?" Stormy said, looking around her, her eyes trying to pierce the darkness. "Coyotes?"

"Beautiful, isn't it?" Ki said, stirring the beans bubbling in a small pot. "No, that wasn't a coyote. The wolves are slowly making a comeback in the wilderness."

Ki looked at her friend and colleague and smiled. "Relax, Stormy. They won't hurt you. The big bad wolf is a myth. There has never been a documented, proven account in the United States of a healthy, full-grown wolf ever, unprovoked, attacking a human being. Wolves shy away from contact with humans. They've learned, over the centuries, that humans are not to be trusted to behave in a rational way."

"I forgot about your working with Craig. That was a good series you did. Some beautiful film."

"Wolves are important. I disagree with Craig about hunters. He thinks all hunting should be banned. That will never happen and it shouldn't happen. But the wolf certainly should have a place in the wild."

"I think hunting is cruel and barbaric," Stormy said, pouring a ready-mixed martini from a small can. She'd bought a case of the ready-mixed drinks to take along.

The outfitter had shaken his head in disbelief at all the equipment the women had bought. Took three packhorses to tote it all. Very gentle packhorses.

"It serves a purpose, Stormy. A very important purpose. I hunted as a kid. I've killed deer. I can dress out a deer just as well as anybody."

This was a side of Ki that Stormy did not know. "Why did you stop hunting?"

"I no longer needed the meat to survive. I came from a very large family, Stormy. A very large family on a very small farm. A lot of times, we wouldn't have had meat if we hadn't hunted.''

"Did you have the heads of deer mounted to hang on the wall?''

Ki laughed. ''No. Daddy wouldn't permit that. He said that was just as barbaric as a soldier mounting the heads of the enemy he'd killed. Daddy taught us to respect the animals we hunted, and the land we lived on. He said nobody could really own land; we were just taking care of it for a time. And we'd damn well better take care of it, for God wasn't making any more of it.''

"I didn't know there were wolves in Missouri.''

"There aren't. Not anymore. Daddy said there were red wolves when he was growing up. Until a bunch of stupid bastards killed them all out. They trapped them, they shot them, they poisoned them.'' Ki cut loose with a string of cuss words that would awe a barroom filled with sailors.

Stormy poured Ki a martini and handed it to her. ''You really get all worked up about wolves, don't you? I've never seen this side of you.''

Ki said, ''Let me tell you something about Craig. He's a top reporter and a gentle and good man. He loves animals. But there is a side to him that most people don't know. He was a marine in Vietnam. More than that, he was Marine Force Recon. Back in the Second World War, those guys were called Raiders. When we were winding down the story on wolves—up in Alaska—we were sitting in the hotel lounge having a drink when this bunch of dipshits came in and started bragging about the wolves they'd killed that day. Stormy, they shoot them from planes and helicopters. They chase the animals until they're exhausted and then shoot them. For sport. That's the type of hunter my daddy taught me to despise. They kill just for the sake of killing. Well, Craig had a few words to say about that, and the man invited Craig to step outside. Stormy, we were in Alaska for five more days, and that guy was still in the hospital when we left. Craig stomped him into the ground. One of the loudmouth's buddies stepped in to take up for his friend, and Craig broke his arm—at the elbow—with some sort of martial arts move. Craig is an easy-going man; you know that. Just don't make him mad.''

Stormy sipped her martini for a moment and then asked, ''You don't believe in gun control, do you, Ki?''

''No. Absolutely not. I know you do, but you're wrong.'' Ki smiled across the small and carefully built fire. While Stormy was blond, Ki's hair was as black as midnight. Stormy was tall; Ki was almost petite. But Ki had been raised on a working farm, and was strong for her size. ''You really want me to get wound up this evening, Stormy?''

''I withdraw the question, Ki. Let's save it for another time. Right now, let's eat. I'm ravenous!''

At dawn, the mercs split up into six two-man teams, spread out, and began working their grids. But they were still miles away from Darry's cabin. It was slow work for the manhunters, for they did not know what Darry looked like, or really, even if he was in the area. The one thing they did know was that he lived alone. The hunt was on. The mercs thought they were alone in this hunt. They were very wrong.

The man who had outfitted Stormy and Ki drove up to the ranger station. ''Don't send any more people to see me, Rick,'' he said. ''I'm nearly out of ridin' horses and pack animals. I never seen so many people gettin' outfitted for the wilderness.''

''Really? So early in the season? Hell, we're just into spring! We're not ready for the influx yet.''

''Tell me about it,'' the outfitter said drily. ''But these

ain't tourists, Rick. I don't know exactly what they are, but they ain't tourists.''

''You want to explain that?''

''Can't. It's just a hunch. They're all armed, Rick. Pistols, mostly. Carried in shoulder rigs or high up on the belt, like the feds do. They got fancy communications equipment. I never seen nothin' like it. Little bitty portable fold-out satellite dishes. And money ain't no object.'' He spat on the ground. ''That's what leads me to believe they're government people.''

Rick looked pained. ''I work for the government, Chuck.''

''That's different. You're one of us . . . in most ways. I figure at least three of these people are military types. Haircuts, bearing, and mannerisms. Something is goin' on in the wilderness, Rick. And I don't like it.''

''They could be moving against Sam Parish and his bunch.''

''That's possible, but I don't think that's it. I just get the feeling these people come from a lot of different federal agencies. And I don't think they're workin' together. I think they're workin' at cross-purposes.''

Rick studied the older man's face for a moment. ''You're not telling me everything, Chuck. Come on, give.''

''Ever' goddamn one of these feds, and that's what they are, goddamn feds, asked the same type of question. Is there a man between twenty-five and thirty years old, five-ten to six feet, livin' alone near here? I didn't tell 'em jack-shit! I hate the fuckin' feds, Rick. No offense, but I ain't got no use for them. You work for the government; you have to cooperate with 'em. But I don't. They can all kiss my ass! If a man wants to live alone or with his family out in the big lonesome, long as he don't break no laws, he's got a right to be left alone with his beliefs. The goddamn government ain't got no business stickin' their goddamn fuckin' noses in his business.''

''I agree with you,'' the voice came from behind the men and spun them around.

''Where the hell did you come from?'' Rick asked.

The man smiled. ''My truck developed a flat tire about a mile down the road. I find that my spare is also flat. Careless of me. Do you have any sort of portable compressor?''

''Are you another goddamn federal agent?'' Chuck demanded.

The man laughed. ''No, 'fraid not. I'm a wildlife photographer. The name is Johnny Mack.''

Darry left his hybrids at the cabin and went for his weekly romp with the wolf pack that had settled into the area. But they were tense and nervous, and they signaled danger to him. Darry walked among them—being careful not to get between the alpha male and female—and they all began to settle down. Normally, a pack would not tolerate an outsider. But with Darry, they knew he posed no threat to them; indeed, he was an asset to the pack, for when he was as them, he warned the pack what areas to stay out of and which were safe for a night hunt. The alpha female signaled ''follow me,'' and the pack took off in single file, with Darry bringing up the rear.

They ran for several miles, staying in the brush and on safe trails the pack had checked out and scented as their own. The female led the pack up a grade and behind some rocks on a ridge overlooking a long valley. She bellied down, and the others followed suit, Darry beside her. Darry had named this female Rodica, after a girl he had known back in the village where he was born. Both Rodicas were lovely.

Neither the wolves nor Darry were winded. Darry had not even broken a sweat during the several mile run.

Darry looked out over the valley and immediately saw why the wolves had told him there was danger. He could see two teams of men working slowly through the wide valley. He uncased his binoculars, adjusted for view, and studied the men. He had never seen them before. They moved like hunters. Not game hunters: man hunters. Professional warriors.

He lowered the glasses and put his hand palm down on the ground. Rodica laid her muzzle over his hand in a sign of trust, then raised her head and gently bit at his chin. Wolf affection. Darry pressed his face against hers and signaled her to take the pack away, to safety. Two seconds later, there was no trace of the wolves on the ridge.

Darry lay alone on the ridge and studied the teams of men. Now they had been joined by a third team of two men, and Darry had a strong suspicion there were more of them working on the other side of the timber-covered far ridge. There was no doubt in his mind what they were looking for. They were looking for him.

Darry sighed and cased his binoculars. He lay for a time with his forehead on the cool ground. He was so tired of running. Centuries of running. An endless roll of years, unable to establish any sort of permanent home or relationship. And it just got worse as technology advanced. It hadn't been so bad before the telegraph and telephone and the industrial revolution; life was slower and easier, and it had been much simpler to lose one's self. It was getting more difficult each year.

Darry raised his head and gazed down into the valley. Two more men had joined the others, and Darry felt sure there would be still more. The men had gathered in a small circle and were squatting down. One was pointing toward the west. That was all right, for Darry's cabin lay to the south of the valley. But they'd get around to it, sooner or later.

He wondered just how good these men were. That question was answered a heartbeat later when a voice said, ''Mike? You copy this?''

Darry tensed, not moving a muscle. He didn't even

blink. How in the hell could a man get this close to him without his knowing it?

"Yeah, Mike. You can see for several miles up here. There are no cabins in this valley. No signs of human life at all. None."

How close was the man? Not more than three or four yards at the most, Darry guessed, for the voice was clear.

"Yeah, okay," the man radioed. "I see Doolin and Blake. They're comin' out of the timber to the north of you. Okay. Right. I'll start workin' my way down to the valley floor. Jenkins has already started down. Sure. Let's give Mr. Roche his money's worth. Right. Webb out."

Mr. Roche? Who the hell was Mr. Roche?

Darry listened as the man turned to leave. He moved well, his boots making only the tiniest of whispers. If the rest of the manhunters were as good as this one, Darry was in for a time of it.

Six teams of two each. At least twelve men were hunting him. Damn! And the reporter and her camera-person. He'd have to run. He'd have to pack up what he could, put the hybrids in the bed of the truck and leave. He had no choice in the matter. None at all that he could see.

Or did he?

Darry lay on the ridge and thought it out. His cover was as good as it had ever been. His driver's license was valid. It would take some organization like the FBI to discover that his past was nonexistent—at least on paper—and it would take them several days to do it.

These men hunting him were not government hunters. He was sure of that. Someone named Roche was paying them. But why? He could not remember anyone named Roche in his past.

Roche Industries? The words popped into his consciousness. Robert Roche, he had read somewhere, was the richest man in the world. Worth billions and billions of dollars. He owned all sorts of factories and construction companies and real estate and . . . hell, Darry couldn't remember all of the article. But Robert Roche's holdings were vast. Worldwide.

Could that be the Mr. Roche the manhunter was referring to?

Probably.

But why?

Darry had no answer to that question. But then, people had chased him before without any real reason. But mostly those had been in the bad old days, back when he was a gunfighter.

Darry made up his mind. He was not going to run. Not just yet. He was weary of running. He'd stick around as long as possible. Maybe he could bluff his way through. He'd done it before.

But the manhunters didn't worry him nearly as much as the TV reporter. He could not allow his face to be shown nationwide. Somebody in his past would recognize him. Then there would be hell to pay.

Darry stood up and checked the valley below. The manhunters had moved on, tiny dots in the distance slowly working their way west.

He looked up at the sun. High noon. What was it that Afrikaner had told him during the Boer War? Yes. It was always high noon in Africa. The same could be said for Darry's situation.

Then Darry remembered something about the manhunters. They all had a short, tubelike object carried on a strap. What the hell was that? What was inside that tube? Some sort of weapon? He'd better find out. He decided to pace his predators. They had to camp somewhere. And when they did, he'd be there.

7

Both damaged tires on Johnny's truck held air. No nails or tacks or bits of stiff wire had punctured and flattened them. Odd, Rick thought. Very odd. If Chuck had noticed, he said nothing about it, and Rick kept his suspicions to himself. But warning bells were ringing silently in the ranger's head.

Rick, Chuck, and Johnny McBroon sat on the front porch of the one-man ranger station and drank coffee and chatted for a time after the "flats" had been inflated.

"So you're here to photograph wildlife, hey?" Chuck asked.

"Yes. I heard that the wolf is making a comeback in this area and wanted to see if I could get some on film."

"Odds are, you won't," Rick told him. "They'll see you, but your seeing them is iffy. Wolves tend to shy away from human contact."

"And you sure can't blame the critters, neither," Chuck said. "They've been hunted and poisoned damn near to extinction. And they sure as hell don't deserve the bad reputation they got hung on them."

Rick was one of only a handful of people who knew that Chuck was not exactly what he appeared to be. Chuck was a descendant of the Lost Tribe. Several years back, a group of not-quite-human beings had been found in the wilderness of Idaho, many of them caught midway in the evolutionary chain. The government had promised to protect them, but as so often happened whenever the government got involved in anything, everything got all fucked up. A handful of scientists from the U.S. and Canada quietly moved the Lost Tribe out and into a new area. Few people knew where they had been relocated. But many descendants of the Lost Tribe still lived in the area.*

"You seem to know a great deal about wolves, Chuck," Johnny remarked.

"I been close to them a time or two," the older man said drily.

Rick smiled at that.

"Am I apt to run into many people out there?" Johnny asked, waving a hand toward the wilderness area.

"A few live there year-round," Rick said. "But it's a little early in the season for many tourists. The nights still get chilly."

"I see," Johnny said. He looked at Chuck. "You say you're all out of riding horses and pack animals?"

"Oh, I reckon I could outfit you, Mr. Mack. You seem like a right nice fellow." He told him how to get to his place and said he'd be right behind him. After Johnny had left, Chuck said, "He's another goddamn fed, Rick. But at least he ain't as arrogant as some of those others."

Darry had worked in close to the manhunters' noon camp and was listening as they rested and talked. Their location was a good one, with plenty of shade and water. But it also showed the men had no idea they were being trailed. Darry had slipped up on them with relative ease.

"What's the matter, George?" one asked. "You're sure quiet."

The Indian looked up, his expression giving away noth-

*Watchers in the Woods—Zebra Books

ing. "I felt eyes on me this morning. I don't like this place. Terrible things have happened here."

"Now how the hell do you know that?"

"I feel it. Sense it."

"I think," a big merc named John Webb said, "that you are full of shit, Indian."

"And I think," George Eagle Dancer said, a cruel smile playing on his lips, "that you are a fool."

Webb started to rise to his boots. "Sit down, John," Tuttle said. "You tangle with George and he'll kill you." Webb hesitated. "Sit down!" Tuttle barked.

Webb sat. He stared at George. "Me and you, Indian, will settle up when this op is over."

"I think not," George said evenly. "I think you will die in this wilderness. But not by my hand."

Darry studied the men. None of them were kids. Darry guessed their varied ages to be between thirty-five and forty-five. And to a man they looked very capable of handling any situation that might confront them.

An ex-army ranger named Joel Bass said, "I've worked with you many times, George. But I've never seen you like this. What the hell's got you so spooked?"

"What we're doing is a mistake," George replied. "There is no clear-cut right or wrong here. We are chasing a man who has broken no laws. If this is the man I think it is, he was a friend to my people. I told you all, Indian nations from Canada to the Mexican border still sing songs about this man who will not die. If we push him, he will be forced to fight. He does not want to fight. But he will, and he is the greatest warrior to ever walk the face of Mother Earth. I agreed to this operation, yes. But I wish I had not. This is not democracy against tyranny, not peaceful people against bandits. What this is . . . is wrong."

"We're not here to hurt this man, George," Tuttle pointed out.

"No. Just kidnap him. Chase him down, drug him with

these guns"—he tapped the tubelike object by his side—
"and take him away against his will."

Tranquilizer guns, Darry thought.

"Let's don't get all moralistic about this op, George,"
Miles Burrell said. "Let's just do the job, collect our
money, and move on."

"Speaking of moving," Tuttle said, glancing at his
watch. "Police this area and let's get cracking. We've got
a lot of daylight left."

The mercs buried their ration containers and left the
area as they had found it, splitting up and fanning out,
moving toward the west.

Darry watched them for a time, then worked his way
out of the area and started jogging back to his cabin. He
wanted to take a bath, then fix a whiskey and water and sit
for a time. He had a lot of thinking to do.

"I'm gonna burn that son of a bitch's cabin down and
kill his goddamn dogs," Willis Reader said.

"No, you're not," Sam Parish told him. "Just leave
him alone for the time being. You'll get your chance at
him. I promise you that. But now would be a real bad
time."

"You mean that, Sam?"

"I mean it, Willis."

"Then I'll wait. Just don't make me wait too long."

To an observer, it would appear that the man was simply looking at his dogs. But there was much more to it
than that. Thoughts were passing between the human
form and the hybrids. When Darry was certain the two
wolf-husky mix understood, he averted his eyes and
rested for a time. It was very tiring communicating with
them for any length of time while in his human form, but
he could make them understand and obey better this way.

Like so many other aspects of his double personage and never-ending life, Darry didn't know why that was so; it just was. But Pete and Repeat now knew they must be very careful and alert for trouble constantly.

Upon returning to the cabin, Darry had done several hours work around the place, then bathed and shaved and silently spoke to his hybrids. It was now approaching twilight. Darry had a stew simmering on the outside stove, under the dog walk, and had just fixed a whiskey and water and sat down on the porch, waiting for the person or persons who had been stomping around in the brush and timber for several minutes to announce their presence.

"Hello, the cabin! Anybody home?"

"The last time I checked, I was," Darry called. "What's the matter, are you lost?"

"Frankly, yes," the voice admitted.

"Well, come on in and rest."

A young man and young woman stepped out of the timber. They looked to be in their mid-twenties. Both of them dressed in the height of outdoor fashion. They both carried side arms on their belts. 9mm or the new .40 caliber; Darry wasn't sure. He waved to chairs on the porch.

"Get out of those packs and have a seat. You both look beat."

"We are," the woman said. "I'm agent Kathy Owens; this is agent Jack Speed. We're FBI." They both showed him their credentials.

"Very impressive. I'm Darry Ransom. You're only about a thousand yards from the river trail. That way." He pointed. "If you listen, you can hear it. The ranger station is about six and a half miles away—in that direction." He pointed. "But it's easy to get off the trail."

The young man sat down wearily. "Our horses ran off—saddle horses and packhorse. Luckily we had made up these backpacks before that happened."

"Did you rent them from Chuck?"

"Ah . . . yes. That was his name," Kathy said.

"They'll go back home. You two can bunk here tonight, and tomorrow I'll take you back to the ranger station."

"That's very kind of you, Mr. Ransom," Jack said.

"Darry. Call me Darry."

It was then the two huge hybrids chose to stand up and approach the FBI agents, almost scaring the crap out of both of them.

"Good God!" Jack said, his hand dropping to the butt of his pistol.

Darry moved; moved so fast he was a blur to Kathy. Darry's hand closed around Jack's arm and paralyzed the move to draw his gun. There was no pain associated with the grip; Jack just could not move his arm

"Don't even think about hurting my dogs," Darry said softly. "Miss Owens, if you make a move toward your side arm, one of those hybrids will have your throat torn out before you can draw. Now just settle down. If you don't make hostile moves toward them, they won't hurt you." He released his grip on the agent's arm. "Let them smell you and they'll go on back and lie down."

Pete and Repeat smelled the agents, then looked up at Darry. "It's all right," Darry assured them.

The hybrids backed up and lay down on the porch.

"They're *wolves!*" Kathy said.

"They're half wolf, half husky, miss."

Jack looked down at his arm. He could now flex his fingers and move the arm. "How did you do that?" he asked, no hostility in his voice.

"Pressure points," Darry told him. "It's a painless, harmless, and very effective way to disarm an opponent."

"My whole arm went numb," Jack said. "No pain, just no feeling."

"Let me give you both a bit of advice. You probably won't take it, but it's free, so what the hell? There are men, and women, living back here in the wilderness, who would have shot you stone dead if they'd been in my boots a moment ago. So go easy on grabbing for guns.''

''Those wolves startled me,'' Jack said, a bit defensively.

''They're hybrids. And they won't hurt you unless you make some sort of threatening move toward them.''

''So there are a lot of armed survivalist types living back here?'' Kathy asked.

Darry smiled. ''I don't know what you mean by survivalist, miss. There are people living back here who grew weary of the rat race of city life; people who wanted to simplify their lives and get away from a pressure-cooker sort of existence. There is a small commune of what used to be called hippies living not too many miles from here. They're good people who never cause any trouble.''

The two federal agents exchanged glances in the dim light coming from a lantern in the cabin. Darry read the look accurately: we'll look for marijuana patches. That amused him.

''What other types of people live back here, Mr. Ransom?'' Jack asked.

''Darry. My name is Darry. We're not very formal around here. What other types? There are a few families who decided they didn't like the way their kids were taught in school, so they moved out here to get away from that; teach their own kids. There are some who believe the United States is going to hell in a hand basket. You'll find a few of them scattered around.''

''Before we came in,'' Kathy said, ''we were briefed about a large survivalist group who train in this area. Sam Parish and his Citizen's Defense League.''

Darry jerked a thumb. ''They're over that way a few miles. Not too far away. They're not the most likeable people I have ever encountered. But as far as I know, they haven't broken any laws.''

''They're racist,'' Jack said.

"Is that against the law?" Darry stood up. "Excuse me, I have to stir the stew. I hope you like stew."

"We have rations," Jack said.

"Keep them for an emergency," Darry called over his shoulder as he stood under the dog walk. He stirred the rich-smelling mixture and returned to the porch.

"What do you do for a living, Mr. Ransom?" Jack asked.

"Darry. I keep telling you my name is Darry. I have a small monthly income that is sufficient for my needs."

That was true. A few decades back, Darry, working under an assumed name, had set up a fund for a fictitious nephew named Darry Ranson. The father of one of his present lawyers in San Francisco, now dead, had done the paperwork. That would stand a check, and Darry felt sure these federal people were going to check him out.

Kathy was studying Darry in the faint light, but not studying him solely through agent's eyes. She was a woman first. Darry Ransom was a handsome man, in a rugged sort of way. He was no pretty boy. It appeared that he cut and trimmed his own thick shock of hair and did so skillfully. But it was his strange eyes that fascinated her; she'd never seen eyes quite like them. They were . . . almost animal in appearance, except for the color. He was in excellent physical condition, and could move very quickly. She also noted that he appeared to have some knowledge of unarmed self-defense, judging by the way he had handled Jack's move toward a gun. He was a man possessing some education, and he appeared to be about thirty years old. So why was he living out here in the wilderness as a near-hermit?

She would request a background check on Darry Ransom.

Such was the power of big government.

* * *

About two miles to the north of Darry's cabin, Johnny McBroon sat near a hat-sized fire and cooked his evening meal. Less than a mile from where Johnny sat, Al Reaux was eating his dinner out of a can. Just to the north of Al, Major Pete Cooper had made his camp and was settling in for the night. To the west of him, although separated by about a mile, Major Lew Waters was cooking his supper and Lt. Commander Jay Gilmore was dubiously feasting out of a packet of MREs—Meals Ready to Eat.

Nearly all the principal players in this soon-to-be Orwellian tragedy were in place, but as yet unknown to each other, except perhaps by reputation.

Come the dawning, all that was about to change.

8

The two FBI agents insisted upon sleeping outside that night, under the dog walk. While they slept, Darry went through their packs and personal articles. He found the copy of the fax ordering the two to investigate the report of the man who could not die, taken from the *National Loudmouth*. He put everything back as he'd found it and returned to his bed.

After breakfast, he led them to the river trail to the pair of agents. "About four and a half miles down this trail, you'll see a well-used and wide trail leading off to the northwest. It will turn to your right," he added, blandly and straight-faced. " 'Bout four and a half more miles and you'll come to the ranger station."

"Perhaps we'll intercept the rescue party," Jack said.

"What rescue party?"

"Our horses returned to their stable yesterday afternoon. Riderless. Surely that was reported and a rescue party sent out."

Darry slowly shook his head. "Let me tell you two something: About thirty-five or so miles from here, there is a small town with a branch bank and a post office and a few stores. There might be some people in that town who care what happens to a couple of federal agents. A few people. That is, if Chuck reported your riderless horses returning. Which I doubt. But out here, you're on your own. Most of the people who move into a wilderness area to live year-round do so to *get away* from government interference and meddling, snooping federal agents prowling around in their lives. Memories are still fresh about an incident that happened up in the northern part of this state a few years ago. A boy and his mother—who happened to be holding a tiny baby in her arms—were shot to death by federal agents. Most of the people who live around here don't trust the federal government, and they don't like federal agents. So don't expect them to welcome you with open arms.''

''Thank you for being so, ah, candid with us, Darry,'' Kathy said. ''Perhaps if the people knew the facts about that case, they might feel differently.''

''Oh, they know the facts, Kathy. They know all the facts. That's just one of the reasons they don't like federal agents.''

''We'd best be going,'' Jack said. ''Perhaps we'll see you again, Mr. Ransom.''

''I'm sure you will,'' Darry said drily.

When Darry returned to his cabin, he found a man sitting on the roof of the shed, holding a pistol in his hand. Pete and Repeat sat on the ground, looking up at him, not in a friendly manner.

''Call off your dogs,'' the man ordered. ''Or I'll shoot them. That's the only warning I'm going to give you. I'm an agent of the federal government.''

Darry got mad. He pointed at the man and said, ''You just stay put for a minute.'' He walked into the cabin and stepped back outside carrying a lever action Winchester .375. ''Screw you and screw the federal government,'' he called to the man, levering a round into the slot. ''The next move is up to you.''

Al Reaux recognized the weapon in Darry's hands, and knew one round from that big game rifle would blow an irreparable fist-sized hole in him. ''Can we just calm down for a minute?'' the NSA man called.

"I am calm," Darry said. "If I wasn't calm, you'd be dead meat on the ground." He called for his hybrids and pointed to the porch. They hopped up and lay down. "Now you can shove that pistol back in leather and climb down."

"Put that rifle away, mister."

"Go to hell!"

Al was a brave man, but he sure wasn't a stupid one. He knew he was in a no-win situation. He holstered his 9mm and climbed down. "Now will you put that cannon away?"

Darry eased the hammer down and lowered the muzzle. Al breathed a bit easier. So far, he'd found the people around here the unfriendliest goddamned people he'd ever encountered . . . and that included the Viet Cong. What the hell was the matter with these folks?

Al approached Darry cautiously. He didn't like the look in the young man's eyes. "I don't suppose you want to shake hands and start all over?"

"You suppose right. What are you doing on my property?"

"I wanted to ask you a few questions, that's all. I didn't know you had wolves running around loose."

"One: they're hybrids. Two: they wouldn't have treed you if you hadn't made the first hostile move. And finally, I don't feel like answering any questions."

It was Al's turn to get mad. "Hey, mister! Don't get too damned cute with me. I can have your ass in a jail cell before you can blink."

"Get off my property and don't come back," Darry said.

"I'd do what he says were I you," the voice came from the north side of the men facing each other. "That .375 Winchester can drop a cape buffalo in its tracks."

Darry and Al cut their eyes to the man with the camera hanging from a strap around his neck. "Who the hell are you?" Darry asked.

"The name is Johnny Mack. I'm a wildlife photographer. But I used to hunt with a rifle, and I know something about guns."

Al pointed a finger at Darry. "I'll leave. But I will be back, hot shot."

"I'll be around."

When Al had picked up his small backpack, shrugged it on, and walked off, Johnny said, "You made a mistake, my friend. You made a bad enemy there. I heard him say he was government. Big government can cause you a lot of grief."

Darry smiled. How well he knew the truth in those words . . . a truth that spanned centuries and dozens of kings. "You came along at a good time. I thank you. Would you like a cool drink?"

"I'd love one."

Johnny and Darry introduced themselves and shook hands. Johnny met Pete and Repeat, and the dogs took to him immediately, allowing the man to pet them and scratch behind their ears. He drank a glass of cold water from the well and set the glass down on the porch. "Why the government interest in you, Darry?"

"Oh, I don't think they're all that interested in me. But they might be getting ready to move in on Sam Parish and his survivalist bunch."

"He's a bad one, huh?"

Darry shrugged. "They've never bothered me."

Johnny asked no more questions, and after a few moments more of casual conversation, he lifted his camera in a gesture of "gotta go to work," said his goodbyes and see you again, and left.

When the man had disappeared from view, Darry said aloud, "He's a fed, boys. A smart one, but still a fed. I guess it's about to get real interesting around here."

* * *

"Something's up, Sam," one of Reader's men reported. "We've got strangers all over the area. And they don't behave like tourists."

"That ain't all we got," another man walked up and reported in.

"What do you mean?"

"Reporters are in the area."

"Local people?"

"No. Big shots, out of New York City. Stormy's here."

Sam cursed aloud. He'd seen the interview Stormy had done with the leader of a survivalist group back a year or so. The bitch had made the guy look like a fool even though he was a reasonably intelligent man. Stormy was so liberal Sam didn't understand how she could walk around without leaning to the left.

Sam looked at Willis Reader. "Pass the word around the camp. No one, *no one,* talks to reporters. I'll handle that end of it." He was silent for a moment, his face a frown. "I think the government is finally going to move against us, people. They know we pose a real threat to them, and they're going to wipe us out. Just like they did those people in Arkansas and Texas and up north of here, and God only knows where else." He fell silent; then the frown was replaced by a smile. "Lynn, you go find the reporter. Invite her to our camp. If she accepts the invite, I want all weapons out of sight. Everybody cleaned up and shining and on their best behavior. Put the words 'nigger' and 'spic' and 'kike' and 'wop' and 'slope' out of your heads. Don't even think the words, much less say them aloud. If we can pull this off, we can turn the tables on this goddamn rotten government."

"Sounds good to me, Sam," Willis said. "Damn good."

The next day.

* * *

Mike Tuttle and Nick Sharp lay on the ground, at the edge of the clearing on the east side of Darry's acreage, and studied him through binoculars.

"What do you think, mate?" Nick asked softly, lowering the binoculars.

"He fits what little we know about him," the team leader replied, lowering and casing his long lenses. "But so do ten other people, including some of those hippie types."

The two mercenaries were unaware that across the way, on the west of the clearing, Lt. Commander Jay Gilmore was studying *them* through binoculars. The ONI man was likewise unaware that he was being observed from the north side of the clearing by Major Pete Cooper from Air Force Intelligence.

It was at that moment that Stormy and Ki came riding up and dismounted by the side of Darry's cabin. The hybrids immediately came around to investigate, and the women got back into the saddle faster than they had ever done before.

Darry stepped around the corner of the cabin and was amused at the antics of the women. "Take it easy, ladies," he said. "They won't hurt you. They're just curious, that's all."

"What are those damn things?" Stormy asked, not about to exit the safety of the saddle, as much as her butt would like for her to leave it.

"They're hybrids, ladies. Step down and let them smell you. They won't hurt you."

Stormy and Ki exchanged glances and swung out of the saddles, allowing the big breeds to sniff them for a few seconds. Then the hybrids jumped back on the porch and lay down.

"Come on around to the porch and have a seat," Darry said. "What can I do for you?"

Stormy was unaccustomed to not being immediately recognized, and she was a bit put out by the man's casual air. Then she realized there was no electricity out here. She shuddered at the thought. Why would anybody choose to live under such primitive conditions? She was still amazed at the number of people she and Ki had found living in this area.

The women sat down in chairs on the porch and accepted with thanks the glasses of cold well water Darry brought them. After they had drank their fill, Darry said, "I'm Darry Ransom."

"Ki Nichols. This is Stormy Knight." She waited for the smile that always brought and was not disappointed.

"My father has a weird sense of humor," Stormy explained. "And so does my mother. She must; she married him," she added drily.

"What can I do for you ladies?" Darry repeated, knowing full well what they wanted.

"We're looking for a person," Stormy said. "He would be about your age; someone who has lived around here for several years. We actually don't know much about him."

Darry shrugged his shoulders. "Believe it or not, there are a lot of people who live around here. Many of them year-round. I don't know ninety percent of them because we almost never socialize."

Stormy leaned forward. "Do you know who I am, Mr. Ransom?"

"My name is Darry. No. I don't know who you are."

"I'm a reporter. Broadcast journalism." She named the network and it was a biggie.

"Congratulations. But I don't have any TV." He smiled. "No electricity. Some of the people who live out here—a few—have portable generators, and they do receive TV by satellite. I don't."

"Don't you miss it?" Ki asked.

"Not really. I used to enjoy watching the cartoons as a

kid, but that was a long time ago.'' He hid his smile at that. Darry loved dark humor.

"Now, you're not *that* old,'' Stormy said with a smile.

Darry smiled and shook his head. "You're right, I'm not. But watching TV is like so many other things. I used to play sports.'' He remained straight-faced, thinking: *sports that you never heard of.* "But if you get away from them, after a time you don't miss them.''

That made sense, of sorts, to the women. But they had both been raised in the electronic age. Neither could visualize a world without TV and computers.

"The TV reporter,'' Nick Sharp said. "And that must be her camera operator with her.''

"Good-looking birds,'' Mike said, lowering his binoculars. "But that blond bitch is cold-looking.''

"I could warm her up.''

"Now, that is interesting,'' Lt. Commander Gilmore said to himself, lowering his binoculars. "The Ice Queen is here.''

Stormy had the nickname Ice Queen hung on her after rebuking a number of sexual advances from other reporters—male and female alike—over the years. Stormy was anything but cold toward sex; she just had very definite ideas about the type of man she allowed in her bed.

"The hot-shot reporter,'' Major Cooper muttered, after seeing the women ride up. "Interesting.'' Since he was on the north side of the cabin, the porch was obscured from view.

"Do you read the *National Loudmouth,* Darry?'' Ki asked.

"I've seen it in supermarkets. But I don't ever recall actually buying a copy.''

Ki cut her eyes to Stormy and received a slight nod.

She dug in her knapsack and took out a copy of the *National Loudmouth* and handed it to Darry. The magazine was opened to the story.

Darry scanned the article and chuckled. He lifted his eyes. "You have got to be kidding!"

Stormy's smile was a strange one. Ki picked up on that immediately. "I spoke at length with the woman who wrote that article. She did a lot of research before writing it. The man in that story is real. Back in the sixties he was known as Dan Gibson. In the forties he called himself William Shipman. Between the years of 1914 and 1918 he was known as Billy Wilson."

Ki was thinking: she didn't tell you any of this, Stormy. I was there, remember?

"Billy Wilson served in the army during the First World War, first in the British Army, then in the American Expeditionary Forces. After the war, he vanished. In the forties a man fitting his description right down to the color of his eyes won a lot of medals as an American soldier in Europe. Then he vanished. There is no trace of him serving in Korea, but the military did launch a very extensive search for Sergeant William Shipman. They wanted to recall him. He was never found. Then during the Vietnam era, a man calling himself Dan Gibson served as an army ranger in 'Nam. Same description as the others, the same color of hair and eyes. In 1969, he was discharged and vanished. Just dropped off the face of the earth. During the mean years of the Ceausescu regime, a number of agents from Romania were dispatched to this country to find a Rumanian national named Vlad Dumitru Radu. One of them sought political asylum; that was granted after he told a very interesting story. I have a good friend in the State Department . . . now retired. He told me the story. You want to hear it, Mr. Ransom?"

"I enjoy a good tale, Miss Knight. It's a way to pass the day. Go ahead."

Ki was sitting with her mouth hanging open.

"Beginning about 1318, a bounty was placed on the head of Vlad Dumitru Radu. It was said he was a were-wolf and those in power wanted him dead. It is documented fact that Vlad Radu lived with, ran with, and hunted with . . . packs of wolves. About 1350, Vlad Radu was almost captured by soldiers. He suddenly vanished right before their eyes and became a wolf. The men were so frightened they threw down their weapons and fled in terror. But one looked back and saw the wolf change into human form. He saw a young man, in his mid-twenties, standing there."

"Folklore," Darry said, reaching down to pet Pete.

"In 1375 he was spotted again, and once again, he shape-shifted into a wolf and ran away. The young man, before he turned into a wolf, fit the description of Vlad Radu . . . to a T. He was now seventy-five years old, and had not aged. There were a dozen or more sightings of Vlad Radu, in both human and wolf form, over the next fifty years or so. Then, in the fourteenth century, Vlad Tepes, known as Vlad the Impaler, placed an enormous bounty on the head of Vlad Dumitru Radu. But he was never caught."

"Because he doesn't exist," Darry said.

"Oh, I think he does, Mr. Ransom," Stormy persisted. "Vlad Radu left his native country for the last time about 1460. He may or may not have been back since then; that is unclear. It's since been almost positively documented that a man fitting Vlad's description fought by the side of Jeanne d'Arc. The Church has denied for years that they had an affair. A man fitting Vlad's description fought with Napoleon Bonaparte. But I'm getting ahead of the story. A man fitting Vlad's description was seen in Japan, years before the first recorded mention of a white man setting foot on that island nation. There are stories of a man fitting Vlad's description in Africa. Toward the end of the 14th century, a man fitting Vlad's description was the leader of a gang who operated around South Yorkshire in England. Many believe this man was the real Robin Hood. There was a mountain man in America's West who fit Vlad's description——he was there fifty years before any other mountain men arrived. Then there was a scout and finally a gunfighter in the 1870s in the Wild West. Both the scout and the gunfighter fit Vlad Radu's description.''

''How the hell do you know all this, Stormy?'' Ki finally blurted, amazement in her eyes. ''You never told me any of this.''

''I've been quietly researching this story for years,'' Stormy replied. ''I started back in high school. I've been fascinated by it. This story is, I believe, the most important story of the millennium.''

Darry said nothing, but his mind was racing. A school girl, he thought. A mere school girl finally put it all together, doing what others have been unable to do over nearly seven centuries. Incredible.

''You have anything to say, Mr. Ransom?'' Stormy asked.

''Quite a fairy tale, Ms. Knight.''

''Oh, it's no fairy tale, Mr. Ransom. It's real. Do you know who this Vlad Radu looks like?''

''No.''

''You, Mr. Ransom. He looks exactly like you.''

9

During a rest stop to catch their breath, let weary muscles relax, and to allow their clothing to dry off a bit after racing through white water on the scenic river, Dr. Collier told his family, "We'll be at our camping spot mid-morning tomorrow. We're right on schedule."

"All right!" Terri said. "A whole week of solitude. Awesome!"

Paul smiled at his sister, and Karen squeezed her husband's hand, both of them thinking how fortunate they were to have two fine kids. The family was counting on seven full days of hiking and exploring and fishing and relaxing before continuing on their adventure of running the white water. They had carefully planned all the activities for each day. It was going to be quite an adventure. But they hadn't counted on tragedy being included.

Major Lew Waters of Army Intelligence, and Al Reaux of NSA came face-to-face on a trail. They stood for a moment without speaking, just looking at each other.

"Nice day for a walk among nature, isn't it?" Lew broke the silence.

"Yes, it is. Been out here long?"

"Couple of days."

Al nodded his head. "Me, too."

Both men took in the other's clothes and boots. Al wore expensive hiking boots. Lew wore "Go Devils" army mountain boots. Each man could see the telltale bulge of a shoulder holster on the other. Neither man knew who the other was, but each man suspected what the other was.

"See you around," Al said.

"Yeah. Probably," Lew replied.

The men moved on, each one thinking of the other: Spook.

"Rick," Tom Sessions said when the receiver was lifted. "I've got to go to Washington for a meeting. I'll be gone ten days to two weeks. You hold the fort down, all right?"

"Sure. What's up?"

"The budget. Fiscal year ends in a few months, and we want to get our gripes in before it's too late. I'll see you when I get back."

"Try to get me a raise, will you?"

"You still believe in Santa Claus at your age?"

Rick laughed. "Have a good trip."

The hybrids felt Darry's tension, and they lifted their heads, staring intently at the women. Ki was watching the big breeds, and her hand moved inside her bush jacket toward the butt of her holstered .38.

"I wouldn't," Darry said softly. "As long as the gun's in my hand, the dogs are all right. They don't like guns in the hands of other people."

Ki slowly pulled her hand back.

Darry cut his eyes to Stormy. "You've done your homework."

Stormy sighed, as if a great weight had been lifted from her shoulders. "So the search is finally over."

"I said nothing of the sort. I just said you've done your homework."

"You are Vlad Radu, aren't you?"

"Ms. Knight, you're here for a story. I am a man who seeks only to be left alone and live in peace. Assuming that I am who you believe me to be, don't you think I've earned some peace?"

Stormy was forced to think about that, but not for very long. "The public has a right to know," she replied, almost automatically.

Ki said nothing, but she didn't agree entirely with her friend. Ki was a conservative in much of her thinking, while Stormy was an avowed liberal. Not quite as bad as some of her take a punk to lunch colleagues, but close. Ki also knew that sometimes the press was wrong to print or broadcast a story . . . solely for the sake of getting a story. Lives could be adversely affected forever. But Ki wasn't sure about this story.

Then Stormy surprised her by saying, "But this could be the chance for you to rest, Darry. You wouldn't have to run anymore."

Darry was silent for a few heartbeats. There was no longer any point in denying who he was. Stormy had him cold. "Oh, you're certainly right about that. I would just have to endure being studied for the next seven centuries . . . or longer. Put on exhibit like some poor caged animal. Poked and prodded and questioned forever."

Ki was watching Darry's eyes. They had changed. The strange, slightly slanted pale eyes held a savage glint. Stormy seemed not to understand just how much danger the two women could well be facing.

Stormy, Ki thought, are you even remotely aware that we might not live to broadcast this story.

"Hello, the cabin!" a woman's voice sprang out from the timber's edge. "May I come over?"

"Sure!" Darry called. "Come on in."

When the woman stepped out of the timber and began

walking across the clearing, Darry recognized her as being part of Sam Parish's group.

"You know her?" Stormy asked.

"Not really. She's part of Sam Parish's Citizen's Defense League."

"Mr. Ransom," the woman said, stopping in front of the porch. "Please pardon this intrusion."

"No problem. What can I do for you?"

"I came over to invite Ms. Knight and her companion, and you, too, of course, to come over and visit our camp. We would very much like to explain what we are and what we aren't to a member of the press."

"Aren't you forgetting that I was ordered to leave your camp and not to come back?" Darry said.

"We got off to a poor start, Mr. Ransom. We'd like to make amends if you would allow us."

Darry shrugged his shoulders. "Fine with me."

The woman, attractive in a rough sort of way, shifted her gaze to Stormy.

The reporter slowly nodded her head. "All right. Tomorrow evening?"

The woman smiled. "Tomorrow afternoon would be better. That would give you a chance to get back to your camp before dark."

"We'll see you then."

The woman lifted a hand and turned and walked away.

"Do you trust those people, Darry?" Ki asked.

"About as far as I can see them."

"Are you going with us tomorrow?" Stormy asked him.

"Maybe."

"You could take that opportunity to leave."

"There is always that possibility."

Stormy had wanted to shoot some film, but Darry nixed that immediately. "I'm tired of running," he had told her.

"I want an end to it. But for right now, the instant the camera comes out, I'm gone. You've got to give me a little time to think about this."

Surprising both Darry and Ki, she had agreed. And then with a smile, added, "But we would like your permission to stay here until after we meet with the survivalists."

"We would?" Ki blurted.

Darry returned the smile. "Don't trust me, huh?"

Stormy shook her head. "That isn't entirely true. But I am suspicious as to why you gave in so easily."

"I wanted to give you time to think about what you're going to do to my life."

Ki winced at the words. Darry had given Stormy a real low blow with that remark. And looking at Stormy, Ki knew the words had hit home.

Stormy said nothing for a time, sitting on the front porch. Finally she said, "That's not fair, Darry. I have a job to do."

"You were a human being before you became a reporter," he reminded her.

And for just a few moments, Stormy slipped out of her reporter role. She stared at Darry for a moment, then said, "I'm still a human being. Sometimes maybe we forget that chasing after a story. But I've paid my dues," she added softly.

"I'm sure you have," Darry agreed. "But so have I. For a lot longer."

Stormy shifted in her chair to face him. "Darry, I don't think you fully understand one aspect of going public with your life. In a very short time, you're going to be enormously wealthy. You're going to be so rich, you can buy all the security you need to maintain some degree of privacy. Have you given that any thought at all?"

"I've been rich, Stormy. And I've been poor. Don't you think I've made investments down through the long years?"

"I'm sure you have. But look at how you're living! You live like a hermit, without any modern conveniences. Darry, you've lived through seven *centuries*. You can verify or refute events. You can write, lecture, teach. You know so much about the past."

Maybe she's right, Darry thought. It just might be fun to try.

I don't believe any of this! Ki thought. I just fucking don't believe it!

The next day.

"You think it's Darry Ransom?" Jack asked.

Kathy shook her head. "I don't know. I tend to doubt it. He's living too open and he's too friendly. I think it's someone in the survivalist camp."

"I think it's the hippie, Jody Hinds. All my alarms went off while talking with him."

"Yeah," she agreed. "I caught the same vibes. Hinds sure is hinky about something. I've asked for a make on Darry Ransom, but nothing's come back yet."

"So we've narrowed it down to two, possibly three people. Let's start zeroing in."

"Where's the starting point?"

"Darry Ransom."

"We're not that far from his cabin. Let's go."

The search had intensified, with all the recently sent in government people now on horseback, to cover more ground in a shorter time. Jody Hinds had, that day, ordered Major Lew Waters off his property at the point of a gun. Setting up his portable satellite and using high-speed burst transmission, Lew felt he had found his man and called in for help. It was then he learned that federal agents had been watching Jody for some time, and Lew linked up with them. Kathy and Jack received the word at about the same time, and they were ordered in to assist. They immediately forgot all about Darry and joined the surveillance teams around the cabin of Jody Hinds, his wife, and her sister and boyfriend.

Yet another colossal government SNAFU (Situation Normal All Fucked Up) was about to take place.

Jody Hinds was not a criminal, nor was he a hippie. He was a man with strong beliefs, and they included the right to be left alone and the right to keep and bear arms. Jody, his wife, Linda, her sister, Pam, and her boyfriend, Jeff, all shared the same beliefs.

"We found a patch of weed over there," a BATF man said, pointing. "It belongs to Hinds."

He was wrong. The patch of marijuana did not belong to Jody Hinds. It was planted—and until recently, occasionally tended to—by two ne'er-do-wells who lived in Salmon, Idaho, some distance away. The two men were now cooling their heels in the county jail, being held for peddling cocaine to school kids. Jody knew about the patch of grass, but since it didn't belong to him, he figured it was none of his business and left it alone.

"He's also a separatist and racist, and he's tied in with Sam Parish and that bunch of crackpots," another federal agent told the FBI people and the Army Intelligence agent, who by now was in way over his head and wished to hell he could figure out some way to vacate this area . . . he had no business meddling in civilian affairs.

That informative federal agent was full of shit. Jody was no racist. If they had done a bit more checking, they would have discovered that Jody's wife, Linda, was half Nez Perce Indian, whose mother still lived on the Nez Perce reservation. And Jody Hinds' opinion of Sam Parish was just about on the same level as his desire to bed down with a rabid skunk.

"And they're all well armed," another fed said.

At least the feds got something right. Jody and those with him were sure as hell well armed. All legal weapons. But they included those nasty, terrible, awful so-called "assault rifles." The weapons that made liberal democrats pee their lace-trimmed drawers in fright and go dithering about, stomping on hankies.

"We should have arrest warrants in hand by this time tomorrow," another fed said. "Then we'll make our move and cut the head off another dangerous snake."

Yeah. Right.

"At the same time, another team will be moving against Sam Parish and his Citizen's Defense League. They're getting into position as we speak."

"What's Sam Parish done?" Major Waters asked, rapidly reaching the conclusion that he was in the midst of a bunch of heavily armed government zealots who didn't know peanut butter from horse shit.

"He's preaching sedition. He believes in the violent overthrow of the government."

"So do about twenty-five million other Americans," Lew replied. "At least. Are you prepared to move against them, too?"

"Whose side are you on, Major?" the team leader questioned.

"I'm on the side of reason. You people are about to screw up real bad here."

"Listen up, Major. Jody Hinds has a portable radio in that cabin. He listens to Rush Limbaugh."

Lew couldn't believe what he was hearing. Had America really come to this? "Is that right?" he finally found his voice.

"Yeah, and he also reads the Ashes books. We've had that author under surveillance for a long time."

"*I* read the Ashes books, you idiot! I'm outta here. I want no part of this fuck-up."

"Don't blow our cover."

Lew shook his head in disbelief. "Do you actually

think Jody Hinds doesn't know he's being watched? Man, Stormy Knight is not three miles from here. She'll be on this story like white on rice.''

''That's a racist remark, Major,'' a black agent said. ''I resent it.''

''Oh, shit!'' Lew said, and got the hell gone from there, thinking that Orwell had only missed the mark by about ten years.

10

Willis Reader came up to Darry and stuck out his hand. He was smiling, but Darry sensed it was forced. The smile did not reach his eyes. "We got off on a bad footing the other day, Darry. I apologize for running off at the mouth. What do you say we shake hands and put it all behind us."

"Suits me," Darry said. He returned the smile and shook the man's hand. As Willis walked away, Darry glanced at his watch. It was eleven-thirty on the morning his life was to be forever changed.

Stormy and Ki had gone over to a huge barbecue pit, where steaks were being cooked. The aroma was marvelous, wafting around the camp.

It was a meal that would not be eaten.

Darry suddenly tensed and looked around. But everything seemed normal. Except that no one was armed, and Darry thought it strange for these people. Then it dawned on him: the absence of weapons was for Stormy's benefit.

Darry again experienced a moment of anxiety and wondered why. Then he began listening beyond the voices in the camp. He could hear no birds singing, no chatter of squirrels. Darry began sensing real danger all around him.

He walked over to where Stormy and Ki were standing for the moment, alone together, and whispered, "Don't argue with me. Just slowly walk toward the timber to your right. Do it. Something is wrong. Very wrong. Move.''

Ki was carrying her camera, a vest and belt harness containing tape cartridges fitted around her. Stormy opened her mouth to protest, and Ki said, ''Do it, Stormy. Just do it.''

The women began strolling toward a V-shaped notch in the timber surrounding the camp. Darry headed in the same direction, but at an angle. They had just reached the timber when a voice sprang out of a bullhorn.

''Federal agents! Stand where you are. Don't move. We have a warrant to search your camp.''

Far in the distance, Darry was certain he could hear gunfire.

Willis Reader spun around and spotted Darry and the two women. ''They set us up!'' he yelled. ''Those bitches set us up.''

''Don't move!'' the electronically magnified voice boomed. ''You are all under arrest.''

It had to happen. It was overdue. Push people long enough, and some of them will fight. Darry had long suspected that was the real reason for the slow disarming of the American people. Certain factions within the government were running scared. Those factions knew that millions of Americans were fed up and pissed off at the government and their constant interference in citizens' lives. Those same factions also knew this nation had been born out of bloody revolution and that the same thing could happen again—but not so easily if the people were disarmed.

''You go straight to hell!'' Sam Parish yelled. ''We're under attack, people. Arm yourselves!''

Darry jumped at the two women and rode them down to the ground just as the camp erupted in gunfire.

* * *

Jody Hinds' wife, Linda, was the first to die. A federal agent shot her in the face as she was standing in the doorway and splattered the back of her head all over the cabin wall. Roaring out his rage, Jody jerked a mini-14 from the wall rack and triggered off a full thirty-round clip in the general area from which the killing shot had come.

A federal marshal took two .223 rounds through the forehead and was dead before he hit the ground.

In two miles-apart locations, the pristine wilderness erupted in gunfire, and the government-instigated carnage began.

Ki was filming even as Darry rode her to the ground. The camera witnessed a mob of men dressed in camouflaged clothing and wearing ski masks come charging out of the woods, automatic weapons clattering. The camera recorded graphically the sight of an unarmed woman taking a three-round M-16 burst to the chest and being flung to the ground, her blue-and-white-checkered shirt suddenly blossoming in crimson.

"Jesus Christ!" Stormy said. "What's happening here?"

"Your government at work," Darry said. "Crawl into the timber. Stay low. Move, dammit, move!"

Just inside the trees, Ki turned and shot a full three minutes of very damning film before Darry grabbed her by the belt and literally dragged her deeper into the safety of the thick brush.

"Those are *our* government agents?" Stormy questioned.

"They sure as hell aren't from Libya," Darry said. "Move. Quickly now. We've got to get back to the cabin and get the hell gone from here. They'll be after us."

That stopped the woman. "After *us*? But *why?*"

"Because we just witnessed a federal government

fuck-up," Ki answered her. "And I got about three and a half minutes of it on tape. They'll want that tape, and I suspect they'll do anything to get it."

"You got that right," Darry said. "And I think I heard shooting coming from the other side of my cabin."

"What the hell is our government *doing?*" Stormy demanded, anger rapidly overcoming her fright.

"Declaring war on dissidents, I suspect" Darry said grimly. "I saw it coming months ago."

With unlimited and unchecked power, big government could be a frightening monster out of control, especially when many of its enforcement agents were young zealots—politically left or right—with the fires of fanaticism burning brightly in their eyes.

Jack Speed and Kathy Owens were young, but neither was a zealot or a fanatic. The two FBI agents exchanged glances and silently agreed to get the hell gone from the area around Jody Hinds' cabin.

This is madness! they both thought.

Jack crawled to his hands and knees and a round from a rifle slammed into his shoulder, knocking him sprawling to the ground. Kathy quickly scurried to his side, and another bullet grazed her head and sent her spinning into darkness. One-handed, fighting the pain in his shoulder, Jack grabbed Kathy's shirt at the back of the neck and began pulling her away from the wild shoot-out. He dragged her a good quarter of a mile from the cabin before they both tumbled over the edge of a ravine and dropped to the rocky ground. Jack lost consciousness and drifted into oblivion. Neither agent would be witness to the carnage that took place a few minutes later.

Kevin Carmouche, a Vietnam veteran who, after serving two tours in 'Nam, came back home to Louisiana, married his high school sweetheart, Niki, had then immediately joined the hippie movement and moved to a commune in Idaho. They had been living in the wilderness area for over twenty years. They had raised four children, and only one remained at home, their youngest daughter, Beth, now sixteen years old.

Of the original sixty or so members of the commune, only a handful now remained. Vincent Clayderman and his wife, Anna, and their fifteen-year-old son, Jerry, and Todd Noble, his wife, Betsy, and their sixteen-year-old daughter, Ginny. Like Kevin, Vince and Todd were combat-tested veterans of the Vietnam war. They were peaceful men, seeking only to live and let live and be left alone.

Many people had terrible misconceptions concerning hippies. Many believed they were cowards and drop-outs from reality. Nothing was farther from the truth. Push a hippie hard enough, and the person doing the pushing was going to have a hell of a fight on his hands, for many of the "back to the earth" crowd were hard-assed military veterans, with some hairy ops behind them.

Vince Clayderman was an ex-SEAL and Todd Noble ex-Marine Force Recon. Kevin had been a Ranger LRRP.

The three families stepped out of their cabins and stood together, listening to the sounds of hundreds of rounds of ammunition being expelled.

"What the hell is going on?" Vince said.

"Sounds like Tet to me," Todd replied.

"Whatever it is, it probably isn't going to be good for us," Kevin summed up much more accurately than he could possibly know at the moment. "You remember I told you I saw Old Buckskin Jennings a couple of days ago, and he told me the place was filling up with federal agents."

Vince spat on the ground; his opinion of federal agents.

Another hard burst of gunfire reached the families. "That's coming from Jody and Linda's cabin," Anna said. "I don't like this at all."

"I'll take a walk over there and see if everything's all right," Kevin said. He turned, hesitated, then went into his cabin and returned with a Winchester model 94, .30-30 lever action rifle. He looked at his friends. "Get ready for a shit-storm," he told them. "I've got a bad feeling about this. I think all hell's about to break loose."

Seven men and five women of Sam Parish's Citizen's Defense League lay dead or dying on the ground. Four more were badly wounded. The rest were being held under guard in a barracks building.

"What the hell have we done?" a woman had screamed at a BATF agent.

"Shut up," he told her, his voice shaky.

"Fuck you!" she responded, and that got her a not too gentle kick in the ribs.

The agent instantly regretted doing that, but he was scared. Really scared. This op had gotten all out of hand. Government agents from several different enforcement agencies had fired into an unarmed bunch of men and women who were doing nothing more than having a cookout. No matter if they were on the list for dangerous groups. They were, at the time, unarmed and offering no resistance. You can't shoot somebody for cussing at you, he thought. This wasn't supposed to have happened. Goddammit, it wasn't supposed to happen. He walked outside and carefully locked the door. He joined the other agents.

He looked around him. The others all had the same silent question in their eyes: What in the hell are we going to do?

The federal agents gathered in a group in the center of the survivalists' camp. They stood silent for a moment, each waiting for the other to say something.

(The question that begs to be answered is: How would *you* react if a group of heavily armed men wearing camouflage and ski masks suddenly invaded *your* home or property?)

One hundred government agents had struck the survivalist camp, and fifty government agents had attacked the cabin of Jody Hinds. Federal marshals, BATF personnel, and members of a special Justice Department unit were involved.

It was a total, colossal, unforgivable, out-of-control government fuck-up. Now it had to be covered up.

A badly shaken federal marshal who had been physically sickened by what he'd seen and taken part in at the cabin of Jody Hinds met Kevin Carmouche on the trail. ''Drop that weapon!'' he shouted.

''Who the hell are you?'' Kevin asked the cammie-clad and ski-masked man.

''I said drop that rifle, goddammit!'' the agent shouted. ''I'm a federal agent.''

Kevin didn't know if the man was a fleeing bank robber or kidnapper or murderer or child molester or just exactly what the hell the man confronting him was. But he damn sure wasn't going to hand over his rifle to this stupid-looking person. ''Go to hell!'' Kevin responded.

The agent cursed, lifted his M-16, and Kevin shot him. The agent was wearing a protective vest, but he'd been standing sideways when Kevin fired. The bullet entered just under his left armpit and exploded his heart, dropping him dead on the trail.

''Oh, shit!'' Kevin said. He stood for a moment over the dead body of the man. Then he picked up the man's M-16 and clip pouch, and took his 9mm side arm and extra clips. He did not search the body for any ID. Kevin walked on. He had to find out what had happened at Jody's cabin. But he thought he knew. Just the supposition made him sick.

* * *

Jody Hinds had made it out alive. He knew his wife was dead, and was certain her sister and boyfriend were also dead, all of them shot by federal agents.

Now Jody was killing mad.

The Collier family had lost one rubber raft on the last stretch of wild white water before reaching their prearranged camping destination. They were low on supplies and fresh water. They had lost half their tents and clothing. They were just slightly discouraged.

It was about to get a hell of a lot worse.

Johnny McBroon did not have any idea what was taking place. He had not gone in the wilderness with all the fancy electronic equipment that the others had. When he had something solid to report to his field reports officer, he'd planned on hiking down to the ranger station and using the pay phone.

When the sounds of shooting reached Johnny, he was sitting with his back to a tree, his boots off, smoking a cigarette and rubbing his aching feet. "Jesus Christ!" Johnny said, as the sounds of the lopsided battles drifted to him.

He was lacing up his boots when he spotted the two running men heading his way. He whistled at them, and they stopped, paused, then trotted over to him.

Lt. Commander Jay Gilmore, from ONI, had linked up with Major Lew Waters of Army Intelligence. Lew had told Jay what he believed to be going down, and the men had ID'ed themselves.

"You're no happy camper out here bird watching," Lew said to Johnny, after identifying himself and Jay.

"We've got ourselves in the middle of a shit-storm. Now who the hell are you?"

Johnny paused. "Let's just say I'm under government contract."

"The goddamn CIA is out here, too?" Jay blurted.

"I didn't say that," Johnny said.

"You didn't have to," Lew told him. The men squatted down, and Lew told Johnny what he knew to be fact and what he suspected was happening.

"Holy Jumpin' Christ!" Johnny said. "We gotta get the hell out of here."

"That may be easier said than done," Jay said. "We just might get shot on sight. Those cowboys I left over at the Hinds' cabin are pumped up and trigger-happy. By now, if it's gone down like I think it has, they've figured out they screwed up bad. Let's do a little careful reconnoitering and try to work up some assessment of this situation."

"I suggest we stay together," Lew said.

"Yeah," Johnny agreed. "This is real bad, people."

"And it could get a lot worse," Jay said, a grim note behind his words.

When the faint sounds of the twin battles reached the twelve mercenaries, they immediately hit the ground and stayed low.

"What the hell is all that?" Bobcat Blake threw the question out.

"It's gunfire," Ike Dover said with a smile. "How soon we forget."

"Knock it off," Mike ordered. "Two major firefights, about two miles from us in either direction."

"Do we assemble our heavy weapons and make a stand?" Al asked with a grin, pointing to his cased tranquilizer gun.

"That's not funny," Billy Antrim replied. "We could be in real deep shit here."

Mike Tuttle's face held an odd expression. Nick Sharp picked up on it. "What are you thinking, Mike?"

"I am thinking that we abort this mission and get the hell out of here," the team leader said. "We cache these side arms and dart guns and split up into pairs. We'll attract less attention that way. We make our way back to the vehicles and head for motels. We don't return until this . . . whatever it is . . . is over."

"I agree," John Webb said.

"I will stay," George Eagle Dancer said. "The rest of you go."

"That's not smart, George," Mike told him.

"Go," George said. And with that, he stood up and walked off, leaving his cased tranquilizer gun on the ground, hidden from view by weeds.

"Strange duck," Nick remarked.

"Let's get gone," Mike said. "George can take care of himself."

Darry whistled for Pete and Repeat, and they came running across the clearing to flop down beside him in the timber. Darry looked behind him and motioned for the women to come forward.

"The cabin is secure," he told them. "But I don't know for how long. Both of you wait right here with the dogs. I'll get your gear and some of mine and we'll clear out. The feds are sure to visit this place. Stay put."

He was back in less than fifteen minutes, after turning the horses loose and gathering up some supplies. "The shooting over there"—he pointed—"came from around Jody Hinds' cabin. Jody's got a bad temper. He's no troublemaker, but he is a man that is best left alone. If the feds struck his cabin—although I don't know why they would—he put up a fight. Bet on it. Let's go check it out.

Now listen to me, ladies. You stay behind me, and you do exactly what I tell you to do, the instant I tell you to do it.''

"This is the work of our government," Stormy said. Darry suspected she was still in some sort of mild shock. "We're not supposed to be afraid of our own *government!*"

"Wake up and smell the coffee, Stormy," Ki said, adjusting the straps on her pack. "We just witnessed federal agents shooting down unarmed men and women. Worse yet, they know I got part of it on film. You think those hot dog cowboys are going to risk, at the least, loss of careers, and at the worst, long prison sentences or maybe the gas chamber? No way. They've got to shut us up, Stormy. And that means they've got to kill us."

Stormy shook her head. "That's . . . unconscionable. It's unthinkable. I . . .'' Her voice trailed off, and her eyes glazed over. She looked lost.

Ki slapped her. It was a hard, open-handed blow that rocked the taller woman and left a red mark on the side of her face. Stormy's eyes flashed.

"Don't lose it now, Stormy," Ki said. "I'm sorry I had to do that, but you've got to come back to reality and stay with it. You've got to understand that we're in greater danger here in the good ol' U S of A than we ever were in Bosnia or Beirut or Central America or Somalia. Those goddamn government jerks out there''—she waved a hand—"are hunting us. And what they've got in mind sure as hell isn't flowers and chocolates. They're going to kill us, Stormy. We're going to have a tragic accident out here in the wilderness. So you get mad, Stormy. Right now. You get mad and you stay mad. And we'll stay alive and blow the lid off this thing. Okay?''

Stormy slowly nodded her head. "Okay, Ki. Okay. Let's do it.''

"Let's get out of here," Darry said. "I think we've worn our welcome a little thin.''

11

"We don't have any choice in the matter," the team leader of this op was saying. "I don't like it any better than any of you. But we just don't have a choice."

"Makes me sick," one agent muttered.

"You want to go to prison?" another asked.

"What about the prisoners?" a young federal marshal asked.

"It's their word against ours," an older man said, walking up. "Who the hell is going to believe anything they say?"

"Wilson said that Jody Hinds guy got away."

"He won't last long. I just spoke with Washington and told them what happened out here." He smiled. "Sort of. I told them about our own dead and got a free hand in dealing with this situation. As for the others . . . we got this area blanketed. We'll find them."

"Max?" a young agent said. "What if . . . ?"

The team leader cut him off. "There is no 'what if,' Jerry. It's the only way. As soon as those reporters understand what we can do to them, they'll hand over the film. We can intimidate the guy with them—we're running a make on Darry Ransom right now. Don't worry. We've got a hundred and twenty-five people out there looking and more coming in. The roads are being watched. It's just a matter of time before we find them."

"Santo's body was just found," the call reached the knot of agents. "He took one through the armpit. Whoever did it took his weapon."

Max Vernon kicked at a rotten limb on the ground. "Five people dead. Two missing." Jack Speed and Kathy Owens had not been found. "All because of a bunch of goddamn survivalist crap." He cussed for a moment. "Has that nose candy arrived yet?"

"We got three kilos of cocaine coming in, Max. Be here late this afternoon."

"All right. Peter, you tell those guys over at the Hinds' cabin to leave everything just as it is. Preserve the scene. Have all the weapons in this camp been found?"

"We think so." He was wrong. There was a hidden cache of weapons and ammo and food and water under the floor of the barracks where Sam Parish and his people were being held. "Pretty standard stuff. Mini-14s and AR-15s. Nothing illegal," he added softly.

"Hey, fuck that!" Max yelled. "These people are subversives and seditionists. We were sent in to secure this area, and by God that's what we're going to do."

Sam Parish and those able to fight had opened the cache of weapons and armed themselves. Very heavily.

"Shirley just died, Sam," a woman told him, pulling the blanket up to cover the dead woman's face.

"Those ass-kissin' government goons!" Sam cussed softly. "They'll get theirs. This is war, people. War!"

Outside, the agents were getting into gear and preparing to move out. Twenty-five teams of five each. Every road and trail had been blocked off. There was no escape for those inside the armed circle. Rick Battle knew nothing about what was going on. A young couple had been reported lost in the far northern reaches of his area, and he was up there, directing a search party of volunteers.

* * *

"Oh, my God!" Kevin whispered. He lay on the crest of a small hill, overlooking Jody's cabin. He could make out what he thought was the body of Linda, sprawled in the doorway. The bodies of four dead men were lined up in a row in the front of the house, covered with ponchos. Using the binoculars taken from the man he had shot, Kevin pulled the scene closer.

It was Linda lying still in the doorway.

"Shit!" Kevin said.

He backed away and headed for his cabin and his friends. He had a sinking feeling in the pit of his stomach that his family and their friends were next on the list. He also knew who had done this: government agents. Kevin had been aware that he and his friends had been under surveillance for some time.

On the trail back to what was left of the commune, Kevin carefully wiped his prints off of the weapon taken from the dead agent, and the binoculars, and cached them. Then he returned to his cabin and broke the news to his wife and daughter and his friends.

"Hello, the cabin!" Dr. Ray Collier called.

The remaining rubber raft had been pulled onto shore, tents pitched, and a small fire built. Dr. Collier knew there was a hiking trail that ran along the river bluffs here, and hoped to find someone who could point the way to the ranger station, some miles away. Then he'd spotted what appeared to be a cabin set back several thousand feet from the river. What Ray was not aware of was that the hiking trail had been closed and this area sealed off by federal agents.

Dr. Collier looked rough. He had not shaved in several days, and his clothing was wrinkled and, unfortunately for him, army surplus. Ray Collier was not a small man.

He was a shade over six feet and through regular exercise was in very good physical condition. While normally a very even-tempered and easy-going man, Dr. Collier could, when angered, have a very short fuse. He played football in high school and college, had his share of fist-fights—until he learned that it was very unwise to strike a solid object with one's bare hand. Lots of little bones in there that were easily broken and very painful and slow in healing. For the past fifteen years, Dr. Collier had been working out twice a week in an unarmed combat class. He was black belt certified. But he had not deliberately hurt anyone in two decades.

All that was about to change.

"Get on the goddamn ground, you asshole!" the hard voice sprang out from a shed beside the cabin. "We're federal officers."

Ray looked around him. "I beg your pardon?"

"I said, belly down on the ground, you ass-wipe! Do it, goddamn you!"

Dr. Collier's fuse suddenly shortened and was lit. His eyes found the cammie-clad and ski-masked man, holding what appeared to be some sort of machine gun in his black-leather gloved hands, and he very slowly and evenly said, "I don't know what kind of game this is, buddy. And I don't believe you're federal officers. I don't have very much money on me, but you're welcome to it."

Ray did not see the man rush up behind him. He heard him just at the last second and started to turn. Then his world went black as the butt of a rifle slammed into the back of his head, and Dr. Collier fell to the ground, unconscious.

"I say," Nick Sharp said with his best smile, approaching the five-man team with his hands raised. "What is all this to-do about?"

"Get on the goddamn ground, buddy."

"Oh, I think not," Nick said. "I've done nothing wrong."

"You either get on the ground or we'll put you on the ground. Both of you."

Nick and Dennis Tipton exchanged glances. The federal agents had no way of knowing it, but they were about to tangle with one of the toughest men on the face of the earth. As a matter of fact, they were about to anger a number of the toughest men on the face of the earth.

Nick Sharp and Dennis Tipton had been friends for years. Each of them had enlisted in the French Foreign Legion before his sixteenth birthday. After serving their hitches, Nick had joined Britain's SAS, and Dennis had returned to the States and joined the American Army, finally ending his career as a sergeant in 7th Special Forces. They had spent the last ten years as mercenaries, fighting all over the world. They were extremely difficult to impress, and these agents standing before them did not inspire much confidence in them at all. They looked to be sloppy in appearance and handled their weapons very loosely and unprofessionally.

"Might I ask why we are being so rudely accosted?" Nick inquired.

A federal marshal and a young BATF man both cursed, then made another very bad mistake. Their first mistake was in sticking guns in the faces of men who had done nothing wrong (that tended to piss off a certain type of person), their second mistake was in cursing the men (that also tended to piss off a certain type of person), and then they got too close to the pair of mercenaries.

The federal marshal suddenly found himself unable to breathe because of a crushed larynx, and the BATF agent could not see because Nick had used his fingers to blind him. The other three feds had only a micro second to react, and they blew that chance.

When the smoke cleared away from the guns that had

five seconds before been in the hands of federal officers, Nick looked at Dennis with a slight smile on his lips. "I say, Denny, do you suppose the shit's in the soup now?"

Dennis laughed. "I reckon it is, Nick."

"Help me!" the blinded agent cried.

"Not likely," Nick told him; then he and Dennis took all the weapons and walked away.

"We stay here," Darry told the women.

"Here" was a cave midway up a rocky ridge, the front of the cave brush-covered. Even people who had lived in the area for years did not know of its existence. The cave wandered for about a hundred yards, ending at a small pool of cold, pure spring water.

Stormy and Ki sank wearily to the cave floor. Pete and Repeat drank from the pool of water and then returned to lie down beside the women. Darry bellied down at the pool and drank (neither woman could see that he lapped at the water like an animal), then filled the canteens and went back to the mouth of the cave.

"I wonder what that brief bit of shooting just a few moments ago was all about?" Stormy asked.

"Bad luck for somebody," Darry replied.

"What if they bring in tracking dogs?" Ki asked, after taking a sip of water.

Darry smiled. "They won't bother us." He uncased his binoculars, slipped outside, and bellied down behind the thick brush that covered the front of the cave entrance. He wriggled through the brush and scanned all the terrain that he could see. He could spot nothing. He slipped back into the cave and sat down.

"What do we do now?" Stormy asked.

"We wait."

* * *

"Oh, Jesus Christ, Richard," the agent said, after taking Ray's wallet out of the small plastic bag Ray used to keep it dry. "The guy's a doctor from Los Angeles."

"He should have followed orders," Richard said. "Done what he was told to do. Besides, what is a doctor from L.A. doing out here, dressed as he is. Fuck him. He's a goddamn survivalist. He's tied in somehow with all these armed groups living and training out here."

"Ransom's gone," an agent called from the front porch of the cabin. "Looks like he grabbed some supplies and split."

Richard nodded. "Let's get out of here. We've got to find that damned reporter and get that film."

"What about the doctor?"

"Leave him. He didn't see our faces."

"I'm blind!" the agent screamed into his handy-talkie. "I'm blind. All the rest of my team is dead. Come in, come in."

"Hang on, Ron," the welcome reply finally came out of the tiny speaker. "We're on the way. Just don't move from your location. Who did it, Ron?"

"I don't know," Ron said, calming down. "Two guys. Bad-looking men. One of them spoke with an English accent."

The rescue team members exchanged glances. Two guys took out five agents? Surely they must have ambushed them?

Army, Navy, and CIA came up on the body lying a few feet off the trail. "I saw this guy over at Darry Ransom's cabin," Johnny McBroon said, kneeling down beside the body. "Said he was a government agent."

Johnny removed the wallet and opened it. "He's National Security Agency. Al Reaux."

"Don't shoot, boys." The voice spun the men around, guns in their hands. "The man stood with his hands in the air. I'm with Air Force Intelligence. Pete Cooper. ID's in my back pocket."

That was verified, and the four spooks stood in silence for a few heartbeats.

Pete said, "I came up on the body just before you guys arrived. There isn't a mark on him. But I think his neck is broken."

"His weapon's gone," Johnny said. "Al seemed to me a pretty tough customer. I wonder who took him out?"

Jody Hinds.

Wild with grief over the loss of his wife and friends, Jody was killing mad and on the prod. He'd come up on Al's tracks and trailed him. When Al stopped to rest, Jody had slipped up behind him and snapped his neck as easily as breaking a toothpick. Jody had been part of a very elite air force group, innocuously called Combat Controllers, and he'd been well trained in the art of unarmed combat.

Jody had made his peace with God and was fully prepared to die. But he was going to take out a lot of federal agents before he met the Man.

Just before twilight darkened the land, Sam Parish and his bunch made their move. They suckered the guards in close and poured on the lead from automatic weapons. They left no one alive. They quickly prepared packs and made ready to take off. Racists and separatists they might be, but they were well trained and had planned for such an eventuality.

"You all know what to do," Sam told them. "We don't have a snowball's chance in hell of getting out of here alive. By now the government is pouring in agents. There'll be several hundred of those bastards in this area by dawn. We go down shooting, people. They'll not get away with this cover-up. Let's make damn sure of that. Good luck and God be with you. Power to the white race!''

The others shouted their slogan and split up, taking off in all directions.

"Mother! Come quick!" Paul shouted down from the bluff. "It's Daddy. He's been hurt."

When Ray Collier had not returned, Paul had gone looking for him. Karen grabbed the first aid kit and took off at a run, Terri right behind her.

Ray was groaning and trying to sit up when Karen reached his side. "You know better, Ray," she admonished him. "Just lie still and let me take a look at you."

While his wife bathed the small cut on the back of his head and then applied antiseptic, Ray told them what had happened. As much as he knew.

"Federal officers?" Karen questioned. "That can't be. They wouldn't do something like this."

Neither mother nor father saw the look that passed between brother and sister. The kids were much more "with it" than their parents. They both had friends whose homes had been raided by cops, local and federal, looking for drugs in the much overused and abused "Anonymous Tip" bullshit in the nation's so-called War On Drugs. In the cases that Terri and Paul knew about, no drugs were found, but the house had been wrecked by the cops: stuffing pulled out of sofas and chairs, commodes torn loose, paneling ripped down, mattresses cut open, and pistols and cash taken. Paul and Terri were rapidly joining the ever-growing ranks of people who distrusted the cops and had absolutely no use for federal agents.

"I lost consciousness more than once," Ray said. "Drifted in and out. I heard snatches of conversation. I really believe they were federal officers. They were talking about survivalists. There must be some sort of survivalist camp close by, and they thought I was one of them.''

Karen picked up her father's wallet and plastic bag from the ground where it had been contemptuously tossed. ''They didn't take any of your money, Daddy.''

''This is outrageous!'' Karen said, the attorney in her surfacing. ''By God, somebody is going to answer in court for this.''

''It happens all the time, Mother,'' Paul said softly.

Ray sat up and looked at his son. ''What do you mean, Paul? 'It happens all the time'?''

The young man shrugged his shoulders. ''Just what I said, Dad. About fifty or so percent of the paper money now circulating is tainted, to some degree or the other, with cocaine residue. A lot of people who carry large amounts of cash have been stopped and searched in airports and had their money seized. Sometimes they get it back; sometimes they don't. The way I understand it, the cops don't have to prove you were going to make a buy; you have to prove you weren't. Innocent people have died from heart attacks when the cops kicked in their front doors in the middle of the night and manhandled them. All in the name of law and justice . . .''

The parents were both staring in disbelief at their son. Karen had not practiced criminal law in years, but until she specialized, she had worked all sorts of cases for a few years.

''The people who choose to live out here in the wilderness,'' Paul continued, waving a hand at Darry's cabin. ''Say . . . they're racist or just believe in anything that goes against what the current Washington administration believes in, why, they get investigated by government agents. Sometimes the federal agents kill them.''

''Kill them?'' Ray questioned, sitting on the ground. ''*Kill them!*''

''Sure,'' Terri picked it up. ''I've seen specials on TV about that. There are survivalists all over the nation, arm-ing themselves and stockpiling food and water and medicines and stuff like that. The government is going apecrap about it.''

''Why?'' Karen asked, enthralled and amazed that her children were so well-informed on a subject she knew practically nothing about.

''I guess the government is scared these people will start some sort of revolution,'' the young woman answered. ''But they seem to forget that this nation was built out of revolution. What's the difference between then and now?''

12

Kathy had come out of it with a raging headache. Using water from her canteen, she cleaned her slight head wound and then went to work on Jack. The bullet had gone right through the fleshy part of Jack's shoulder, and the bleeding had stopped. That was good. She bathed the wound, front and back, and applied antiseptic from her small first aid pouch, then bandaged the wound. Jack was awake, his eyes shiny with pain.

"Did we really see what I think we did?" Jack asked.

"We sure did. We've got to get out of here and report. This is a cluster-fuck, Jack."

With a small groan of pain, Jack got to his boots and fumbled around for his compass. He took their bearings and pointed. "That way. But we'll never make it to our camp before full dark. We'll find a place to hole up."

"That woman back at the cabin, Jack. She wasn't armed."

"I know it. Those guys killed her in cold blood."

"Some of those men back there were Bureau people," she reminded him.

"I know that, too."

"What are we going to do?"

Jack shook his head. "I don't know, Kathy. I just don't know."

* * *

George Eagle Dancer found the tracks of Darry, the two women, and the dogs. But the animal tracks were slightly different from those of a dog. Hybrids, George thought. Part wolf. He followed the trail until it grew too dark to see; then George ate from a packet of MREs, wrapped a blanket around him, and settled in for the night.

Johnny McBroon, Pete Cooper, Lew Waters, and Jay Gilmore settled in for a cold night after eating field rations and washing them down with water from their canteens. They did not dare risk a fire for fear it would draw gunfire. They had heard about the escape of Sam Parish and about thirty of his followers over a small receiver Jay had in his pack. Nighttime was not the time to go blundering around in the wilderness.

Kevin and his friends bunkered in with lanterns and candles out and weapons ready. They had no way of knowing what the night would bring with it . . . but they were ready for trouble.

Paul Collier, after helping his father down the bluff and to his tent, went back up to Darry's cabin and found a Winchester lever action rifle chambered for .22 magnum. He rummaged around and found three boxes of ammunition and a cartridge belt. "If I can't get the rifle back to you, mister, I'll pay you for it, and that's a promise," he whispered to the empty cabin.

He filled the cartridge belt and buckled it around his waist, pulling his shirttail out to cover it. He wrapped the rifle in a piece of torn tarp and hid it in the rocks halfway down the bluff. Paul was still in the Boy Scouts—although he seldom went to meetings anymore—and he had been trained in how to handle a rifle. He had made up his mind that nobody was going to rough up his dad again. Nobody.

Nick Sharp and Dennis Tipton caught up with the other team members and told them what had taken place back in the now bloody little spring-flowered meadow where the federal agents had confronted them.

"The hell you say!" Bobcat Blake said. "Did the bastards give you a reason why they were bracing you?"

"Not a clue," Nick replied. "They were just arrogant and rude as hell."

"Give me that H&K," Ike Dover said, holding his hand out for the 9mm submachine gun taken from a dead federal agent. "Nobody runs me out of a place."

"You guys serious about this?" Mike asked. "You're blowing off a lot of money—not to mention risking your lives and a long prison term." He nor any of the others mentioned the dead agents, for they simply didn't care about them.

Mess With The Best And Die Like The Rest was their philosophy.

"Fuck it!" Joel Bass said. "I don't like federal turds waving guns in the faces of my friends."

John Webb said, "Let's go pick up some more weapons. We're going to need them if we're planning on starting a war with the feds."

Miles Burrell nodded his head in agreement.

"Oh, hell with it, then!" Mike said. "Count me in. Finding a good war nowadays is getting harder and harder anyway."

* * * *

"We have any press in on this?" Max Vernon was asked by a man from the Justice Department who had just flown in from Washington.

"Not a peep, sir."

The official stared hard at Max. "I find all of this very hard to believe."

"It's the truth, sir. Every word of it. Look." He walked over to a camp table that had been set up and lifted the edge of a poncho. "Three keys, sir. Three keys of high-grade cocaine. We found these in Stormy's camp, tucked away in her things. We found what was left of a laboratory in a shed behind the cabin belonging to a Jody Hinds. He burned the lab during the shoot-out." A shed had been burned, but Jody hadn't set it on fire. "We're sure that Agent John Santo was killed by another member of this dope ring. A hippie-type name of Kevin Carmouche and two of his friends. We've got his place surrounded and will move against him tomorrow."

"Who is this Darry Ransom person?"

"We're not sure. He may be the go-between."

"Any idea who ambushed those agents and blinded Ron?"

"Friends of the hippies running this dope operation, we're sure. We don't know if they're still in the valley, or managed to slip out. We think they're still in the area."

"God, this is touchy, Max. Real touchy. Ms. Knight is a big-time TV journalist. There isn't a blemish on her anywhere. Even in college she was known as unapproachable when it came to drugs. And Ki Nichols is the same. Highly respected camera-person; won lots of industry awards."

"They're dopers and worse, sir."

"Worse?"

"They were fraternizing with a known and very dangerous survivalist group. We have pictures of her laughing and big time buddy-buddying with Sam Parish. She was the guest of honor at the cookout when we arrived and they opened fire on us.''

The official nodded his understanding. ''Max, we don't want another screw-up like Waco. We can't stand the heat. No play on words intended.''

''I understand, sir. There will be no mistakes on this one. We've got them cold. We have the evidence that will stand up in court.''

''How many civilian dead so far?''

''Eleven.''

The official winced at that. ''Any kids?''

''No, sir.''

''Thank God for small favors.''

''Yes, sir.''

''I've got to get back to Washington. Max, you're in charge. I don't want any screw-ups. You understand?''

''I understand.''

''I want this operation neatly wrapped up with a nice big pretty bow on top. The evidence looks good. Wrap it up, Max.''

''Consider it done, sir.''

When Darry was certain the two women were sound asleep and not likely to awaken until their bodies had been refreshed by rest, he stepped outside of the cave and became his Other. He padded silently down the ridge until he smelled man-scent. He stood for a moment, staring and smelling the night. He walked on silent paws to stand a few yards from the sleeping George Eagle Dancer. He sensed this man was not a federal agent. His manner of dress and hair style was all wrong, and he wasn't pretty enough to be a fed. This man was a warrior, a hunter of men. But Darry sensed that this man was no enemy of his.

If he had been, Darry could have easily killed him with one crushing snap from powerful jaws. Darry did not like to kill, and seldom did in his Other form; only a few times in this century. But sometimes it was necessary.

Darry let him sleep and moved on through the night, running effortlessly and soundlessly. He scented blood and moved in that direction. He stood on the crest of a small slope and looked down at the two FBI agents who had visited his cabin, Jack Speed and Kathy Owens. The man had been wounded in the shoulder. But by whom?

He did not know.

Darry moved on, running for several hours, circling the area. He found the sleeping mercenaries and a dozen or so camps of federal people—the smell of nervous sweat and fear and indecision was strong there. He found several camps of Sam Parish's people—the smell of sweat and hate was strong there.

Darry went to his cabin and knew instantly someone had been there. A rifle was gone. He picked up the scent and loped over to the river bluffs and looked down. A family unit was sleeping on the flats. He scented out where his rifle was hidden and left it.

Everywhere he'd been that night stank of trouble. It hung in the night air like a strong poison.

Tragedy everywhere, Darry thought, as he began the run back to the cave.

Max Vernon learned early the next morning that he'd lost two more agents during the night. Someone had slipped up on them while they slept and cut their throats with a very sharp and a very large knife. Boot prints showed the man to be big, about two hundred pounds. The cabins of Kevin Carmouche and his family and friends were surrounded by dozens of agents, and they could not have broken out to do this. Max just thought Kevin and his friends were trapped. Even a rabbit had more than one hole, and Kevin had had more than twenty years to dig his.

"Jody Hinds," a man said.

"Yeah," Max grunted. "Jody Hinds. Did we get anything back from Records on this guy?"

"Air Force Commandos, among other things," Max was informed. "Silver Star in 'Nam. The guy is good." He did not add what many of the agents already knew: Jody Hinds was clean, he'd never even received so much as a traffic ticket in his life, and he certainly didn't do drugs.

"The son of a bitch is not 'good,' Johnson," Max snapped at the man. "He's killed federal agents."

"We started it," another agent muttered, being very careful that Max Vernon did not overhear his comment. He wished desperately that he could find a way out of this ever-growing mess. But he was in too deep for that. Just too goddamned deep to get out of it.

Most of the now several hundred agents in the area had been helicoptered in. The people in the tiny surrounding towns (and they were miles away from the hunt area) knew absolutely nothing about the massive manhunt going on. When Rick Battle returned from the north, having found the missing young couple, he was astonished to find the road leading to his station closed and blocked and guarded by federal agents. He had a hell of time just getting past them. Then he found his station being used as a command post.

"What the hell is going on?" Rick demanded.

"You don't have a need to know," he was bluntly informed. "Pack up a few things and go find a motel to live in until this is over."

Rick kept his cool . . . barely. "I will find out what is going on," he said tersely. "One way or the other. This is my station, this is my area and you don't have the authority to order me out. You might be able to *get* it. But until you do, I stay."

"Mr. Battle," another man said, stepping in to defuse the anger-building situation. "I just got here a few hours ago. So I really don't know all the particulars of this operation. But I'll tell you what I do know."

Rick had not noticed a man and a woman, both neatly dressed in civilian clothing, standing off to one side. The man was a senior inspector and the woman an experienced special agent from the FBI. They were from the FBI's Internal Affairs Division. And as far as they were concerned, this whole operation was stinking to high heaven. They sensed something was very wrong. Now they just had to prove it.

The newly arrived man talked, Rick listened, and by the time the federal man had finished, Rick was flabbergasted. "You're not serious!" he finally found his voice. "Don't you think I know the people who live in my district? I've had them all checked out. Every one of them. They're clean. They're good folks. You *killed* Linda Hinds? Jesus Christ! Have you lost your minds? There is no cocaine lab around here. I've been to Jody's place dozens of times. I've been in that shed. I was there about two weeks ago. He tans hides and does taxidermy work out there."

"Mr. Battle," the fed said. "Just calm down, sir."

"Calm down?" Rick shouted. "Calm down's ass! You raided his place and killed his wife, his sister-in-law, and her boyfriend and you want me to fucking *calm down!*"

The inspector and the special agent exchanged glances.

Rick caught his breath and was off again. "You're going to raid the cabins of Kevin Carmouche and his friends? Why? They haven't done anything. They've been here for years and done nothing but good all the while. They've gone on search-and-rescue missions, they've fought forest fires, and never asked for a dime for doing it. Stormy and her camera-person are here to do a story. They interviewed me; they interviewed Darry Ransom. They're not involved in any dope ring. There is no dope ring around here. I knew Sam Parish and his bunch were under loose surveillance, but hell, they haven't done anything either, except hold some rather weird views. I don't believe they opened fire on you people. But it might have been the other way around.''

Again, the inspector and the special agent exchanged glances.

''What the hell are you implying, Ranger?''

''You figure it out,'' Rick told him, then spun around and walked off to his living quarters.

Inspector Henry ''Hank'' Wallace and Special Agent Carol Murphy left to change clothes. They had a lot of work to do. Out in the field.

''Hank Wallace is here,'' Max Vernon was informed.

''Damn!'' Max said. ''Is that bitch Carol with him?''

''Yes.''

''They smell something. Attack that goddamn hippie commune. Do it right now.''

''Yes, sir.''

By now there were over four hundred federal agents involved, very nearly a mob. Over a hundred agents from several federal agencies attacked the cabins at the old hippie commune. That proved to be a very costly mistake. A dozen agents went down, dead or seriously wounded, in the first fifteen seconds of the attack. Kevin had told Vince and Todd that the agents would be in protective gear. So the men and their wives and kids all went for head shots. Living in the wilderness, and having to rely on game for much of their food, all were expert shots, as the agents tragically discovered almost immediately. To compound the tragedy, more than half of the agents now involved were under the impression this was a legitimate operation, and had no idea it was a government foul-up and attempted cover-up and that they were attacking innocent men and women and kids.

After the first attack was thrown back, the men sent their wives and kids out the back, using tunnels they'd dug years before, back when the peace and love and hippie movement was heavily infiltrated with government agents looking for members of the SDS or the Weathermen. But the reports detailing the construction plans of communes had long since been destroyed after the movement died out years back.

"We'll hold our fire while you get your wounded out of there!" Kevin shouted from his cabin. "Go on, do it. We won't fire on you if you won't fire on us."

"What the hell?" a federal marshal muttered to a friend. "That doesn't sound like hard-core drug dealers to me."

"Something's very strange about all this," a Bureau man said to a buddy who was with the BATF.

"It stinks," the Alcohol, Tobacco, and Firearms man replied. "I have not seen one word of intel on these people. And I have to say that Max Vernon is unstable."

"I agree. But you didn't hear that from me."

"Then how in the hell did he get where he is?"

The Bureau man grunted. "Luck and ass-kissing."

"You believe that crap about Stormy Knight and her cameraman?"

"No. And it's camera-person."

The BATF man grinned. "Right." His grin faded. "Then what are we doing here?"

The team leader of this unit of the FBI's Hostage Rescue Team looked over at the two men. "What are you guys suggesting?"

"It's a set-up, a fuck-up, and a cover-up," his colleague said bluntly.

The TL gave that some thought. Then he shook his head. "No way. We wouldn't fuck up that bad. We're under orders to shoot to kill."

"Yeah," the special agent said drily. "Just takin' orders. And how many times have you heard that?"

Jack Speed and Kathy Owens knew what they should do, but didn't know how to go about doing it. They quickly realized they were caught up smack in the middle of a free-fire zone. They didn't know code words or passwords and had no safe way of learning them. During the shooting, the wounding, the frantic crawling and the dragging of Kathy, then tumbling down into the ravine, they had lost their ID folders and radios.

"We're fucked!" Kathy said.

Jack smiled through the burning pain in his wounded shoulder. "This is no time to be thinking of sex, Kathy."

Three men suddenly appeared at the top of the knoll. "Freeze, goddamn you!" one shouted. "We're federal agents."

"So are we," Jack said.

"Sure," another man said, unable to see how Jack and Kathy were dressed due to the shadows where they lay. "And Santa Claus humps reindeer. Get your hands up."

Kathy raised both her hands, and Jack held up his one good arm.

"Both hands, goddammit!"

"I can't. I've been wounded. Look, I've got my wallet right here. I have ID." Jack stuck his hand inside his jumpsuit, and the third man on the knoll shot him.

Screaming her rage, Kathy pulled iron and emptied a full clip into the men, killing two and wounding the third. He dropped his M-16 and went staggering off, holding his bleeding neck.

Kathy turned to Jack. But his face was covered with blood, and she could not find a pulse. She cussed and then scrambled up the hill, retrieving the M-16 and a magazine pouch from a dead agent. She picked up a handy-talkie, only to find that one of her bullets had shattered the transceiver.

"You stupid, cowboy, hot-dog, trigger-happy sons of bitches!" she cussed the dead men. Then, fighting back tears, she started trailing the man who had killed her partner.

A team of federal agents spotted the mercenaries moving across a meadow and, believing they were part of Sam Parish's bunch, opened fire on them.

Al Jenkins went down, a bullet taking him in the center of his forehead.

The mercenaries suddenly vanished in the tall grass and brush, and the killing stalk began. The federal officers would lose.

13

"We stay right here," Darry told the women, after hearing gunfire coming from all directions. "I have a hunch that the worst is yet to come."

"I just wish I knew what was going on?" Stormy bitched.

"The both of you are wanted for questioning about drug trafficking and subversion," Darry informed the women.

Stormy and Ki sat on the cave floor, on their bedrolls, and stared at him in utter disbelief. Stormy found her voice first. "You have got to be kidding!" she exploded, waving her hands in the air.

Darry shook his head. "No. I heard some agents talking last night."

"You went out there last night?" Ki questioned.

Darry smiled. "Yes."

Stormy read the smile accurately. "But not in human form." It was not a question.

"You have a very vivid imagination, Stormy," Darry said, not losing his smile.

"What about this drug crap?" Ki said, anger in her voice. "And subversion? That's nonsense."

"Sure it is. But they've got three keys of cocaine to back up their story. They found it in your camp."

"They found *shit!*" Stormy practically shouted the

words. "I've never used dope in my life. I don't even like to take a pill for headaches."

"Oh, you don't have to convince me. I believe you." Again, that odd grin. "But now, ladies, you can share a sensation with me. Tell me: how does it feel to be hunted like an animal?"

Sam Parish had taken transceivers from the dead agents in his camp and passed them around. He and his people could now listen to everything that was going on and stay one step ahead of the feds.

Sam Parish had talked about someday overthrowing the government of the United States. But like so many of his ilk, all that had been so much hot air. However, the government did take those types of remarks quite seriously and had sent a man in to infiltrate the Citizen's Defense League. Sam had never quite trusted the infiltrator and had not told him about the cache of weapons the CDL had used in their escape. The infiltrator had feigned being shot when the attack started and was now (after having his butt chewed on by Max Vernon during a debriefing) once more a part of the agent team searching for the CDL.

But he wouldn't be for long, and neither would the men and women with him. The agents had made the mistake of attacking Nick Sharp and his mercenary team, and they now found themselves encircled by the highly experienced group; and the noose was slowly tightening.

Max Vernon was about to lose another team of agents.

"You were attacked by men claiming to be federal officers?" Henry Wallace asked Dr. Ray Collier.

"Yes," the doctor replied. "I've still got a knot on the back of my head where one of them struck me."

Carol Murphy looked and nodded her head. "He took a hard lick, Hank. No doubt about that."

The inspector sighed heavily. ''I apologize for that, Doctor. I know that doesn't help much, but I want you to know the Bureau is not in the habit of assaulting innocent people.''

Ray held up a hand. ''I don't know if these people were from the FBI. They were all wearing camouflage and ski masks. I thought they were outlaws.''

Carol shifted her gaze over to the doctor's son. She did not like the look in the young man's eyes. He was obviously angry clear through and clearly was capable of doing something very foolish if the rogue agents returned. She looked at the doctor. ''Do you have any weapons in camp, Doctor Collier?''

''What business is that of yours?'' Karen snapped the question.

''None, Mrs. Collier,'' Carol quickly assured her. ''None at all. I was just curious.''

''We don't own any type of firearm,'' Dr. Collier stepped in.

''But all that is probably about to change,'' Karen said.

The doctor cut his eyes to his wife, not quite sure what to make of that.

But Henry knew. He'd seen it before . . . too many times of late. Another law-abiding citizen getting ready to arm himself because of the excesses of the federal government. ''Might I make a suggestion, Doctor?''

''Certainly.''

''Move your camp on several miles. Get out of this area for safety's sake.''

''I think that is a very good idea,'' Dr. Collier said.

''I don't,'' Karen said. ''I like it right here.''

''Me, too,'' Paul said. ''Why should we move? We haven't done anything.''

''There is a manhunt going on in this area,'' Carol pointed out. ''It just isn't safe to stay here.''

''I've already discovered that,'' the doctor said drily. ''Rather painfully. But we'll consider your suggestion.''

"Please do," Hank said. "If at all possible, we'll be checking on you from time to time, Doctor. Tell me, since you've been here, have you seen the owner of that cabin set back from the bluffs?"

The doctor shook his head. "No. Since the, ah, incident, we've seen no one."

"Be careful," Carol warned the family. "Very careful."

And keep your powder dry, young Paul thought, remembering a line from an old western movie.

Kathy found the agent she'd been trailing. He was lying dead, having bled to death from the neck wounds she'd inflicted with her 9mm. She did not know the man, and as she looked down at him, she felt nothing. She searched the body looking for ID, and found it. BATF. She tossed the ID by the side of the body and stood up, trying to get her bearings. With a sigh, Kathy realized she was as lost as she could be. She had absolutely no idea where she was.

She looked up at the leaden-colored and cloudy sky. She could not see the sun. She took the dead agent's canteen and water purification pills and walked on. She didn't realize it, but she was heading deeper into the wilderness, straight toward George Eagle Dancer, who was less than a half mile away.

Johnny McBroon, Pete Cooper, Lew Waters, and Jay Gilmore had found a secluded spot to make camp and stay put. A small spring was close by and all four men had had the forethought to carry emergency rations that would last them for a couple of days. They planned to sit this one out until the shooting stopped.

*   *   *

Jack Speed moaned and stirred and tried to sit up. He could not manage it. He had taken a bullet graze on the side of his head that had bled copiously and left him with a terrible headache, and another bullet had hit and gone through the meaty part of his wounded shoulder, exiting out his back, just under the collar bone.

Jack managed to claw and crawl his way to the top of the small knoll and was shocked to discover the bodies of two cammie-clad men. He did not know who he was, where he was, or what the hell had happened to him. He passed out between the bodies of the dead agents.

The mercenaries gathered up all the weapons and ammo of the dead agents, took their transceivers, and then buried the body of Al Jenkins. They left the bodies of the agents for the varmints and moved on. Their original mission was forgotten. This was personal now. They had been first accosted and then attacked, and one of their own was dead.

The ten highly skilled warriors moved out.

The war was on.

Rick Battle suited up in uniform and Smokey Bear ranger hat, provisioned up, made sure he had plenty of ammo for his side arm and rifle, and saddled up, over the protestations of several of the federal agents.

"Ranger, it's a war zone out there!" one said.

"By God, the people who live here didn't start it, now did they?"

The agent had no come-back to that.

Rick lifted the reins and rode out, his packhorse trailing on a lead rope.

*   *   *

George Eagle Dancer saw Kathy approaching and hit the ground. Several moments later she passed within only a few yards of him and was oblivious to his presence. George lay still and watched as a man seemed to spring out of nowhere and shout to the woman. The shape-shifter! he thought. He was one with the earth and I did not sense his closeness.

Kathy lifted her M-16.

"I'm friendly!" Darry shouted. "I mean you no harm. I am not armed. I have Stormy and Ki with me. They are as confused as to what is going on as I am."

Through the pain in her head (she still had a headache from the bullet graze), Kathy recognized Darry and breathed a sigh of relief.

"Has the whole damned world gone crazy?" she asked, walking toward him.

"I've seen it a lot crazier," Darry offered, with that strange, almost mystical smile.

"I don't know what that means, but we can pursue it later." She walked up to him. "Stormy and Ki with you?"

"Yes."

"Jack is dead."

He stared at her until she grew uncomfortable under his gaze. She got the strangest feeling that he was looking into her soul. But that was a crazy thought. She shook her head. "What is it?" she finally asked.

"Where did it happen?"

"With Jack?"

"Yes."

She pointed. "Over there. I have to admit, I'm lost."

"Easy to do out here. I knew the other agent was wounded, but I didn't know how seriously."

"How did you know?"

"I was there not too many hours ago, looking at the both of you. Come on. Let's get you settled. And your friend."

"My . . . friend? You were over there . . . *looking* at us?"

"Yes. Your friend is the Indian who is hiding in the rock and brush over there," Darry said, pointing.

"I don't know any Indians!"

George Eagle Dancer stood up. "I come as a friend," he called. "It was not that way originally, but I left the others. I want you to believe that."

"I believe you. But if I find you are lying, I'll kill you."

"I believe that, too, shape-shifter."

Kathy looked at Darry. "So you are . . ."

"We can talk about that later," Darry cut her off.

"He is immortal," George said. "My grandfather was a great medicine man. The last of his kind. When I returned to live on the reservation, he would tell me about the shape-shifter, the immortal who led many lives. The man who came from the east. The first white man to come to us. He was a mountain man, scout, gunfighter, soldier, and he was a good friend to the Indian. He has been called by many names. So many names that no one can remember them all."

Darry turned without replying, and the FBI agent and the mercenary looked at one another and then followed him up the hill.

In the cave, Darry did the introductions and then said, "I'll go see about your friend, Jack."

"I just told you, he's dead."

"Perhaps. Perhaps not. We'll see." He looked at George. "See that nothing happens to the ladies."

"I will do that." He smiled. "I almost said, 'be careful.' But what could harm you?"

Darry did not reply. He left the cave without another word.

Several miles away, Kevin Carmouche stood with his friends and looked down at the body of Vince Clayderman's wife, Anna. She had been shot in the back by a long-range shooter and managed to stagger on for several hundred yards before collapsing. Their fifteen-year-old son, Jerry, was fighting back tears as he stood beside his father.

"Go on," Kevin told the others. "I'll bury her."

"We can't take the time for that," Vince said. "The feds will be here any moment. They'll body-bag her. Anna would understand. We've got to get these kids clear and safe. Then we'll map out some tactics."

Still, no one made the first move to leave the body of Anna Clayderman.

"When we're sure the kids are safe, we'll take the fight to them," Todd said.

"Yeah," Vince said, his voice choked with emotion. "Those federal bastards want a war, we'll give them one."

But no federal agent had killed Anna. The shot had come from a member of Sam Parish's CDL.

The three young people could not hold back their tears, finally allowing their emotions to flow freely.

The Vietnam vets and what was left of their families turned away from the cooling body and slipped into the thick brush. Kevin took the drag, erasing all signs of their passing. The group was only about a half mile from the river and the camp of the Collier family.

"Tell Sam I got me one of them federal bastards!" Sid Dalton said. "It was a bitch agent."

"That was a damn good shot, Sid," a friend complimented him. "Had to be at least four hundred yards."

"I can't believe it," another CDL member said. "The war is really on. It's really on."

"Sam always said the day would come when we'd have to fight the government," Sid replied. "Now it's here." He slung his rifle. "Come on. God, guts, and guns took this country from the savages two hundred and fifty years ago. Now let's go take it back from the feds."

14

Rick Battle left the saddle a micro-second after the slug passed by his head, coming so close he could feel the heat from the lead. On the ground, he yelled, "Hold your fire, you trigger-happy hot dogs! I'm Ranger Battle. Doesn't this hat tell you anything? Who do you think I am, the reincarnation of Sergeant York?"

"Sorry," came the call. "We thought you were one of them."

"Who the hell is *them?*" Rick said, getting off the ground and brushing at his clothing. He began rounding up his spooked horses.

A man stepped out of the brush and walked up to him. "We just got in from the Los Angeles area last night. We were told this entire area is infested with armed radicals and survivalists and dopers." A dozen more agents left the brush to join him.

Rick was angry to the core. "You people better go easy with those triggers. There are a lot of good people living out here. There are campers and white water rafters. Jesus Christ! Are you going to shoot everybody you see?"

"Hey, Ranger!" the team leader of this particular bunch of feds flared. "We've lost half a dozen agents, at least, during this op. Anyone carrying a gun is suspect."

"You're crazy," Rick said bluntly. "Just plain nuts. Most of the people out here are armed. There is no law against it. The boundaries here are ill-defined. Some of this land is private; some is government-owned. A lot of it is leased to timber groups. Other parcels are under a ninety-nine-year lease to private citizens.''

"We've ordered everybody out," the TL said. "If they don't go, that's their problem."

"The government's gone crazy," Rick muttered, swinging into the saddle. He looked at the knot of heavily armed agents. "Let me tell you something, people. A lot of the men and women who live out here year-round are tough as wang leather. You point a gun at them, and they'll kill you. There are paths and trails leading into this area from three directions that you people couldn't cover if there were five hundred times your number in here. This is Thursday; starting late this afternoon, there'll be people from towns all around this area coming in here to fish and camp and boat and relax. And they won't be using the roads you've got blocked. They'll be backpacking and floating in. This is a *wilderness* area, people. Some of those coming in will be armed for self-protection. You shoot some private citizen, and I will personally come after you."

"Are you threatening us, Ranger?"

"No. I'm just telling you how the cow ate the cabbage, that's all. Now get out of my way, you assholes!"

Rick rode on, leaving behind him some angry and rather confused federal agents, who really did not know exactly what the hell was going on.

Just following orders.

Darry took his time getting to where he'd seen Jack and Kathy in the ravine, moving swiftly but carefully, utilizing every bit of cover he could find. He counted a dozen big transport helicopters circling to land as he made his way to the ravine. He was correct as he thought, Some of these agents are going to be shooting each other before this is over.

As the sun dropped to signal mid-afternoon, there were now more than six hundred federal agents in the area, with more coming in.

All of them just following orders.

"Hello the camp!" Kevin called to the Collier family camped on the riverbank. "Don't be afraid, we're friendly."

"That would be a novel experience," Dr. Collier called, his eyes taking in the young people with the group. "Come on down. We don't have much, but we'll share."

The remnants of the old hippie commune climbed down and introduced themselves. Kevin said, "We're not going to stay here. You'd be in serious trouble if we were found here. But you people better clear out of this area. The damn feds have gone crazy."

Ray pointed to a log. "Sit down, have some coffee and tell us what's going on."

"I'm an attorney," Karen said. "And I have seen just enough to know that our government is out of control. Consider yourselves represented."

"You might not want to do that once you've heard our story," Todd said.

"They killed my mother!" Jerry blurted out, once more close to tears.

"That settles it," Karen said. "Terri, get some cups and pour us coffee."

Darry found Jack and the dead agents. He found a pulse and then picked up the man and carried him about a quarter of a mile from the site before stretching him out on the ground and seeing to his wounds. Over the endless decades, Darry had seen and tended to all sorts of wounds, and he did not believe these to be serious; but they did need immediate care. He had a first aid kit back among his supplies, but out here, he more often than not used natural medicines to aid and promote healing.

Darry found a small spring and soaked his handkerchief and the one he'd removed from Jack's pocket in the cold water, then bathed the agent's face, removing all the dried and caked blood. The bullet had cut a groove in the man's head, but Darry could find no bone movement. He would certainly have a raging headache when he did come out of it.

Darry did not want to sling the man over his shoulder to carry him, for fear that would reopen the two shoulder wounds. He took Jack's canteen to the spring, emptied out the tepid water and filled it up with cold spring water, then poured it over Jack's face. Jack moaned and opened his eyes.

"Easy now," Darry cautioned. "Just lie still while I go refill the canteen. You've lost blood and need water to drink. You also need food in you."

"Where . . . ?"

"Be quiet. I'll be right back."

Darry lifted Jack's head so he could drink and then gave him a piece of jerky to chew on. "Don't try to swallow the meat, just chew on it. It isn't much, but it'll give you some nourishment."

Jack chewed on the jerky and drank some more water. "In my jumpsuit side pocket. A high-energy bar."

Darry found the chocolate bar and removed the wrapper. Jack carefully took the jerky from his mouth, laid it aside, and bit off a hunk of the high-energy bar.

"It's dried venison." Darry anticipated the question. He smiled at the man. "You like it?"

"It's . . . interesting," Jack said, his voice growing stronger. "But I wouldn't want a steady diet of it."

"You think you can walk?"

"I can damn sure try. What the hell is going on?"

"It's a long story, Jack."

Dr. Ray Collier had never seen his wife so angry. She was livid with rage. After Kevin had related all that had taken place, she paced up and down on the riverbank, visibly calming herself down. She returned to the group and sat down on the ground.

"Now tell me the truth, all of you," Karen said, looking at each member of the old hippie commune. "Do you grow or sell marijuana?"

To a person, they shook their heads. Kevin said, "No, ma'am. None of us. Not in years. When we got out of the service and moved out here, we used to smoke. We all had our little patches of grass. But when the kids were born, we quit. I'll bet you it's been a good fifteen years since any of us toked on a joint. And Jody Hinds, to my knowledge, never used drugs of any kind. Tom Sessions—he used to be the ranger around here, before he became head of the district—he checked us all out. Then when he was promoted and Rick Battle took over the station, he checked us out."

"We never minded that," Todd said. "We know we live a lifestyle that is very different from what others live. But we've never bothered a living soul. All of us were shot up pretty bad in 'Nam, and we all draw disability checks. Out there"—he jerked a thumb—"it wouldn't be enough to live on. But it's plenty in here. We grow a lot of our food, and we all hunt and fish. Our wives are college graduates and have teaching certificates . . . that's how we could get by teaching our kids at home. And they've received a good, balanced education. The older ones have all gone to college and graduated." He smiled as he looked at his wife. Betsy picked it up.

"They're not geniuses," she said. "Although we all like to think that of our kids. But they all graduated with three-point-two and three-point-three or -four averages. And they're all working now and paying taxes and so forth. Helping to pay the salaries of those who attacked us,'' she added bitterly.

''And killed my wife,'' Vince's words were softly offered.

''And wiped out Jody's family,'' Kevin added. ''But we sure wasted some of the bastards. Excuse my language.''

''That's all right,'' Karen said. ''I certainly understand your feelings. After they knocked my husband to the ground, I can share a little bit of your emotions.''

Paul was looking at the weapons the men and women had brought with them. The weapons were not new, by any means, but they were well cared for. Mini-14s, he thought, with twenty- or thirty-round clips. The kind of weapons called assault rifles. And at that moment, the boy—almost a man—knew why there was such a great hue and cry to disarm the American public: unarmed citizens could not fight back against government excesses and brutality such as these people in camp had faced. And Paul also thought, as he studied the men and women, that the government better be very wary of men and women such as these, for their spirit of independence and self-reliance was strong, and not likely to be broken. If enough men and women like Kevin and his friends could get together, they could *force* the government to toe the mark. That's why the government was coming down so hard on men and women the media called survivalists. They were scared of them.

Paul didn't realize it yet, but he had just become a survivalist.

''Spotters report an entire team down and dead up here,'' the agent said, pointing to a spot on the map. ''Ten agents. Eight men and two women. Their weapons and personal gear taken by whoever hit them.''

Max Vernon threw his tin coffee cup to the ground. ''All right, people. We've sealed this area off . . .'' Not true. Several dozen hikers and campers and fishermen (excuse me, fisher-persons) and nature lovers were now in the area, and they did not have the vaguest idea they had walked into a free-fire zone. It would take two full divisions of troops to seal off over a thousand square miles of wilderness; and even then, someone would probably slip through. But Max Vernon was impressed with his gold badge and government-authorized near-dictatorial powers, so he was too stupid to realize that. He had attained his position by ass-kissing and carefully placing himself in the right places at the right times. And never having the courage to question directives or orders. Just following orders. Don't blame me, I'm just following orders. ''. . . we've evac'd everyone who isn't aligned directly or who we think doesn't secretly support these terrorist bastards . . .'' (Anyone who didn't blindly follow the Washington party-in-power's dogma like a bunch of lemmings to the sea. They used to be called free thinkers—but now they were referred to as terrorists, traitors, much-to-be-feared survivalists, seditionists, separatists, or whatever else some of the elected nannies and ninnies could hang on them.) ''. . . so it's shoot-to-kill time, people . . .''

A number of those agents standing close to Max exchanged very wary glances at that remark. Those looks held one unanimous and silent comment: they would shoot only if they were shot at, and if Max Vernon didn't like that, he could go suck an egg.

''. . . those orders are being radioed to all teams. Draw equipment and provisions. Let's secure this area, people. Move out!''

*   *   *

A dentist from Boise and a schoolteacher on spring break from out of state were to be the first real outsider casualties of the American government's armed and dangerous Thought & Speech Police. Both of them had entered the wilderness area the day before, and were only a few miles from the meadow where the mercenaries had done battle with the federal agents. As Darry was helping Jack to the cave, the dentist and the schoolteacher met on one of the many trails leading into the wilderness area. They chatted for a few moments, then walked on. A half hour later, the dentist was dead, shot through the head by a government sniper. The woman's left arm had been shattered by a bullet, and she was running away in a blind panic, believing she had been set upon by outlaws.

Just about the same time the dentist and the schoolteacher were ambushed, Mike Tuttle and his mercenaries sprung the trap on a five-man team of federal agents. The mercenaries took no prisoners and left no one alive. One member of the team did manage to get off a short radio message before he died, giving position and status, which was grim.

"The whole area is filled with highly trained and motivated paramilitary troops!" the agent frantically radioed. "They're armed with automatic weapons and sure as hell know how to use them. We've had it, Max. I—"

The radio went silent.

Max's face turned hard as he realized what had happened to that team of agents. "Get the word out to all our people: the password is 'tails,' response is 'wagging.' Anyone who doesn't know the correct response is to be considered an enemy. Shoot to kill. Send that out in code, by burst transmission. The enemy now has our radios, and they'll be able to listen in on open transmissions. And get word to Washington that it looks like this area is the central hotbed for insurrection. I want federal marshals in here to completely seal off the area. No troops. That would tip off the press." He turned to a map and using a grease pencil marked the hot area. "This area. Get it done right now. No one in, and no one out unless they are with us. Understood?"

"Yes, sir."

Max Vernon turned to face the map. "I'll crush you all," he promised in a whisper. "I'll break the back of insurrection, and I'll be a hero."

Max had dreams of being promoted as soon as this operation was successfully concluded. Parties in his honor. His name in gold letters on his office door.

The only thing Max was going to get his name on was the marble of his tombstone.

15

While Jack was being made as comfortable as possible in the cave, Darry went outside again to wander through nature's garden, collecting plants and herbs to make a poultice to hasten the healing of the agent's wounds. He was back shortly and had a camp pot filled with water heating over a small fire.

"I thought you were dead, Jack," Kathy said. "I couldn't find a pulse."

"Those dead agents?" Jack asked.

"I killed them," his partner admitted. "I guess I'm in deep shit, right?"

"I doubt it. They opened fire on us, remember?" Jack's memory was slowly returning.

"Some one is moving out there," George Eagle Dancer called from the mouth of the cave. "I think it is a woman, and I think she is hurt."

Darry peered out through the brush that covered the mouth of the cave and nodded his head. His eyesight was far superior to the average human's, and he could easily see that the woman was hurt and in considerable pain. "I'll go get her," Darry said.

Kathy had moved to his side. "She's going to be frightened out of her wits, Darry. I'd better go with you."

Darry gave that a few seconds thought. "You may be right. Let's go."

It took the pair about fifteen minutes to carefully climb down the rocky and brush-covered slope, then make their way across the basin of the small valley. The closer they came, it was apparent to both of them that the woman was suffering a gunshot wound.

As they approached the staggering woman, she spotted them and panicked. "Don't run away!" Kathy called. "We're friendly." She started to add that she was a federal agent, then thought better of that, since the odds were pretty good it was federal agents who had shot her.

"Please!" Darry called. "We won't hurt you. Let us help you. There are half a dozen of us who have taken refuge in a cave across the valley."

The schoolteacher, who looked to be in her mid to late twenties, paused, turned around, then began walking slowly toward Kathy and Darry. She started crying. "My God, what's happening around here? A man I met on the trail was shot to death by masked men, and then they turned their guns on me. There was no warning. Nothing. The bastards just opened fire on us!"

Darry took her good arm. "Come on. Your arm looks like it's broken. We can patch you up and make you comfortable."

As they started walking across the valley floor, Kathy asked, "Were they wearing ski masks and dressed in camouflage?"

"Yes."

"Federal agents," she told the woman.

"*Federal agents!* I'm a schoolteacher from Kansas, dammit! This is my fifth trip out here. I come out here once a year. Why the hell would federal agents shoot me?"

"They shot me and my partner," Kathy replied. "And we're FBI."

"You've got to be kidding!"

"It's a very long story," Darry said. "And I'm afraid it's not going to have a very happy ending."

"You let me get my hands on a gun, and I'll show you a happy ending," the schoolteacher from Kansas said grimly.

"Freeze, goddamn you!" the BATF man shouted from the top of the bluff overlooking the Collier camp. "You're all under arrest."

Seventeen-year-old Paul was out of the agent's line of sight, crouched under an overhang on the worn path. He reached for the rifle he'd taken from Darry's cabin and carefully cocked the hammer. He knew there was a live round in the slot, for he'd levered one in after loading up the tube upon finding the rifle.

"Don't be ridiculous!" Karen snapped at the two agents standing above them. "I'm an attorney from Los Angeles, and my husband is a doctor. We've done nothing illegal."

"You're harboring fugitives. Aiding and abetting them. Now stand up and get your hands in the air!"

Paul inched backward and could just see one agent's head, from the shoulders up. He slowly lined up the head with the iron sights.

"I've had all this nonsense I'm going to tolerate," Karen told the federal agent "You go right straight to hell!"

"I'll kill you, bitch!" the agent said, jerking his M-16 to his shoulder. He had lost two close friends this day, ambushed by the mercenaries, and was in no mood for any type of resistance.

Paul shot him, the tiny .22 slug, pushed by a magnum powder load, striking the man in the eye and exiting out the back of his head. Before the agent dropped his M-16, his finger tightened on the trigger, and he blew off half a clip. The weapon discharged upon hitting the ground, nearly taking off his partner's foot, the .223 round blowing a hole in the man's ankle. The wounded man screamed in pain and lost his balance, doing a header off the bluff. He landed on his head, and all heard the neck snap.

Paul climbed up the bluff and stood for a moment over the body of the federal agent he'd just killed. Then the teenager knelt on the ground and puked up his lunch.

"We've got to get out of here!" Kevin said, rising to his feet. "All those shots will attract attention."

"We can take the big . . . raft," Ray said, his voice trailing off as he turned and looked toward the raft. The rounds from the agent's M-16 had all torn into the rubber. It was flattened and ruined.

"I had to shoot him!" Paul called from the bluff. "He was going to shoot you, Mother!"

"Yes, I think he was going to do just that," Ray Collier called up to the boy on the bluffs. "You did the only thing you could. It's all right. Stay up there and keep watch, son. Keep your eyes open."

"Where did he get the rifle, Ray?" Karen asked.

"Probably from the cabin."

"Ballsy kid," Kevin remarked, off-handedly. "I wasn't that much older when I was in 'Nam." He turned to his group. "Let's pick up those M-16s, people, and the walkie-talkies and the ammo. We've got to get the hell gone from here and do it damn quick."

"Where do we go?" Karen asked, her eyes on her son on the bluffs.

"I know a place," Kevin said. "If we can make it, we'll be safe for a time. But we're goin' to have to hurry. We don't have that much daylight left."

"Time just might be running out for all of us," Todd said.

"What do you mean by that?" Dr. Collier asked.

"Dead men don't talk," Kevin replied. "I've got me a hunch that this government operation has been one mistake after another right from the start. There is no telling how many innocent people have died due to this fuck-up.

You can't bear witness against the government if you're dead.''

"I can't believe our government would allow anything like that to happen," the doctor said.

"Wake up and smell the coffee, Doc," Vince told him. "Open your eyes. Our government sucks. And it has been that way for a long time. You've been too busy making money and hobnobbing with the country club set to realize that. You and your wife and family live way up here on such a lofty plane"—he extended his arm as high above his head as he could reach—"you're totally unaware of what's been taking place around you. Our government, through its enforcement agencies, is ruthless. Hell, Doc, even living out here like we do, we know more about the obscene practices of the government than you do, and you said you live in L.A. You think what is happening out here is something new? No way. Goes on all the time. Most of the time people don't get killed; they just get the crap scared out of them. Their doors are smashed open; they're dragged out of bed in their nightclothes . . . just like the Nazis did to the Jews when Hitler was in power . . .''

Karen had stopped her packing and was listening intently, the lawyer in her now running on all eight cylinders.

". . . we've been rousted before over the years," Niki Carmouche picked it up, as she helped Terri Collier put a few things in a backpack. "But never this violently. The government and the local cops, everywhere, have gone bonkers about drugs . . . as well they should, for drugs are helping to destroy many of the nation's youth . . .''

Gas escaped from the dead agent lying only a few yards away. Niki cut her eyes to him. ". . . but they should use some common sense in enforcing the law. Now it seems that people who are into survivalism are being treated in the same manner that druggies are treated. The government is scared, Doctor. And they're overreacting.''

"You see, Mr. and Mrs. Collier," Betsy Noble took the verbal ball. "We know so much more than you about the abuses of big government because we subscribe, in a very round-about way, to so-called 'underground' publications. I say 'round-about' because government agents regularly intercept the mail of people they think are practicing any type of 'subversive lifestyle.' Whatever the hell that means." She smiled. "We have friends over in Washington State who used to use pigeons to deliver short notes between family and friends. Naturally, the government got word of it and would occasionally shoot down the birds. One note read: 'Big G going under next week. Country will never be the same. Don't miss it.' Naturally, the feds thought it meant a plot to overthrow the government . . . hippies are such dangerous people, you know? So about a hundred agents surrounded the farm and moved in, machine guns ready. What they found was that 'Big G' meant Big George Wilson. He had finally accepted Christ and 'going under' meant he was being baptized in a small creek that ran through the land. To say that our government is paranoid is slightly understating the obvious."

"They shot down the birds?" Terri questioned. "That's grotesque!"

"So is our government," Kevin added.

Inspector Hank Wallace and Special Agent Carol Murphy, from the Bureau's IAD, decided to use Darry's cabin as an HQ for their operation. Darry would be compensated for the use of his cabin and, should he return, the IAD people would move out posthaste. The pair of IAD agents quickly let it be known to all the agents in the field (now numbering over seven hundred) that any gunshots around the cabin would be met with dire consequences.

Just before dark, a team of federal agents walked up to

the cabin and asked if they could have a drink of water from the well.

"Of course you can," Carol told the BATF personnel. "Any luck out in the field?"

"We don't even know what we're looking for," one of the men replied.

"We were choppered in about six hours ago and assigned this sector," another said. "We were told that a large bunch of very dangerous and heavily armed survivalists were on the loose."

"Well," Hank said, "that much is probably true. But from what we've learned so far, although we can't prove it, one way or the other, the survivalists didn't start the fight. We did."

"The hell you say!"

"That's right. They were having a cookout, no arms in sight, when a team from Max Vernon's bunch raided the camp and started shooting. To date, we have nine dead civilians and several others badly wounded from that camp."

The BATF men exchanged glances.

"In addition, the cabin of a man named Jody Hinds was raided, his wife and her sister and boyfriend were killed."

"That's the guy who had a drug lab, right?"

Carol shook her head. "So far as we have been able to determine, no drugs or drug paraphernalia were found, nor any signs of a drug lab. No illegal weapons were found."

"Jesus H. Christ!" another BATF agent whispered.

"Oh, man," his friend said. "We don't need this."

What Max Vernon and the other federal agents did not know was that Hank and Carol were not the only IAD people working the area. There were other IAD people among the field teams posing as field agents.

"A very reputable doctor from Los Angeles was roughed up by government agents," Hank said. "He and his family are on vacation, doing some white water raft-ing. They were right over there.'' He pointed. ''We haven't heard or seen them since we set up HQ here, but we've only been here for a short time.''

''Two dead agents over here!'' the words burst from a walkie-talkie. ''By the river.''

Gathered on the bluffs, the federal people looked at the bodies of the two agents.

The BATF men looked at Hank and Carol . . . hard looks. One said, ''It would appear that your doctor and his family aren't as innocent as you were led to believe.''

Hank and Carol exchanged glances. ''Maybe,'' Carol said. ''And just maybe Sam Parish and his bunch were here.''

''That's a thought,'' the team leader said. ''But I want a make on this doctor and his family. Radio it in, right now.''

When darkness settled over the wilderness, nearly all human movement ceased. No one wanted to get shot blundering around in the dark.

The mercenaries, having fought in wars all around the world, were used to field conditions. Mike Tuttle set up a guard schedule, and the men made a cold camp and went to sleep.

Inspector Hank Wallace slept on the porch of Darry's cabin while Special Agent Carol Murphy used the bed-room.

Sam Parish and the CDL people with him were bedded down only about a thousand yards from a team of federal agents. Both groups were in for a very ugly surprise come the dawning.

McBroon, Cooper, Waters, and Gilmore stayed put in their little hidey-hole and waited.

Dr. Ray Collier and family, and the people from the old hippie commune, got away from the river safely and walked deep into the timber, Kevin Carmouche leading the way. He led them to a ravine that was almost impossible to see unless one was right on top of it, and there they made camp for the night.

Rick Battle set up camp and made a small fire to heat his food and coffee. He wanted people to see him.

Jody Hinds, certifiably insane from grief after seeing his wife and friends murdered, and dropping deeper into madness, killed again just as the sun was blood red and going down. Jody took a few moments to use his knife and camp axe to rig some man-killing booby traps before moving on and finding a hole to sleep in that night.

Max Vernon did not sleep well that night. He was fully aware that his cover-up was getting more and more complicated and stood a good chance of falling apart. Of the hundreds of agents now involved in the manhunt, only about six or seven percent of them knew the awful truth, and some of them were very uncomfortable with that knowledge. They did not know how to put an end to this growing fatal absurdity. But some of them sure wanted out.

"Stay here," Darry said to the group gathered in the cave. "It'll probably be very late when I return. Don't worry about me. Just get some rest and change those poultices on Jack's shoulder and Beverly's arm in about an hour."

"Bring me a cheeseburger and a chocolate shake, will you?" Jack said with a feverish smile.

"Sure," Darry said; then he stepped out into the darkness and was gone.

George Eagle Dancer smiled as he placed a hand gently on Pete's head. Repeat was lying beside Stormy.

"You find something amusing about all this?" asked Beverly Stevens, the schoolteacher from Kansas, seeing the smile.

"Amusing, no. Fascinating, yes."

"How good are those men you came in with, George?" Kathy asked him.

"The best in the world. If for whatever reason they became involved in this conflict, your people will have no chance against them. They have no fear of death. They have seen too much of it. But I am through with war. No more for me."

"What will you do?" Stormy asked, sensing yet another story unfolding.

"I don't know," George Eagle Dancer spoke softly. "Return to college and get my degree. Perhaps go back to the reservation and try to help my people. I don't know, really. But first we have to live through the next few days of madness. And for mortals, that might not be so easy to do."

"What are you talking about?" Beverly asked. "Mortals?"

But George would not reply. He stretched out on the floor of the cave and went to sleep. He sought a vision, and silently prayed to his Gods to send him one.

16

Alberta Follette (she answered to Al) was highly irritated when she reached the ranger station just before dark. She'd practically had to threaten to shoot some federal marshals in order to get through. This was her first posting, having just completed her training, and nothing, by God, was going to stand between her and her duty assignment. It had almost taken an act of congress to get her into the federal ranger program, for she was only five feet, two inches tall. But what she lacked in height, she made up for in spunk. Alberta was a country girl, having been raised on a farm, and the only girl among five brothers. She was not easily intimidated. She wore her blond hair short, was very shapely, and was now standing as tall as possible in her Smokey Bear hat, looking at the middle button on the shirt of an FBI agent who stood six feet, four inches.

"What in the hell are you?" the agent asked, with a friendly smile. "Or should I say, who are you?"

"Ranger Alberta Follette." She tapped her name tag. "This is my duty station. Now get out of my way."

"Yes, ma'am!" the agent said, stepping to one side.

"What is going on around here?" she asked, dropping her suitcase and duffle bag to the floor.

"I'm Glenn Higgins," the agent said, sticking out his hand.

Alberta took the hand. "Nice to meet you. You wanna answer my question?"

"It's a long story."

"It's been a longer day. Where is Ranger Battle?"

"I don't know. I've only been here a few hours."

"Well . . . let's find the coffeepot and you can bring me up to date."

"As much as you have a need to know," Glenn said cautiously.

Alberta threw back her shoulders and stuck out her chest, the action brightening the early evening for all the males present. You could practically hear the eyeballs click. She was amply endowed for her size. "Agent Higgins, I am assigned to *this* ranger station. I have my orders in my pocket. If Ranger Battle is not present, that means that *I* am in charge. And I *will* be informed as to what is taking place in this district. Is that clear?"

The roomful of newly arrived federal agents, most of them in their late twenties or early thirties, and a good-natured bunch, started applauding.

Glenn grinned, then mock-bowed to Al. "Yes, *ma'am!*"

"Fine," Alberta said, unable to hide a grin. "Then let's get with the program."

Darry, as his Other, covered the distance very quickly, loping along on silent paws. He encountered no other wolves, for the other packs had heeded his earlier warning about the danger of man and were lying low, staying close to the den and hunting only small game.

Darry smelled blood and angled off, coming to the spot where Beverly had been wounded and the dentist from Boise had been killed. His body had been removed, but the blood smell was still strong. Not more than several hundred yards away, he could smell man and hear the murmur of their voices. He edged closer and listened.

"I am not moving from this spot," he heard one say. "I'll be goddamned if I'll be a part in the killing of innocent people. I won't do it."

"Same here," another agent said. "I'm staying put, eating these lousy field rations, and keeping my ass out of trouble. This whole thing stinks to high heaven."

"Look, we're under orders to—"

"Fuck orders!" another agent blurted. "I was up north of here on Ruby Ridge a few years back when we attacked the people in that cabin. It was a goddamn federally sanctioned assassination, and that's all it was. You can call it whatever you like, but it was an assassination of family members whose views went against what some asshole liberal bureaucrat in Washington thought they should be. Shoot a kid in the back and then blow his mother's face off while she's holding a baby in her arms. *Goddamn!* That was a set-up, bait and hook, just like this is."

"You were at Waco, weren't you, Jimmy?" the question was softly asked.

There was a pause of remembrance. Bitter recalling. "Yeah, I was at Waco. I smelled the bodies cooking. Men, women, and kids. I didn't join the Bureau for this. I haven't spent over twenty years in the Bureau to end my career by killing people who don't believe and behave exactly how the government tells them to. Max Vernon is a dick-head. Max has always been a dick-head. How in the hell he got put in charge of this operation is beyond my comprehension. But this is a snafu and getting worse."

"Situation normal, all fucked up."

"You got it."

"You pulling the pin after this one, Jimmy?"

"You better believe it. My last kid just left the nest with a full scholarship, and in a few months I'm out of this chicken-shit outfit and heading for the woods."

"You and Louise gonna become survivalists?" The question was asked with a chuckle.

"We might," Jimmy replied, his tone serious. "We just might. In our own way. I don't like the direction this country is heading. And this fucked-up operation just made up my mind. Spying on people who have done no more than voice their opposition to the current administration. Using the IRS to hassle—"

"Careful, Jimmy," a friend cut him off in mid-sentence. "You know not to even think that, much less say it aloud."

"Who the hell is going to hear me?" Jimmy responded. "Only those who know it's true."

"You could lose your pension, man."

"Are you forgetting I married a rich woman, Ernie? My pension is a drop in the bucket when compared to what our investments bring in. Some are hers, some are mine. Screw my pension. You guys wake me up when this is over. And not before."

Darry moved on, silently leaving the camp behind him. He visited other camps that night, listening to the federal agents, men and women, talk and grumble and bitch about this assignment. He quickly reached the conclusion that about ninety percent of them believed this operation to be a cover-up for Max Vernon's mistakes. But that still left about a hundred hard-core agents who had to kill those civilians involved or face dismissal and/or prosecution.

Darry headed for his cabin.

It amused him to leap noiselessly onto the porch without waking the sleeping man and then to pad silently through the cabin and look at the sleeping woman in his bed. Darry knew without any doubts that he could slip into the camp of this Max Vernon and kill him without notice. But what would that accomplish? Nothing.

No. This had to be handled another way.

Darry padded out of the cabin and down the steps. There, he shape-shifted, to stand in his human form by the sleeping agent on the porch. Darry clamped one hand over the agent's mouth and with his other hand pinned the man to the porch floor.

"Listen to me," Darry whispered. "Don't struggle. I am not here to harm you in any way. I own this cabin; lease these acres. I must talk with you and your female companion. I am going to turn you loose. Please, don't be alarmed. Do you understand?"

Hank nodded his head, as much as the hard hand on his mouth would permit.

Darry released him. "I'm sorry about this. But I didn't want to get shot." Darry could not die; but he could experience pain, and it was not a comfortable sensation. Therefore it was one he tried to avoid.

"You're Darry Ransom?" Hank asked softly.

"Yes. Please wake the woman and we'll talk. This terrible tragedy taking place all around us must be stopped."

"Don't move!" Carol shouted from the doorway. She stood with her pistol pointed at Darry.

"Easy, Carol," Hank said. "Put it away. This is the man who owns this cabin. He's here to talk with us. That's all."

She lowered the pistol. "Let me get dressed and I'll join you."

"Don't light the lamps, please," Darry urged. "There are nervous trigger fingers all around us."

"It's a damn mob," Hank said, sitting up and pulling on his boots. Carol dressed quickly and joined them on the porch.

"Are either of you aware that a dentist from Boise, a backpacker, was shot and killed only a few hours ago and a schoolteacher from Kansas was wounded in the same attack?"

"Oh, shit!" Hank said.

"Are you aware that two federal agents were killed on the bluffs over there?" Carol asked, pointing.

"No. But it doesn't surprise me. When heavily armed men suddenly pop out of the woods, wearing camouflage and ski masks, how the hell do you expect people to react?''

Both Hank and Carol chose not to respond to that question.

''Now, listen to me. Stormy Knight and Ki Nichols are not involved in any drug trafficking. They were at the cookout at the survivalist camp when the camp was attacked. The people there were not armed. Max Vernon planted those keys of dope to cover his own ass. The women are safe, and you won't find them unless I lead you to them. And that is something that is not likely to happen. I also have with me, hidden, two FBI agents, one of whom is wounded, although not seriously. Kathy Owens and Jack Speed. They were both shot by federal agents. Max Vernon's people, I believe. The schoolteacher is also with them, her left arm broken by a bullet fired by a federal agent—''

''Holy Jumping Christ!'' Hank blurted.

''You're holding two FBI agents?'' Carol asked.

''I'm not *holding* anybody, lady. I found Kathy wandering around, lost, and she told me where Jack was. She thought he was dead. He was covered with blood, but he is alive and doing well. Just before I left, he asked me to bring him back a cheeseburger and a chocolate shake.''

Hank smiled. ''Putting up a brave front, is he?''

''He's a good man, I believe.''

''Yes. Go on.''

''Jody Hinds was not operating a drug laboratory in the shed behind his house or anywhere else, for that matter, and Kevin Carmouche and his friends were not involved in the growing, manufacturing, or selling of drugs. Innocent people have been gunned down by federal agents, their reputations smeared, and this whole operation is nothing more than a screw-up that has turned into a cover-up.''

''So you say,'' Carol spoke bluntly.

Darry cut those strange eyes to the woman. "That's right, lady. I say."

Carol held up a hand. "Proof, Mr. Ransom. We have to have proof before we can act."

"You know an agent named Jimmy? He was involved in the shoot-out up in Northern Idaho a few years back, and he was also at Waco. He's about ready for retirement and his wife is named Louise."

"James Harrison," Hank said. "Yes. I know him. Damn good man."

"Talk to him. And there are others . . ."

"How do you know all this?" Carol demanded.

"I visited a dozen camps this night and listened to the men and women talk."

"Oh, come now!" she scoffed. "That is quite impossible."

"I have to agree," Hank said.

Darry's cover was blown, and he knew he would have to go on the run once more. He had sensed it when he read the article about him. But for all his ageless wanderings through time, and all the horrible scenes he had witnessed, Darry possessed a wicked sense of humor.

He shape-shifted on the porch.

Most wolves averaged about ninety to ninety-five pounds, the females running about ten pounds lighter. A one-hundred-and-eighty-pound timber wolf, with legs twice the size of the average wolf and with jaws that could crush the spine of a buffalo with one snap would be an awesome sight. It was.

Carol let out a shriek that would crack brass, and Hank was so shaken he could not speak.

Darry shape-changed and once more stood before the pair in human form. "*That* is how I got so close to the camps."

Hank Wallace was a very moral man, and one who took his religion very seriously. He stepped way, way out

of character when he finally found his voice and blurted,
"You are fucking *real!*"

Carol's hands were shaking so badly she had to sit
down on them.

"Oh, yes," Darry said softly. "I am very real."

"In-fucking-credible!" Hank said.

Max Vernon was shaken out of a fitful sleep. "Post 17
never reported in, Max," he was told. "I sent two men
out there to check it. Now they're not reporting in."

Max cussed as he swung his legs off the camp cot and
pulled on his boots. He had fallen asleep with his pants
on. He glanced at his watch. It would be dawn in a few
hours. He decided to get up and stay up. "Nobody else
goes out until dawn," Max ordered. He thought for a moment. "We'll helicopter the rescue team in. Have one
standing by ready to go at first light."

The mercenary standing the dog watch that morning
was monitoring the walkie-talkie and heard the call go
out, and it was not sent in burst. "Well, now," Tom Doolin said. "Well, now! What do you think about that?"

He walked over to wake up Mike Tuttle and give him
the news.

Ranger Alberta Follette and Agent Glenn Higgins had
talked for over an hour, oblivious to the older, married
agents winking at each other and smiling in the direction
of the pair. Glenn was quite taken by the feisty little
ranger . . . and she liked him. But Glenn was not the only
agent she spoke with. She concluded that most were all-
right guys; only a couple of macho types, all full of themselves and overly impressed with their power. But she'd
had a ranger instructor who shared the same attitude.
There were assholes in any organization.

When it came time for sleep, Alberta chased a couple

of feds out of the newly added second bedroom of the station and closed and locked the door. She sat for a long time at the small desk in the bedroom, writing up a report about her first few hours on the job, concluding with, *Something very weird is going on around here. I get the strong impression that most of the agents I spoke with—although they didn't come right out and say it—don't believe that Stormy and her camera operator are involved with dope. So what is going on?*

She didn't know. But with youthful curiosity, she was, by God, going to find out.

Alberta turned off the lamp and went to bed.

After talking for a few more moments, Darry left his cabin, and two thoroughly shocked agents, and traveled for several miles, then curled up in a small hollow and slept for several hours, awakening about an hour before dawn and making his way back to the cave just as the sun was rising.

"We were all worried about you," Stormy said.

Darry squatted down and poured a cup of coffee. He smiled at the reporter over the rim of the cup. "No need to worry about me. I've been getting along quite well for . . . ah . . . some time."

"I'm sure," Stormy's words were drily offered.

"What did you learn out there?" Kathy asked.

"You have several IAD people working. I spoke with Hank Wallace and Carol Murphy."

"They're top people. Tough, but fair," Jack said, from his makeshift bed. "The only agents who dislike them are the ones who have something to hide. Did you tell them about us?"

"Yes. But not where you are."

Darry ate a couple of dry and tasteless crackers and started salivating at the thought of his Other sinking teeth into fresh-killed raw meat and feeling the salty blood trickling down his throat. Those close to him saw his eyes change, glowing with a fierce light. Then as fast as it occurred, the light vanished, and Darry swallowed the gathering saliva and struggled to push the savage thoughts away.

"What were you thinking just then?" Stormy asked.

Darry smiled, doing his best to keep it a smile and not a snarl, for his Other always lay just a heartbeat away. "Oh, just remembering good things, I suppose."

He remembered playing with Shasta and the pack; all their happy times together. Their "getting acquainted" ritual, which all wolf packs engaged in several times a day: the muzzle biting, the pushing their faces against one another, the rubbing and the tail wagging and joyful playing.

In many ways, the social order of a wolf pack was far superior to any society humans may have developed over the centuries. There was a clear and undisputed leader, and that was that. Only the strong and healthy alpha male and female breeded, once a year, thus insuring pups who had the best chance of surviving in a cruel and unfriendly environment.

"You want to come back to us, Darry?" Kathy asked, jarring the man out of memories. He looked at her, and she added, "You were miles away."

Miles away? he thought. I was centuries away. Running wild and free with the most magnificent animals on the face of the earth. "Yes," he said gently. "I suppose I was."

"Are you back to earth now?" Stormy asked with a smile.

"Oh, I never left earth." And all close to him could sense the weariness in those words, but only a few suspected the reason behind it.

17

The agents in the helicopter never had a chance. Mike Tuttle and his mercenaries hosed them down with automatic weapons fire, killing the search team and the pilot.

There was no reason for any of this, other than the fact the mercenaries had all had run-ins with the FBI before . . . some of the run-ins less than pleasant. The government of the United States didn't like its citizens fighting in other country's wars, although what business it was of big government remained a mystery to many people. Probably the overriding reason for the attack was that mercenaries lived to fight, and good wars were getting harder and harder to find.

The mercenaries stood around the dead for a time, then began collecting weapons, food, and ammo. They took fresh battery packs for their radios, then walked off a few hundred yards and squatted down.

"You boys know that George was right," Mike said. "None of us are going to leave this area alive. Except maybe George. The rest of us will all be carried out in body bags."

"Who gives a shit," Bobcat Blake said.

And that just about summed up the feelings of all the men.

"I have a thought," Mike said. "Let's hook up with this Sam Parish and his bunch. We could not only kick some federal ass, but get some pussy in between fire-fights. Those survivalist cunts just might be very grateful for our help.''

''Some slap and tickle would be nice,'' Nick said.

''Let's do it,'' Ike Dover said, standing up.

The other men silently stood up. Mike turned and walked toward the brush, the rest following.

Another helicopter spotted the downed chopper and radioed in. A special assault team was sent in, and reported back what they'd found. Max radioed the news to Washington. The director of the Federal Bureau of Investigation was out of the country, so what to do next fell on the head of the Justice Department.

''Secure the area,'' the attorney general of the United States said. ''Innocent men and women and children must be allowed a place to camp and play and fish and boat without fear of being shot by those horrible, nasty, survivalists with those awful assault rifles.''

So far, the survivalists hadn't been the ones doing most of the shooting of innocent people. That little bit of news was not pointed out to the attorney general because no one in Washington was aware of it.

The attorney general continued, ''And speaking of assault rifles, they should have been removed from the hands of the American public years ago. For their own good, of course,'' the AG was quick to add.

''I've had all this I can stand,'' Johnny McBroon said. ''I want a hot shower, a vodka martini on the rocks, and a large steak. In that order.''

''Me, too,'' Jay Gilmore said. ''But make mine a gin martini, straight up.''

''I'm low class,'' Pete Cooper said. ''I'll take a beer with mine.''

"Now that we have our menus all planned," Lew Waters said, "I'd be very interested in learning exactly how we're getting out of here with our asses intact."

"Oh, ye of little faith," Johnny said. "Just wait until a patrol gets within hollering distance. Then I'll show you."

"You're going to holler at a patrol?"

"Yeah," Johnny replied.

"Can we dig this ravine a little deeper?" Lew muttered.

Upon awakening, Ranger Battle lay in his sleeping bag and reached the conclusion that he had done a very stupid thing by riding out into a free-fire zone alone. Then he remembered that the new ranger was due to report in . . . yesterday! Al Follette was the name, Tom Sessions had told him, smiling as he did so. Funny that I should recall that smile now, he thought.

Rick crawled out of the warmth of the sleeping bag and pulled on his boots. He coaxed nearly dead coals into flame and filled his battered old coffeepot with water for coffee. Then he found his radio and called in. Somebody would answer the radio at the station. Damn place was crawling with federal agents.

"I think the ranger is still sleeping," a strange voice told him. "I just got here myself late last night."

"Will you take down some map coordinates?"

"Sure."

That done, Rick said, "Have Ranger Follette meet me at that location ASAP—okay?"

"Will do," the agent said.

Rick sat back and poured a cup of coffee, then sliced bacon from a slab and started fixing breakfast. Al should be along in about two hours. He would relax until then.

*   *   *

Highly paid, highly talented, and highly rated by viewers network reporters just simply did not vanish without a trace for days on end without causing some concern back at the network's headquarters.

"Where the hell is Stormy?" a senior VP asked another senior VP.

"I have no idea. Did you call her secretary?"

"I tried. She's out having a baby. Left Monday."

"Let's go see the news chief."

"She's in Idaho," the VPs were informed. "And I'm getting worried about her."

"*Idaho!* What the hell's she doin' in for-Christ-sake Idaho? Interviewin' Big Foot?"

"She would if she could find him. I called Craig Hamilton yesterday. He was wrapping up a story in Montana. Told him about Stormy. He chartered a plane and left immediately. He should be in the area right now. He'll find her."

"Idaho?" the senior VP repeated. "Nothing newsworthy ever happens in Idaho!"

At the sounds of an approaching helicopter, Johnny McBroon stepped out of the ravine and into a clearing. He began waving his arms at the chopper. The pilot spotted Johnny and the others who had joined him in the clearing, circled a couple of times, and radioed in the coordinates.

"This could be a trap," the pilot said. "Approach with caution. I don't like the looks of these guys."

"Roger that. I've got a team on the way. Can you circle?"

"Affirmative."

"Well, that was easy enough," Pete said. "We ought to be out of here before too much longer."

"I guess you were right, Johnny," Lew said.

"Man, oh, man," Jay Gilmore said. "I can taste that steak now."

The four men sat in the meadow for a time while the helicopter circled their location.

Pete looked at his watch. "I musta busted it somehow. What time is it?"

"Ten hundred hours," Lew told him, just as a hard burst of gunfire came from the other side of a hill. The sound brought the men to their feet, into an automatic crouch, and spun them around toward the sound, all of them reaching for their pistols.

The helicopter pilot could not hear the gunfire, or see where it originated due to the thick brush and timber. But he could see the four men in the meadow grab for guns and could see the team of federal agents fast approaching from the east side of the ravine, about three hundred yards from the meadow. The pilot radioed, "All four suspects now armed. It's a trap! You're walking into a trap!"

"Take 'em!" the team leader shouted to his men. "Go, go, go!"

Half a dozen agents went to the north of the ravine; half a dozen went to the south. As soon as the four men in the meadow were visual, the agents opened fire.

When the lead started whistling and humming and howling all around them, Army, Navy, Air Force, and CIA hit the ground and automatically returned the fire. The range was too great for effective pistol shooting, but the returning fire did send the feds scrambling for cover and gave the men in the meadow time to go belly crawling into the timber and brush. The chopper pilot lost them from visual.

But the chopper was in fine range for Jody Hinds and the rifle he'd taken from an agent . . . after cutting his throat. Jody opened up. The lead started pinging and banging and punching through the skin of the chopper, and the pilot wisely got the hell out of that area.

And so did Johnny McBroon, Jay Gilmore, Pete Cooper, and Lew Waters, cursing the very government they worked for as they ran.

*   *   *

Sitting in the brush that surrounded the mouth of the cave, Darry accurately guessed what was happening all around him (although he had no way of knowing the names of those involved), and it was darkly amusing to him. He'd had seven centuries of seeing big, powerful governments eventually turn against their own citizens and knew the United States of America had rounded that corner and was now on a corrupt, twisted, and tortured path . . . and had been for the past several decades.

"What's happening out there?" Kathy called from the cave.

"Chaos," Darry replied. "Bloody chaos."

"This is going to be quite a story," Stormy said, crawling out to join Darry.

"Only if you newspeople will get off your asses and start taking a hard, realistic look at the news," Darry said bluntly.

"I resent that!"

Behind her, Ki smiled.

"You can resent it all you like. It's the truth. You people are the second most powerful voice in America, right behind big government. If you people would start hammering at the government to ease up on its citizens, to drastically cut federal programs, to slash income taxes—which are unconstitutional to begin with, I might add—to return control of their personal destinies back to the law-abiding citizens, to do all sorts of things that would lighten the yoke of government control on the shoulders of American citizens, you people would be hailed and revered as heroes. But as it stands now, in the minds of a large percentage of citizens, you're all right down there in the sewer among the dubious company of snake oil salesmen and politicians."

"Amen," Ki said, and that got her a hot look from Stormy. "I have long supported a straight across the board tax rate for everybody. But those assholes in congress won't even bring it to committee.''

"That would be terribly unfair to the poor," Stormy spewed the tired old liberal cliche.

"Horseshit!" Ki responded.

The helicopter pilot was not hurt, but his chopper was. He was going to be forced to put it down, and there was nothing he could do to prevent it.

"We're going to have company in our little valley," Darry said. "Look."

The chopper pilot managed to set the whirlybird down, after a couple of bounces, and then he jumped out just seconds before the crate blew. The blast knocked him to the ground, not hurt seriously, but unconscious.

"Let's go get him," Darry said to George Eagle Dancer, then smiled. "This cave is going to get crowded."

Rick sat on his rolled sleeping bag and stared as Alberta dismounted from her horse. *"You're* Al Follette?" he blurted.

"Yep. That's me. It's short for Alberta." She walked over and stuck out her hand just as Rick was getting up.

Rick took the hand and held on while Cupid suddenly appeared, flying about them, shooting every arrow in his quiver.

Their stay in the wilderness held promise to be very interesting; in more ways than one.

Mike Tuttle and his mercenaries found and linked up with Sam Parish and his band of survivalists. Sam was both astonished and thrilled that a band of the world's foremost mercenaries would want to join his CDL. Since the CDL subscribed to every known adventure magazine published in the United States, the exploits of Mike and his men were etched in the mind of every member.

"So what's the first thing we do?" Sam asked.

"Attack," Mike told him.

"Well, I thought it was a good idea," Johnny McBroon panted the words.

The four men from intelligence had managed to elude their pursuers—temporarily—and were catching their breath in a clump of woods.

What Johnny did not immediately put into words was his thought that the Agency had set him up to get rid of him. Johnny had been a thorn in the side of the CIA for years. Johnny didn't want to believe they would do it; but he couldn't quite remove that little sliver of doubt. He lay for a time, allowing that little sliver to grow into a full slice.

He finally made up his mind and looked at his companions. "I think you guys better take off on your own. I think it's me they're after."

"How come?" Lew asked.

"Let's just say I didn't always agree with policy or do exactly what was I supposed to do. I lone-wolfed it too many times when I was supposed to be a team player. Take off, guys. It's been nice knowing you."

"You sure about this, Johnny?" Pete asked.

"I'm sure. Besides, even if the Company isn't out to shut me up, I've got the latest copy of the Ashes books in my pack. That automatically makes me a subversive in the eyes of the feds."

"He's right, you know," Jay said.

"Who?" Lew asked.

"Ben Raines."

Johnny chuckled. The fictional character of Ben Raines had gotten the author into all sorts of hot water with the feds. He'd heard that the feds had worked up a psychological profile on him, interviewed his friends, and he'd been told the Bureau had a dossier on him about the size of a Tom Clancy manuscript. Despite all their efforts, and God only knew how much taxpayer money, to date, they had failed to link the author to any dangerous survivalist group or, for that matter, to *any* group that might have the overthrow of the government in mind (they never would because the author didn't belong to any). Johnny had enough sense to know that any writer had no control over who bought his books or sent him fan mail. Also, to date, the author did not have the vaguest idea why the feds had singled him out for such an intense investigation.*

Johnny felt that if the government would stop wasting so much time sending their enforcement agents out to keep tabs on certain musicians and writers, they'd have a hell of a lot more time to catch crooks. Johnny also felt that the time was rapidly approaching when the First Amendment wasn't going to be worth the paper it was written on.

"Okay, if that's the way you want it. We're gone, Johnny," Pete Cooper said. "Good luck."

Johnny smiled and wished his new-found friends well. He shook hands with each man. When the others had gone, Johnny lay for a time reviewing his situation. If the feds wanted him dead, they were going to have to work at it. For Johnny was an old pro at the art of staying alive.

"Come on, you bastards," Johnny muttered. "Now you're going to start *really* earning your money."

After checking on the pilot, and finding him just a bit addled and not hurt, Darry sent George back to the cave to get the others. "This crash will bring the feds in here fast. They'll find that cave eventually. We've got to get out of here and do it quickly."

*September 1994—Shreveport, Louisiana

"Come on, you prick," Darry said to the pilot. "Get on your feet."

"You going to kill me?" the pilot asked.

"Don't be stupid! It's you people who are trying to kill us."

The pilot blinked at that.

"So far," Darry told him, "you trigger-happy federal gunslingers have killed a dentist from Boise, wounded a schoolteacher from Kansas, attacked the cabins of law-abiding and decent people who have lived out here for years, staged an assault against an at-the-time unarmed camp of survivalists, killing and wounding no telling how many of them, roughed up a doctor from Los Angeles, whose wife is a very well known attorney from that city . . . and that's just the people that I know about. God only knows what else you silly bastards have managed to screw up, all in the name of law and order."

The pilot's shoulders sagged. "I felt it in my guts. It just didn't seem right. You know what I mean?"

"Oh, yes," Darry replied, his mind racing back over seven centuries of big governments all around the world running amuck and riding roughshod over citizens. "Yes. I sure do know what you mean."

Book Two

The time is now near at hand which must probably determine whether Americans are to be freemen or slaves; whether they are to have any property they can call their own; whether their houses and farms are to be pillaged and destroyed, and they themselves consigned to a state of wretchedness from which no human efforts will deliver them.

—George Washington

18

It would be difficult to put a political label on Craig Hamilton. On some issues he was very liberal; on others he was archconservative. He could have been a top-flight broadcast journalist, right up there with Stormy and Dan and Connie and Tom and Peter. But he had no burning desire for great wealth and worked on stories that he wanted to do and to hell with the others. But among the things that could light his often very short fuse were abuse to animals and violation of the constitution.

Craig's fuse became lighted when he hit his first road-block. Craig's cameraman (and it *was* a man, so all you political correctness freaks can settle down) had gone back to Los Angeles after wrapping up the story in Montana. But Craig had his own mini-cam and was skilled in the use of it. He backed off from the roadblock and shot some film, then once more approached the line of federal marshals.

The marshal in charge of this roadblock got just a tad nervous, for he had recognized Craig Hamilton immediately. He didn't want to sound like a fool when asked what was going on, but the truth was he *didn't* know what was going on in the wilderness. He'd heard snatches of stolen conversation from other agents and, of course, the inevitable rumors. But by manning this roadblock, he was just following orders, that's all.

Just . . . following . . . orders.

Blind obedience toward the masters.

The marshal held up a hand, palm out. "I really don't know what is going on in there, Mr. Hamilton. And that is the God's honest truth. But we have orders to keep everybody out, and that includes you. Sorry."

"I think I'll go talk to the sheriff," Craig replied.

"I sure can't stop you from doing that, now, can I? It's a free country."

Craig's look was very bleak. "Right. And everybody who still clings to that bit of overused bullshit can stand up and whistle the wedding march from a *Midsummer Night's Dream.*"

"You have a choice," Darry told the shaken-up helicopter pilot. "You can go with us, you can stay here by your chopper and hope somebody comes to find you, or you can strike out across country and hoof it back to your base."

"The hell you say!" the pilot blurted. "Those people out there are shooting on sight! Both sides. We know from running fingerprints that one of the dead men is, was, a known mercenary. One of the highest paid mercs in the world. Interpol has notified us that about a dozen of those guys have suddenly dropped out of sight. We think they're here and have linked up with Sam Parish's CDL. We're looking at a full-blown war in this area. Anybody who goes blundering around out there"—he waved a hand—"is looking for a bullet with his name on it." He looked at the group gathered around him. "I'll stick around here, probably hide over there in that brush. I'll . . . do what I can to help you folks. But I'm just a pilot. I don't have a lot of stroke."

"You're still an FBI agent," Stormy said. "Why don't you demand our surrender?"

The pilot hesitated for a few heartbeats. "Two reasons.

I don't think you people have done anything wrong, and with Max Vernon running this op, I . . . ah . . . would not recommend any of you turn yourselves in. But you didn't hear that from me.''

''He knows I've got film of him and his bully-boys attacking that survivalist camp and opening fire on unarmed men and women, right?'' Ki asked.

''That's . . . ah . . . what I hear, yeah.''

''He's got to kill us, right?'' Darry asked.

The pilot shrugged his shoulders.

Darry handed the man the 9mm autoloader he'd taken from a shoulder holster rig. ''You might need this.''

The pilot took the pistol, very gingerly, and slipped it back into leather. Then he sighed and shook his head. ''Jesus, what a fuck-up!''

Craig drove away from the roadblock for about a mile, then cut off the road and into the brush, following the faint signs of an old logging road. He had rented a four-wheel drive Bronco and made the few hundred yards into the timber easily.

Craig had put together his pack before leaving the motel, and he shouldered into it and started walking into the timber. He had a map that clearly showed the location of the ranger station. He headed in that direction.

Craig was no dewy-eyed, city-born idealist. He was about half liberal (if that term even applied of late), but he'd been raised on a working ranch in East Texas, in what years back was known as the Big Thicket country. He was home in the woods or on the plains, had pulled two tours in Vietnam with Marine Force Recon, and had been on some dangerous assignments during his years as a reporter. Right now, every nerve in him was screaming out *danger*.

Craig stopped by the side of a tree and carefully and slowly looked all around him. He stood quite still for several moments before he finally spotted what he had suspected was out there; and only then because the man moved. The man was in full-body blind leaf camouflage.

It's big, Craig thought. And dangerous. But he had heard nothing on the radio or TV about any manhunt. There had been nothing in the newspaper. None of the people he'd spoken with in the town where he'd spent the night had mentioned anything about roadblocks or escaped killers or massive manhunts. So what the hell was going on? And where were Stormy and Ki?

Craig eased his way back toward the Bronco. On his way in, a few miles back, just off the road, he'd passed an outfitter's place. He'd stop there and see what he could find out. But Craig had a bad feeling about this. A real bad feeling.

"I'm not going to jail for shooting that man, Mother." Paul Collier finally spoke of the killing. Up to now, he had said very little about the incident on the bluffs. "That man threatened to kill you, we all heard him, and I defended you. That's all there is to it."

"No, Paul," his father said, his voice firm. "You most definitely are *not* going to jail."

"Ray," Karen cautioned. "Don't make promises you can't keep. He will have to turn himself in. That's the way our system works. You know that."

"No, goddammit! I'll send him out of the country. I've got friends in Argentina that will take him in. I'll—"

She put a hand on her husband's arm. "Ray, don't talk foolish. Even if he does go to trial, no jury will convict him. He'll have the finest legal representation in the world. Once all the evidence is heard, there is a good chance no charges will be brought. But we've got to do this by the book."

Kevin, Vince, Todd, and families exchanged glances at that. Despite all of Karen's legal experience, the aging hippies probably knew more about government excesses than she did, due in part to the underground newspapers that made their way to them . . . and most of them did not come by the U.S. mail. Several times a week all would gather at Kevin's cabin. Kevin would crank up the generator outside his cabin, aim the satellite dish, and pull in television programs that the majority of Americans never watched because they preferred to sit with their noses stuck up the asshole of some athlete or sit like zombies, viewing a program of extremely dubious quality rather than know what was taking place within their own government.

And an alarming number of Americans don't read. They can read, of course, they just *don't* read past the sports page . . . and they never read a book. A large number of Americans (and probably, taken per capita, an equal number of citizens of other countries) get their news from TV reporters, most of whom seem loath to take a firm stance against the growing excesses of government and the disturbing number of personal liberties that are being stripped away from citizens by the very government those same citizens are *forced*, through income taxes, to support.

And many Americans are so afraid of their own government, they simply will not do or say anything against it for fear of reprisal directed against them. They are astute enough to know (or at the very least, *suspect*) that the power of the Internal Revenue Service can be used against them very, very vindictively. More than a few Americans are keenly aware that the federal tax system is now nothing more than oppressive tyranny under the guise of revenue gathering. Citizens of America are aware of midnight raids on homes by heavily armed, ninja-suited and masked police (city, county, state, and federal) sometimes with bogus warrants whose charges come from jailed informants wishing to make a deal in order to lessen their own time in the bucket or to have pending charges dropped or reduced. Sometimes the warrants come after a tip from a disgruntled neighbor; sometimes, many suspect, the warrants are a means to harass and silence a too vocal critic of government policy. (Occasionally the national press will report on such midnight raids, but they seldom follow up on those stories even though they should be aware that their own First Amendment rights are slowly being taken from them.)

"You allow that kid to turn himself in to this bunch of trigger-happy bastards," Kevin said, "and he won't live long enough to reach the main highway."

"You don't know that for sure!" the mother snapped at him.

"Open your eyes, Karen." Betsy Noble spoke the words softly. "If you get out of this mess alive, start reading between the lines . . . so to speak."

"What do you mean?" Karen asked.

"Organize a group of people to openly protest income tax. Get a large group of people together—if you can find enough people with the courage to do it—and go public. But be sure you get someone who is a skilled polygraph or PSE operator. See how long it takes before you're infiltrated by government agents. You won't be in business six months before some of you will be audited by the IRS or visited by IRS field agents with thinly veiled threats. If you're self-employed, you really better look out, for this government has declared war on the self-employed . . . that's being done to force more people to be subservient to the government."

"I simply cannot believe that," Doctor Collier said.

"I'll bet you will before this mess is all over," Vince told him.

"What do you mean, Craig?" the news chief back in NYC asked.

"I mean the whole goddamn area is blocked off by federal marshals and FBI and BATF and God only knows what other federal agency. And Stormy and Ki are right in the middle of it. They're being hunted on some bogus charge of selling dope.''

''*What?*'' the news chief screamed the one-word question. Craig held the receiver away from his ear as the man two thousand miles away roared, ''That is fucking absurd!''

''Of course, it is. It's bullshit. I got this info from an old guy named Chuck something-or-another. I'm calling from his place right now. He's an outfitter. He rented Stormy and Ki horses to go into the wilderness. He says he's been hearing gunshots day and night for the last three days or so. He says some fed came to see him and told him to keep his mouth shut about anything he might see or hear. The old guy told the fed to go fuck himself. Look, I'm on my way to see a man called Buckskin Jennings. I've got a note from Chuck to show him. Chuck says Buckskin will guide me in and keep me out of trouble. I've got to find Stormy and Ki.''

''No. You stay right where you are. I'll have crews out there by late this afternoon,'' the news chief promised. ''Craig? You blow the goddamn lid off this operation, you hear me? This network will back you one hundred and ten percent, and I'm having that put into writing as soon as you hang up. And if the boys and girls in the legal department don't like it, they can stick it where the sun don't shine.''

Craig laughed. He and the head of network news were old and good friends, and if the man said he'd back you, he'd back you all the way. ''I'm going to find Stormy, Boss. She might really be in trouble.'' He hung up on a sputtering news chief back in NYC and headed for his Bronco. He had to get to Buckskin and find Stormy.

*   *   *

"There they are," the agent said to his team leader.

George Eagle Dancer was leading the small group across a clearing.

The TL lowered his binoculars. "So it is," he said.

The agent looked at him. "We have to stop them, Will."

"Do we? Thomas, do you really believe that Stormy and Ki are dope dealers and involved with a dangerous survivalist group?"

"Ah . . . well, not really."

"Anybody?" the TL looked around at his group.

The men all averted their eyes.

"That's what I thought."

"Will?" another agent said, lowering his glasses. "That's Jack Speed and Kathy Owens in there! I graduated academy with them."

The TL looked. "They've still got side arms, and Kathy is carrying an M-16. What the hell?"

"This makes it a whole new ball game, Will."

"Yeah, it sure does." He stood up and shouted to the group about a hundred yards away in the clearing.

"Jesus, Will!" Thomas said, astonished. "You're violating procedure."

Will ignored him. "Jack, Kathy! Hold up. We're friendly. The rest of you just take it easy. Don't do anything foolish. Just stay there, I'm coming to you." He looked back at his men. "Stay off the radio until we get this matter straightened out. If I hear one crackle on my radio, I guarantee you the man who sent it will spend the rest of his days operating a one-man station in Death Valley." Will stepped away from the brush, leaving his M-16 behind, and walked over to the group.

"Mr. Augello," Kathy said, remembering the agent from when he lectured at the academy.

"Kathy, Jack," Will said, stepping warily around Pete and Repeat. Biggest damn dogs he'd ever seen—looked like wolves. Hell! They *were* wolves.

"They won't hurt you," Darry said, watching the direction the man's eyes had taken. "Not unless you try to hurt them or me."

"Perish the thought," the senior agent said. "Jack." He took in Jack's bloody clothing. "How hard hit are you?"

"I'm all right, sir." He jerked a thumb toward Darry. "This man saved my life."

"Duly noted. Kathy?"

"I'm all right. It was just a graze."

Senior Agent Augello looked at Ki, still carrying her camera, and smiled. "Young lady, I understand you have some film that might prove rather damaging to some federal agents."

"Yes, I do. And I intend to keep it."

Will slowly nodded his head. "Fine. It's your property. On top of everything else that's happening, I certainly don't plan on interfering with the press."

"Agent Augello," Stormy said. "Neither Ki nor myself are involved with drugs in any way. We—"

Will waved her silent. "I believe you. But don't say any more about it. Not to me, not to any of my men. Not just yet. I'm violating enough procedural rules right now to possibly end my career. For the moment, let's get out of this clearing and under cover." He glanced at Beverly. "What happened to you?"

"I was shot by one of your goddamn agents," the schoolteacher said, very bluntly. "And a dentist from Boise, whom I had just met on the trail, was killed by the same bunch of jerks."

Agent Augello looked heavenward and muttered, "Lord, give me strength."

"Goddammit, Max!" the just rescued helicopter pilot shouted. "I'm telling you, some of these people you're hunting pulled me away from a burning chopper and took care of me. One of them cleaned out and bandaged this cut on my forehead. I'm not harmed in any way. I've still got my side arm. Doesn't that tell you anything?''

"You keep your mouth shut about this," Max warned him. "Don't you say one word. You got that?"

"You go right straight to hell, Vernon! This whole operation stinks. I'm going to find Inspector Wallace and tell him what happened."

"You do and by God your career is over. What do you have to say about that?''

The pilot smiled. "What do I have to say about that? Fuck you very much!''

19

No one would ever learn who leaked what to whom, but the big three networks and two all-news networks hit the area within minutes of each other, all of them flying in by private jet and then chartering prop jobs to take them into a strip in the wilderness area. Other network personnel were coming in by truck and motor home as fast as they could, bringing in food and cots and other supplies. The federal marshals at the roadblock on the only road leading to the ranger station were very nearly overwhelmed by the crush of newspeople.

At FBI Headquarters, at the attorney general's office, at Langley, at Fort Meade, and in the offices of Army, Navy, and Air Force Intelligence, as soon as the networks started cranking out signals, the reaction was pretty much the same.

"Oh, *shit!*"

The White House was just about as eloquent. "God-dammit!" the President shouted. "This is gonna make me look like a fuckin' fool!"

Not that he really needed any help to reach that pinnacle.

*   *   *

About an hour before dark, much to the chagrin of the agents, Craig Hamilton showed up at the federal outpost, guided there by Buckskin Jennings.

"How in the hell did that old fart find us?" one agent asked another.

Actually, the animals told him, for like Chuck, Buckskin sprang from the loins of the Lost Tribe.

Craig embraced first Stormy, then Ki. When he put his arms around Ki, she slipped the canister containing the damning film into his jacket pocket. Then they pulled apart and grinned at each other.

Buckskin had observed the switch and smiled, thinking these newspeople were a devious bunch.

"No film, no interviews," Will Augello warned Craig.

"Fine," the reporter said. "No problem. My main concern is Stormy and Ki."

"As you can see, they are both well."

"Are they under arrest?"

"Not yet."

"Chopper is on its way with Hank and Carol," an agent called.

"Get ready to strobe them in. Daylight is fading fast."

"Right, sir."

"Can you guide me out of here in the dark?" Craig asked Buckskin. "Without both of us getting shot?"

The old man smiled. "You best ride back in that helicopter. If that's all right with the feds."

"I'm sure that will be fine. Mr. Jennings, I would advise against you riding back in the dark. There are agents out there who might mistake you for . . ." Augello paused, searching his mind for the right word. Enemy? So far, he hadn't been able to discern any clear-cut enemy, except for that unknown band of paramilitary people who kept popping up and killing for no reason.

"The enemy, son?" Buckskin asked. "Out here, the only enemy we have is the goddamn federal government. Anybody takes a shot at me this night is gonna be in for a grim surprise.'' He looked at Craig. ''You drop by and see me 'fore you leave. You're always welcome at my place.'' He looked at Will Augello. ''You federal fuckers ain't.'' He winked at Craig. ''See you, boy.'' Then the old man was gone.

''Damned old turd,'' one Bureau man muttered.

''Chopper five minutes away,'' the agent handling the radio called. ''They've got a doctor on board.''

The chopper landed, and Hank Wallace and Carol Murphy stepped down with a doctor. Moments later, the chopper lifted off, with Jack Speed, Kathy Owens, Craig Hamilton, and the schoolteacher.

Back at the ranger station, which had been turned into a command post, Max Vernon was well aware that Hank and Carol had boarded a chopper for someplace. He was in charge of this op, but he knew better than to question or interfere in any way with IAD. Max was arrogant, ambitious, and rather short-sighted in many areas of judgement, but he wasn't stupid. One of his men, who, like Max, was up to his ass in this cover-up, had listened to the radio transmissions from Agent Augello. He walked up to Max and whispered to him.

Max nodded his understanding. ''You can bet Ki Nichols slipped that film to Hamilton. You get some men and be there when that chopper lands, and you get that film. Any way you can. Understood?''

The agent nodded and moved off into the gathering darkness.

Rick Battle and Alberta Follette had returned to the station, and Al had observed the exchange. ''Come on,'' she said to Rick. ''Something weird is about to happen.''

''Something weird has been happening around here for days,'' Rick responded. But he dutifully followed her.

Hank was tape-recording everything. ''And this film, Miss Nichols, you have it with you?''

"No."

"You've hidden it?"

"In a manner of speaking, yes."

Hank Wallace was an excellent interrogator, skilled in picking up on the slightest nuance. He sensed instantly that the film was gone, probably with Craig Hamilton. He cut his eyes to Carol, and she made a circling motion with her index finger, imitating the main rotor of a chopper.

"Miss Nichols," Hank said, "I really wish you had not given that film to your friend. You just may have placed him in very grave danger."

Ki was shaken at that remark. Even though she knew the IAD man was only guessing, she instantly realized the truth behind his words. She cut her eyes to Stormy.

Stormy said, "Inspector, we don't know who is involved in this government . . . well, screw-up, but that film is our only hope of showing why it happened. For all we knew, know, you may very well be involved in trying to cover up this . . . mess. We had to get that canister out."

"I understand," Hank said. "And I can assure you that neither Special Agent Murphy nor I are involved in any cover-up. If this government has rogue agents in its employ, we intend to find them and either recommend dismissing them and/or bring charges against them." He cut his eyes to Darry. "You do get around, don't you, Mr. Ransom?"

"I know the area," was Darry's response.

"I'm sure you do." Hank's reply was dry. He turned to Carol. "Get that chopper on the horn. Tell it to get back here and—"

"Chopper just landed at the command post, sir," Hank was told.

"Damn!" the inspector said. His eyes widened as Ki pulled a short-barreled pump shotgun out of her duffle.

That made the other agents a bit nervous.

"Ah, Miss Nichols," Hank said. "Would you please put that shotgun away?"

"I was just going to unload it," Ki said.

"Why don't you give it to Agent Norris, there?" Hank suggested.

"Why, sure," Ki said sweetly, and handed the shotgun to the agent. She did not mention anything about the .38 she had under her jacket.

"Thank you, Miss Nichols," Hank said, then turned to George Eagle Dancer. "Now, sir, if you would be so kind as to tell me your part in this . . . little drama."

George smiled and began speaking in Cheyenne.

Darry ducked his head to hide a grin.

Hank Wallace sighed and looked very pained.

Craig sensed trouble coming his way as half a dozen men began closing in on him seconds after he hopped out of the chopper. He circled the chopper, found himself in a small pocket of darkness and almost ran into Alberta and Rick. He took a chance that the rangers were not involved in any dirty business and slipped the canister of film into Alberta's jacket pocket. "Don't lose that, and don't let the feds know you have it," he whispered.

"What?" Rick asked.

"They'll kill you for that film," Craig whispered.

"Hey, you!" The shout stopped the reporter and the rangers. "Reporter! Hold up. We want to talk to you."

Craig turned and smiled in the darkness. The main rotor blade had wound down and stopped its ticking. The night was silent. "Why, sure, boys. I want to interview some of you, too."

"No interviews," he was told. "Come on."

Rick and Alberta pressed up tight against the body of the big chopper. The lights on the makeshift pad had been turned off, and neither felt they had been seen.

Craig walked off toward the ranger station with the agents, chatting easily with the men.

"You just might have the shortest career in the history

of the service," Rick whispered to Alberta. "Let's see: interfering with a federal officer, withholding evidence . . . and I'm sure there are about a dozen more charges they could pin on you."

"So are you going to turn me in?" she asked with a grin.

"Don't insult me. Come on. We've got to get that film to a safe place."

"Where?"

"Be quiet. I'm thinking."

A gentle rain began falling as the mist moved in, covering the land.

Ray and Karen Collier had seen the helicopter circle and land, then later, as the night closed in, watched as fires were built. They talked it over and made up their minds to take the family, hike over, and put an end to this nonsense.

"Don't be a fool!" Kevin told the man and wife.

"It has to end," the doctor said. "My son has killed a federal agent. You people were involved in a wild shoot-out where federal agents were killed. If we don't turn ourselves in, we're all going to be hunted down like rabid animals and destroyed. Don't you see that?"

"He's right," Niki surprised her husband by saying. "There is no place left to hide, Kevin. And I don't feel like running for the rest of my life. Those agents attacked us, not the other way around. A judge has to take that into consideration. Karen has said that her law firm will represent us. We've got to think about the young people, love."

"Mother is right, Dad," Beth said. "Come on. Let's get this over with."

Kevin looked at his friends in the very dim light that night allowed. Vince and Todd both nodded their heads in agreement as did the rest of the group. "All right," Kevin said with a sigh. "Let's go. Everybody get a flashlight. Just pray we don't get shot."

The group started walking across the flats toward the camp of the federal officers.

"Look, goddammit!" Craig was rapidly losing what little temper he had left. "I've told you fifteen times, I don't have any film. I don't even know what in the hell you're talking about."

"He must have given it to the guide," Max said, speaking openly now, for he had no intention of letting Craig Hamilton leave this room alive. Max and the agents aligned with him had just stepped over a line from which there could be no retreat. "Alert all outposts that there is a man on horseback who is armed and dangerous. Blow him out of the saddle."

"You're *insane!*" Craig said. "Crazy—all of you. You can't possibly hope to get away with this. Come on, guys. Give it up. Jesus Christ, people, don't dig yourselves in any deeper."

Craig had positioned himself against the rear wall, next to the back door, his back pressing against the panel of light switches. He could tell the door was not locked.

Max looked at an agent he'd called Sonny. "You have the crack."

"In my pocket."

"I've got a cold gun," another agent said.

"Then you know what to do," Max said.

Craig plunged the small room into darkness, jerked open the door, and headed for the woods, running low and doing his best to move like a snake.

Jody Hinds had been so exhausted he had to rest. He'd curled up under some low-hanging branches and dropped off into a deep sleep, oblivious to the rain that fell around

him and on him. He was about fifty yards from where
Major Lew Waters, Lt. Commander Jay Gilmore, and
Major Pete Cooper were resting, huddled under an over-
hang in a small ravine.

Johnny McBroon had seen the bobbing flashlight
beams from his position on a low rise and walked down to
join them, taking a chance that the group was not federal
agents or any of Sam Parish's bunch.

"Hey, you people!" he called, after squatting down
behind some bushes he'd almost fallen over in the rainy
darkness. "Don't shoot. I'm friendly. I just want to get
out of this mess. Put your beams on me if you like. My
hands are in the air. I've got a pistol in a holster."

"Come on out," Kevin called. "And talk to us while
you walk."

"My name is Johnny McBroon. I write under the name
of Johnny Mack. I'm a wildlife photographer and writer.
I've been ducking and dodging gunfire for what seems
like a damned week."

"We do know the feeling," Ray Collier said, as
Johnny stepped up to join the group. He held out his hand.
"I'm Doctor Ray Collier. We're going to take a chance
and turn ourselves in to that group of federal agents over
there." He pointed to the camp fires about a half mile
away. "Hopefully, peacefully," he added.

"Turn yourselves in?" Johnny questioned. "What the
hell have you done?"

"It's a very long story," Karen said.

"Well, we'd better start hollering at those feds now,"
Johnny suggested. "I guess they're not trigger-happy, or
they'd already be shooting at us."

"You people out on the flats," the bull-horn voice
boomed through the rain. "Stand easy with your hands in
the air. We're federal agents. Don't panic. We're not
going to shoot."

"I know that voice," Johnny said, blowing his photographer story.

"This is Inspector Henry Wallace from the Federal Bureau of Investigation."

"Oh, shit!" Johnny said. "He used to be a legal attache at the embassy in Berlin." Then Johnny grinned mischievously. "I heard he went IAD. This is going to be interesting."

"If you're armed, sling your rifles and shotguns and keep your pistols in leather or in your pockets. Come on in."

"Jesus, Hank," Special Agent Augello said. "Are you trying to get us all killed?"

"I'm trying to keep everybody alive," Hank replied. "You think if those were angry survivalists they'd be walking across an open area with flashlights burning?"

"Hey, Hank!" the voice came out of the misty rain. "It's Johnny Mack. What's the matter, Hank? Did some of your Cabbage Patch Kids screw up on this op?"

"Johnny McBroon," Hank muttered. "The damn CIA is in on this. Who else is going to pop up?"

"Cabbage Patch Kids?" a young Bureau man said. "I resent the hell out of that!"

"Believe me, we've called them worse," Carol said. "You know that man, Henry?"

"From way back, Carol. I was le-gat at the embassy in Berlin. Johnny was active then. I heard he got into trouble—which he did almost daily—and resigned before they fired him. He's probably doing contract work."

Johnny stepped into the light from the fires, both hands held up. "Evenin', Hank. Some of your boys and girls screwed up big-time on this one. Al Reaux from NSA is dead. Somebody broke his neck."

"Goddammit!" Hank lost his religion and hurled his half-filled cup of coffee across the clearing. Then Carol stood astonished as Henry "Hank" Wallace did some of the fanciest cussing she'd heard in a long time.

"My word!" Carol said.

When Hank had calmed down, Johnny said, "You've got to call a cease-fire in this area, Hank. There are innocent people being killed, and there'll be more if something isn't done right now. There are Army, Navy, and Air Force Intel people dodging lead out there."

"What the hell does the military have to do with any of this?" Carol blurted.

Johnny shrugged. "They were sent in to find a man. Just like I was."

"Well, we all know who that man is," Hank said, looking around for Darry.

But Darry had silently vanished into the night, Pete and Repeat with him.

"Jesus Christ!" an agent blurted and pointed. "He was standing right there with his dogs five seconds ago."

George Eagle Dancer smiled.

20

The agents blasted the misty night with pistol fire, bringing the entire encampment of agents on the run, startling Alberta and Rick (who had hidden the canister in the barn, stayed in the barn darkness, and were engaged in some kissing and a little friendly groping when the mini-war started), but leaving Craig unscathed as the reporter serpentined through the timber.

Once in the brush, Craig cut on the afterburners and headed for the road, the last place (he hoped) the rogue agents would think to look for him. He quickly reached the roadblock, the lights plainly visible from his position, and stayed in the timber paralleling the gravel road. He had quit smoking upon returning from his tours in Vietnam, years back, and was in excellent shape. He began jogging whenever the terrain and brush would allow it. Chuck's place was not that far from the ranger station, and Chuck liked him and despised the federal government. More and more, Craig was understanding why so many people loathed the government and their high-handed, near dictatorial tactics.

Then he heard footsteps behind him.

Craig dropped to the earth and lay still, listening. What he heard shocked him.

"Hey, Mr. Hamilton!" the stage whisper reached him. "I know you're out there. I'm friendly. I'm a helicopter pilot who was befriended by some of those people Max Vernon is hunting. My chopper crashed and they helped me. Look, I believe this whole thing is a set-up, and I want away from it. Okay?''

Craig had to trust somebody. He raised up. "Okay, man. Come on and let's talk."

"My name is John Ayers. We can talk later. Right now, let's get the hell gone from here. I've still got some wind left. You seemed to have a definite location in mind, let's go. You don't want those guys lined up with Max to catch you . . . and I don't want them to catch me with you."

"What the hell do you mean the AG is out of pocket?" Hank Wallace yelled into the mike.

"Just that. She left on vacation yesterday, by car, with some friends. I don't know where in the hell she is. Back-packing in the Smoky Mountains, I think."

"Try to find her," Hank said wearily. "And get hold of the deputy director for me. He's got to call off Max Vernon and his two-legged dobermans. It's out of control here, Jerry. Just out of control."

"I'll do what I can, Hank."

"Do better than that, Jerry. Just get it done!"

Darry and Pete and Repeat loped effortlessly through the rainy, misty night, staying in the low places, the ravines, and using ancient wolf trails that were older than man. If they were spotted at all, it was only for a micro-second, and the watcher could not be certain his eyes weren't playing tricks on him in the night; he only thought he saw dark, animal-like shadows flitting silently through the wet and gloomy mist.

They covered the miles to the ranger station in an astonishingly short time, for wolves could run for incredibly long distances without stopping for rest, and if sensing danger or closing in for a kill, the average wolf could reach speeds of up to forty miles per hour.

At the ranger station, the three bellied down in the brush and watched the goings-on, which seemed to be frantic.

"Goddammit, find him!" Max yelled. "He's got to be found and silenced."

"Have you lost your damn mind?" Rick Battle came charging up to Max, Alberta right behind him.

"Shut up and stay out of the way," Max warned the ranger. "You don't have the whole picture here."

"The whole picture?" Alberta yelled. "The man is an internationally known reporter."

"I don't give a damn who he is," Max returned the shout. "He's withholding evidence, aiding and abetting two fugitives from justice, and he just took a shot at one of my men. Now, little girl, you just shut your mouth and stay clear of this."

"That's pure crap and you know it!" Rick yelled. "The whole damn country knows that Craig Hamilton is one hundred percent antigun (that was about to change). Don't you ever watch the news?"

"Little girl!" Alberta exploded, drawing herself up to her full five feet, two inches. "Screw you . . . you sexist, chauvinistic big bag of shit!"

Max backhanded the woman, striking her on the side of the jaw and sending her sprawling on the wet ground. Bad mistake on Max's part. Alberta bounced to her feet, blood leaking from a cut inside her mouth, and planted her right hiking boot right in the big man's balls. Max hit the ground, howling and puking, both hands holding his gonads.

One of the rogue agents ran out and threw Alberta to the ground. Rick gave that agent a solid one-two, belly and jaw, knocking him on his butt, before the ranger was manhandled to the ground and both he and Alberta were shackled—with their own handcuffs.

Max was helped to his feet—very carefully—and managed to moan, "Lock them in the storeroom, and make sure they're locked in secure. We'll deal with them later."

Alberta started kicking and screaming and struggling, managing to inflict no small degree of pain on several agents before she was popped on the head with a collapsible steel baton which ended the brief struggle.

Rick kept his cool and his silence. But mentally, he was thinking some dark and dire thoughts about Max Vernon and the other rogue agents.

Before Darry shape-shifted, he signaled Pete and Repeat to stay where they were and then watched as the pair of rangers were led into the house; Rick walking, Alberta being half dragged. Darry left the hybrids in the brush and silently made his way close to the rear of the ranger station. He'd been in the ranger station many times, and knew exactly where the storeroom was and what kind of lock secured the back door.

Darry watched as the agents who had escorted the rangers into the storeroom returned to a still-moaning Max, now sitting in a chair on the front porch. He made certain it was the same agents who had taken the pair of rangers inside who returned to the porch; then he slipped around to the rear of the house.

A guard had been stationed outside the rear door, and Darry took him out with one blow to the neck. It was not a killing blow, for Darry had no way of knowing if the man actually was a part of this cover-up gone sour, or just a man completely in the dark about what was actually taking place and just following orders.

Just . . . following . . . orders.

Blindly and without question.

Darry certainly realized that a country could not function without some form of government, but he had never

seen a government that did not—although the founders
started out with good intentions—eventually become too
large and too out of control, and turn on its citizens . . .
just as the government of America had done. And Darry
had nearly seven centuries of observing behind him. And
many more centuries of doing the same ahead of him.

A government that did not allow dissent was a dictatorship, and that was the status America was fast approaching.

Had it been a dead-bolt lock, that would have proved
difficult, but this was a regular door-knob lock, which
Darry simply broke off. Darry was a deceptively powerful
man, with large wrists and heavily muscled forearms and
upper arms. His shoulders were padded with muscle.

"Keys on my belt," Rick whispered.

"Later," Darry told him. "Right now, let's get clear of
this place."

Alberta was still a bit addled, but able to walk, although
somewhat unsteady on her feet. She looked down at the
unconscious agent on the ground outside the storeroom.
"Is he dead?"

"No," Darry told her. "But he'll be asleep for some
time. Come on, this way."

Darry led the rangers into the brush, and Pete and Repeat silently came to their paws and followed, the hybrids
giving Alberta quite a shock when she spotted them.
"Great God Almighty!" she blurted.

"They won't hurt you." Darry removed the cuffs from
the rangers and told them to keep the shackles; they might
need them later. Then Darry and the rangers and the hybrids walked into the brush.

"Where are we going?" Alberta asked.

"To the FBI."

"Oh, wonderful," she said sarcastically. "You are
aware it was the FBI, along with people from BATF,
DEA, and probably others, who tried to kill Craig Hamilton, bashed me on the noggin, and locked us up?"

"There are a few rogue agents," Darry said. "But the great majority of the others are solid and straight . . . if a bit misinformed about what constitutes a democracy."

"Who are you?" Alberta persisted.

"You wouldn't believe him if he told you," Rick said.

"No more talking," Darry said. "Save your wind and follow me."

Alberta smiled. "Strong silent type."

"The FBI did *what?*" the news chief roared. Due to the time difference, Craig had reached the man at his home.

"Placed me under guard and then, when I broke and ran, shot at me," he repeated, cutting the retelling down a bit.

"I'm talking to our legal department as soon as we hang up, Craig. This is a goddamn outrage."

"It's just a few rogue agents, I'm thinking. So don't start condemning the whole Bureau. Hell, I've got a Bureau man with me now."

"You *what?*"

"Yeah. He smelled a rat and wanted away from the stink."

"Now, you listen to me, Craig. Here's what I want you to do . . ."

Lew Waters awakened to a faint buzzing sound. The first thing he thought of was a rattlesnake. Then he listened more intently and dismissed the snake thought. It sounded like . . . well, someone snoring!

What he was hearing was the very loud snoring of the exhausted Jody Hinds. He shook his buddies awake. "Listen," he whispered. "Tell me what that sound is."

They listened. Jay whispered, "That's somebody *snoring.*"

"Jesus," Pete said. "They must be camped right on top of us." Then he frowned and was silent for a moment. He shook his head. "No. Just one man."

"One man?" Lew questioned.

"Think about it. If it was more than one man, somebody would have shushed that guy by now."

The other men gave that some quick thought and agreed.

"So . . . ?" Jay questioned.

"Let's ease over there and see what we've got," Pete said.

"Hell, why not?" Lew whispered.

Lightning was beginning to dance across the sky now, as a raging storm was only minutes away from unleashing its fury upon this small part of the embattled wilderness area. Thunder rumbled in the distance.

Army, Navy, and Air Force crawled out of the ravine and split up, moving silently toward the exhausted Jody Hinds. Jody, back in his military days, had been known as The Bull. He was a man who possessed enormous upper body strength and used to enjoy wrestling two or three men at a time, almost always winning. Jody was not a man to trifle with, as Army, Navy, and Air Force were about to discover.

"Now!" Pete said, and threw himself on the sleeping form lying in a small depression under some branches. "Whoa!" Pete hollered, as he came sailing back out, a good three feet off the ground. He landed on his butt with such force he saw twinkling stars and heard little birdies singing for a few seconds.

Lew grabbed hold of Jody's legs and suddenly knew how it must feel to grab hold of the world's largest and strongest boa constrictor . . . and try to maintain that grip.

Jody gave Lt. Commander Gilmore a shot to the jaw with one huge fist that almost put the navy man out for the duration.

After several minutes, with both sides in this mini-conflict doing a lot of cussing, slugging, biting, kicking, and hollering, the military intelligence officers finally managed to get Jody's hands secured behind his back, tied with Jody's belt, and the big man's legs tied with a long piece of tent rope that Jay had brought along.

"Goddamn federal murderers!" Jody gasped out the words. "Sorry-assed, no-good, murdering cock-suckers!"

Lightning cut the darkness for a second, and Pete Cooper blurted, "The Bull!"

Jody's gaze shifted, and he stared at the man for a moment, reason overpowering his madness. "Lieutenant Cooper?"

"You know this ape?" Jay asked, rubbing his aching jaw.

"Yeah. He was in my outfit. Sure. Jody Hinds. I didn't put it all together until just now."

"Christ, would you look at the weapons this guy's been carrying around," Lew Waters said, opening two large duffle bags and staring in disbelief. The duffles were so heavy an ordinary man would have had difficulty just picking them up, much less carrying them around.

"We're not your enemies, Bull," Pete said. "We've been ducking and dodging bullets for several days."

Jody started mumbling incoherently and slobbering. He tried to bite Pete.

"He's crazy as a road lizard," Jay said. "Completely around the bend."

"I have a question," Lew said. "Now that we have him, what in the hell are we going to do with him?"

"Bring him along with us," the voice sprang out of the rain and windswept darkness.

21

"It's all coming apart, Max," one of the agents who was very reluctantly aligned with him said. "Not only are the reporter and the rangers gone, but so is John Ayers."

Max Vernon stood silent, waiting for the man to finish.

"You know damn well they'll polygraph us. When we fail it, and we will, IAD will never give up."

"All because of a bunch of hippie trash and hermits," another agent said bitterly.

That agent had conveniently put out of his mind that he had been a part of attacking Sam Parish's bunch, who, at the time, had been unarmed. That agent forgot that others just like him had attacked the peaceful cabin of Jody Hinds and killed his wife and her sister and her sister's boyfriend. That agent forgot that Kevin Carmouche and the other families they attacked had broken no laws, unless defending oneself was against the law. That agent, and the others like him, either could not or would not understand that this was big government gone completely out of control. There had never been a proper symmetry of checks and balances within the enforcement agencies of the federal government. Now that imbalance was coming home to roost.

"There is a way out of this," Max said, thinking fast. Then he laid it out, slowly and carefully.

"Oh, Jesus Christ, Max!" an agent said, after Max had detailed his plan. "No. No, man. No."

"It's either that or prison," Max replied. "And you know what will happen to us in prison."

There were some forty hard-core agents left who had been part of the original bunch who attacked the survivalist camp and the homes of the hippies and Jody Hinds. The others who had taken part in those triple travesties of justice were either dead, killed by the mercenaries or by Jody Hinds (who had been quite busy doing just that), or they had bowed out and joined teams in the field, after vowing to keep their silence.

"We've got Stingers," another agent spoke up.

"How the hell did we get Stingers?" he was asked.

"They're mine," the agent said. "Never mind how I got them. We can bring down Hank's chopper with one, and that will be that. Goodbye Hank and Bitch Carol. Blame the shoot-down on Sam Parish's bunch."

"Good, good!" Max said. "I like that."

"At the same time the chopper goes bang, we hit what's left of the camp and take out Augello and his people," Marty Stewart said. "We know that spic and those in his team are solidly behind Hank Wallace."

"Right," Max said. "Good. Now let's work it out."

"Coming in!" Darry called to the camp. "I've got a crowd with me."

It was after midnight; the rain had ceased, but the night was as black as sin from the low-hanging clouds that covered the area.

Fires were built up and fresh coffee brewed. The entire camp was up, listening to Rick Battle and Alberta Follette tell their stories.

"Incredible," Hank said, when the rangers had finished recounting the events.

"We hadn't done nothing," Jody said, slipping out of

his madness into a moment of lucidity. "Nothing. I haven't used dope since 'Nam. I sure as hell don't grow none nor manufacture any. I don't think I've broken a law in years. I don't poach. The federal cock-suckers just opened fire. They shot my wife in the face. Blew her brains all over the wall." Jody started howling like a wild animal, thrashing around on the ground, snarling and gnashing his teeth, kicking and fighting his bonds.

"Inspector," the agent handling the radio called. "Jack Speed, Kathy Owens, and the schoolteacher are now in the hospital. Jack and the teacher are in the operating rooms now. Kathy was given a sedative and is resting comfortably."

"That's good," Hank said.

"But something is really fouled up, Inspector," he said a few minutes later. "I can't get through. I think we're being jammed."

"Jammed?" Carol asked.

"Yes, ma'am. And the dish is missing. I can't bounce off satellite."

"I want a head count right now!" Special Agent Augello said. "Sound off."

One man was missing.

"Interesting," Hank mused softly. "Max planted one of his people in your team, Will."

"Looks like it."

"Doesn't matter. Max's game is over. We've got a chopper coming in to take us out at first light."

"Don't get on it," Darry spoke. "This Max person has got to be getting desperate by now. And choppers are easy to bring down."

"That *is* something to think about," Carol said.

"Yes," Hank agreed. "Unfortunately."

"Break camp and move out," Darry suggested. "I damn sure intend to clear out of here. Build up the fires and pretend as if we're all going to sleep. Then one by one, ease out of camp. I know a place."

"I'm going to blow the lid right off of this atrocity," Stormy said. "You are witnessing a changed person."

"It's about time," Ki said with a smile.

As with so many hastily conceived cover-ups, by dawn, Max found himself with thirty-five people who would stick by him. An hour later, that number was down to twenty-five as the major networks broke the story and the American people sat at the breakfast nooks and in their dens over coffee and listened to the stunning news that several federal government enforcement agencies had attacked and killed and wounded innocent people and then tried to cover it up. They watched and listened as Craig Hamilton told of being roughed up and shot at. They took in his bruised face where Max and others had hammered on him. By noon, the damning film of the attack on the survivalist camp was on the air, followed by Dr. Ray Collier, Karen Collier, Kevin Carmouche, and his family and friends. Then came Rangers Battle and Follette, telling of being roughed up and locked up by federal agents. Then the schoolteacher had her bitter comments to make in front of the cameras, and certain individuals in Washington cringed at her statements.

Then the cameras showed the shot-up cabins of Kevin and Todd and Vince and Jody, and you could almost hear the groans coming from in and around the nation's capital.

On through the day and into the night it went, and things were so jumbled and confused in that area of the Idaho wilderness, with outposts and roadblocks being very quickly brought down and the agents vanishing like smoke, Sam Parish and his followers were forgotten until it was too late. Parish and the remaining mercenaries slipped out. Max Vernon found himself facing about two dozen different felony counts, and he and fifteen of his rogue agents slipped away into the night, all of them now wanted fugitives and all heavily armed.

Stormy looked around for Darry; but she really didn't expect to find him, and she was not disappointed. At dawn, she went back to his cabin. The cabin felt deserted. She knew that Darry and Pete and Repeat were gone.

"Damn!" she said.

Back at the ranger station, she asked Rick, "Do you think he'll be back?"

"Who?" Rick asked innocently.

"Darry Ransom. Dammit, Rick! You know who I mean."

"I never heard of him," the ranger said.

Miles north of the Salmon River, Darry sat with George Eagle Dancer at a rest stop. Pete and Repeat had been fed, watered, and were now back inside the camper shell on Darry's pickup truck, safely out of sight.

"What are you going to do now, George?" Darry asked.

"Lay low for a time. But I am through with war. I have saved many thousands of dollars over the bloody years . . . more than enough to see me through to the grave. But you, now, that is quite another matter. You realize that Max Vernon and the other agents who went along with his scheme will be seeking revenge, as will Sam Parish and probably those men I came into the area with. And don't forget Robert Roche; he will never give up his hunt for you."

Darry smiled. "I've been chased for seven centuries, George. I wouldn't know how to act if somebody wasn't after me."

"When will it ever end, my friend?"

Darry sighed. "I don't know. Someday, surely."

"We have been listening to the news on radio, and

watching the television at night in our motel rooms; it's very strange that your name has not been mentioned.''

"Stormy will never give up her hunt for me. That is a very determined woman. But there are other, stranger things about this. The government is remaining silent about any charges other than those placed against Max Vernon and his hard-core bunch. And I don't understand that. Big government is almost always very vindictive. Something is going on. I just don't know what.''

"Cutting through all the BS,'' Dr. Ray Collier said bluntly, ''you want a deal, is that it?''

The spokesman from the Justice Department smiled. "That's such a crude term, Doctor. But, frankly, yes.''

The expression on Karen's face was a mixture of disgust and loathing.

"And if we don't deal?'' Ray asked.

"Your son killed two federal agents,'' another Justice Department official said. ''It's not nice to kill people.''

"The second man was shot in the leg by his partner and fell off the bluff,'' Ray replied. ''Paul shot a man who was preparing to kill his mother.''

"You say,'' the first man spoke with a smugness that made Karen want to slap his face.

"That's right!'' Ray popped back, his temper rapidly reaching the redline. ''We say. There were witnesses.''

"Shaggy-haired, dope-smoking, hippie trash. Dropouts from society. We'll tell you right now, they won't testify for the defense. We did a thorough search of their filthy cabins. We found all sorts of dope. Enough to put them all behind bars for years.''

"I don't believe that!'' Karen said.

The two men and the woman from the Justice Department smiled. The woman said, ''I assure you we have the evidence.''

"If you do, you planted it there," Karen said, her eyes burning with anger.

"Now, Mrs. Collier, that is a very serious accusation. Your government does not 'plant' evidence."

"Sick and evil." Terri Collier spoke for the first time. "That pretty well sums up our government."

"Why don't you run along outside and play, dear," the woman said.

"Why don't you kiss my ass!" the teenager popped right back.

Both parents were suddenly very proud of their youngest chick. Three weeks back, Ray and Karen would have been appalled and would have immediately grounded her for saying such a thing. Now they smiled.

The woman from Justice did not lose her composure. She was too skilled a stooge for the government . . . among other things. "Awful things happen to young, sweet boys behind bars. But I'm sure you both know about that."

"You . . . *filth!*" Karen spat out the words. She had sensed immediately and accurately that this severely dressed woman was a man hater from way back.

The three from Justice stood up as if controlled by one mind . . . which, of course, they were. Programmable robots with brown spots on their noses. "Do think about it," the parents were told.

A few hours later, when the mail arrived, Ray and Karen Collier received a registered letter from the Internal Revenue Service, informing them that their assets were frozen and they were under investigation for defrauding the government . . . among other charges.

For several decades, certain members of the government, who belonged to a certain political party, had taken the entire press corps for granted for too long. They became complacent. Certain government officials were well aware that the press was sickeningly over-loaded with hanky-twisting, foot-stamping, boo-hooing liberals who knew just how far to push elected and appointed members of the government . . . unless they were conservative, and then, in most cases, it was open season on them—anything goes . . . humiliate them . . . dig up bones and expose them. And we'll help you do anything you can to shut up those nasty ol' conservatives who don't know when to back off.

Even murder?

Well . . . let's not phrase it in such a vulgar manner.

Extreme prejudice sounds so much more civilized.

After all, one must remember, we're only doing this for the good of the country.

Right?

Stormy gently hung up the phone after speaking with Karen Collier. Karen had called from a pay phone, certain that her own phone in her home had been tapped by the government. Stormy had put the call on speaker so all in the suite could hear.

"It sucks!" she said to Ki and Craig. The three were staying at a Los Angeles hotel.

The camera-person and the network reporter sat and stared at their friend. They both knew they were witnessing a dramatic metamorphosis. They also knew that when Stormy sank her teeth into a story, only death would break the bulldog grip.

"We'll be putting our careers on the line," Craig reminded her.

"So I go back to work in Springfield," Ki said. "Big fuckin' deal. Maybe I'd sleep better at night."

"It'll be us against them," Craig said. "You both better realize that right now."

"Maybe we could get Darry in on this," Ki said.

"Darry hates all governments," Stormy replied.

"Every aspect of big government. And he's had the time on earth to see that they all eventually turn rotten. Don't think for one instant I've forgotten Darry Ransom."

"The problem is—one of the problems, that is—will the network back us?" Craig asked. "Considering the FCC can shut them down at a whim."

"If it's a big enough story, they'll almost have to back us," Ki said.

"We've all got vacation time coming," Stormy said. "So let's take it and get to work."

"I'm in." Ki held up a thumb.

"Me, too," Craig said. "And may God have mercy on our souls, because the goddamn government won't!"

22

"Well, I should be angry, but I'm not," Robert Roche said to Mike Tuttle. "None of us had any knowledge of a government raid in the area." He waved a hand. "It's done with. We won't speak of it again."

Mike and his mercenaries had split from Sam Parish and his bunch shortly after getting clear of the hot zone. Mike had promised to hook up with the survivalists in the near future, and then promptly forgot about them.

"You say you lost one man and one quit?"

"Yes, sir. Al Jenkins was killed and George Eagle Dancer quit us."

"Ten should be sufficient. Five teams of two each. Find Darry Ranson."

"Yes, sir. We're on our way."

"Mike?" Roche's voice stopped him.

"Yes, sir?"

"The Indian . . . he'll keep his mouth shut about this?"

"Oh, you can be sure of that. If it's one thing mercenaries have, it's honor." Mike walked out of the office.

"Indeed!" Robert snorted, and returned to the paperwork on his desk.

"I have it all on tape," Paul Collier said, pointing to an 8mm camcorder placed on a shelf. "I taped over the recording light so they wouldn't notice and turned it on just before they walked in.''

''Is there anything they said that you can use in court, honey?'' Ray asked his wife.

She smiled. ''Just about everything they said. Drive down to a pay phone and call Stormy. Tell her to come out here. She's going to love this.''

Within twenty-four hours of their leaving the wilderness area, Major Pete Cooper was sent to Germany, Major Lew Waters was shipped off to Turkey, and Lt. Commander Jay Gilmore received orders to depart immediately for a long cruise on an aircraft carrier.

Johnny McBroon called in and was told his services were no longer needed. His assignment had been terminated.

Johnny smiled as he hung up the phone. Then he went out in search of a bar; he wanted a tall drink and something to eat. That would prove to be a very bad mistake on Johnny's part.

Stormy sent a fax to Rick Battle: ''Advise Kevin Carmouche and friends to relax. Someone from network will be out to see them in a few days. We'll beat this thing.''

''What the hell?'' Alberta mused.

''I don't know. But it sure looks like Kevin has the press on his side.''

''I don't understand what's going on, Rick. The government can't deny they screwed up big-time in here. What are they trying to do now?''

''Sending signals.'' District Chief Tom Sessions spoke from the open door, for the day had turned warm.

''Welcome back, Tom,'' Rick said. ''This is Al Follette.''

He shook hands with Alberta, but the serious look never left Tom's eyes.

"What do you mean, 'sending signals'?" Rick asked.

"Let's just say that your jobs are secure for the next couple of years. After that . . ." He sighed. "You screw up just a little bit, you're both history."

The two young rangers exchanged glances. "We both talked about the possibility of that happening," Alberta spoke. "But we didn't think it would."

"Think again," Tom said, walking to the coffeepot and pouring a cup. "And it's not just the government who does things like this. So does big business."

"That doesn't say much for the ethics of our country, Tom."

Tom smiled a humorless curving of the lips. "Don't put ethics in the same sentence with big government, boy. The two will automatically clash."

"So you've had the word put on you?" Alberta asked.

"In a manner of speaking. I've been told I'm retiring, effective 31 July of this year."

Sheriff Greg Paige had about as much use for the DEA as he did for the FBI . . . which meant he would rather drink a bucket of buzzard puke than be in the same room with them. He sat in his office and glared at the two men. Greg had called Deputy Don Shepherd in for the meeting. The feds hadn't asked for this meeting; they had *commanded* it.

"Say what's on your mind and then get out of my office," Sheriff Paige told the federal officers.

"There is no need for any hostility, Sheriff," the FBI said. "We're only here to help."

"I don't want your help, I don't need your help, and I didn't ask for your help." Greg's county was huge, taking in part of the wilderness area where the recent "incident" occurred, as the government was now calling the killing, wounding, destroying, burning, and roughing up of citizens. "Haven't you people done enough in this part of the state. Why don't you go back up north and kill some folks up there."

Many people in the state were a bit more than slightly fed up with the government's high-handedness. And if the networks and the major newspapers and magazines would take accurate polls, they would find that a very large number of Americans feared, distrusted, and/or openly hated the federal government. But it was the widely held belief of many that these so-called public opinion polls, while not necessarily rigged, were very carefully conducted. To ask someone who lived in public housing and had been slopping at the public trough for years, then ask the same question of a hard-working, law-abiding, over-burdened taxpayer who was worried about paying the mortgage and putting food on the table and shoes on his kids' feet (without government assistance), the answers would be diametrically opposite.

"We'd like to see any files you might have on Kevin Carmouche, Vince Clayderman, and Todd Noble," DEA said.

"I don't have any files on them. They're good, decent, law-abiding people who chose to live in the wilderness, which, I might add, is their right."

"Large quantities of drugs were found in their cabins," FBI said.

"Horse shit, bull-dooky, and skunk-piss," the sheriff replied. "This is my county, people. I know what's going on in it. And I am fully cognizant of the fact that the federal government is now engaged in a cover-its-ass operation, after another of the government's gigantic fuck-ups. Is there anything else I can do for you . . . people."

The accusations and sarcasm bounced off the feds. "What do you know about a Darry Ransom?" the agent continued.

"He came into this area about two years ago, leased

land from the government, a ninety-nine-year lease, built a very nice cabin with his own hands, and has not, to my knowledge, broken a single law of God or man since arriving. I wish we had more like Darry and less like you. Now why don't you people get the hell out of my office and leave me alone?''

The federal agents had done their homework on Sheriff Paige. They couldn't threaten him with a cut-off of federal money because the sheriff wouldn't take any. Nobody would run against him because the last person who did received only twelve votes. Sheriff Greg Paige was a very good sheriff, who ran a very tight and fair department, and he was a very popular man, due in no small part because he would stand up to the feds and speak his mind.

''We'll be in this area for a time,'' BATF said.

''That news just overjoys me,'' Greg replied. ''I can't tell you how thrilled I am about that. I think I'll drive over to the radio station and get on the air. I'll tell the people they can sleep well tonight with the knowledge their government is in the area protecting them. Of course, should I do that, about half the population would immediately pack up and leave for the duration of your stay. The other half would stockpile ammunition, board up their windows against possible government assault in the middle of the night, and pull in their pets, since you people seem to enjoy killing family dogs.''

FBI, BATF, and DEA stood up as one mind (which they were) and left the office without another word. At the door, DEA turned around and said to Greg, ''Asshole!''

Sheriff Greg Paige solemnly gave the man The Finger.

Darry drove back to the wilderness area, George Eagle Dancer with him.

''I understand why you are doing this,'' George said. ''You do not run because you don't want innocent people hurt. And in here, the odds of any innocent getting hurt is greatly reduced.''

"That's certainly part of it, George. But are you sure you want to stick with me?''

"I am certain. Your hybrids like me, and I them. You will need someone to look after them during the times you'll be gone.'' There was a twinkle in the man's eyes. ''And I think that will be often.''

Darry smiled. ''Let's just say I plan on staying busy.''

The director of the FBI was still furious when his plane landed, and he was quickly hustled off to the Hoover Building. He was no sooner in the car and the door closed behind him than he was on a secure line.

"Who the hell authorized Max Vernon to pull this stunt?'' he demanded.

"Nobody,'' the deputy director said. ''He did it all on his own.''

"That's bullshit, Roger. Bullshit. Stop playing CYA. Max isn't that stupid. He had to have the Go sign from somebody. I don't want this blowing up in our faces somewhere down the line.''

"Max snapped, okay?''

The DIR/FBI cussed, loud and long. His driver could hear him through the glass separation and cringed. ''*Snapped?* Snapped? Is that the story you're handing out to the press?''

"That's it.''

"Great Jesus Christ! How many agents involved?''

"Max had forty bad ones. All agencies included. The rest were just following orders. Of those forty, nearly half were killed during various assaults and by a lone assassin named Jody Hinds. Mr. Hinds is insane and being confined in Idaho. He is a raving lunatic.''

"Is that the man whose wife had her face shot off in front of him?''

"Ah . . . yes, sir."

"Goddammit, Roger! There is more to this."

"When you get here, sir."

A half hour later, the director slammed the door behind the group that had followed him into the office, tossed his briefcase on the floor, and slowly turned to face the men and women. "Who fucked up?" he asked, his voice low and menacing. "And by God, I better get the truth."

The White House was already working damage control on the "incident" in Idaho. But the President did not know about the visit to the Collier family by members of the Justice Department, or of the letter from the IRS and its contents.

The government used to be pretty good with cover-ups, back when its officials would just blandly and very convincingly lie about things. Then somebody got the bright idea to use threats and coercion and muscle by various government enforcement agencies—and the IRS—to whip its dissident citizens into line. Bad mistake. It had to backfire, and in this case, it did. Big time.

Already, the more astute of the American public were beginning to realize that Big Government was developing more and more a bully-boy attitude toward its citizens. By the mid-1990s, even the less astute were no longer wondering about the government's attacks and raids on so-called survivalist camps around the nation (many liberals not included; they thought the raids were simply wonderful). But others began to see them as raids against the right to dissent, to peacefully gather, and a direct challenge to the many hard-fought-for rights of American citizens . . . that were slowly being deliberately and insidiously taken away. Conservative and right-wing radio and TV commentators found themselves targets of the government. Big Government felt the mood of many Americans shift and decided to come down hard (very selectively and as hard as they could without attracting a lot of attention) on any who would not fall in line with the ruling party's tenets. Property seizures under vague drug laws and by the IRS had drastically increased by the mid-1990s. Investigations into the private lives of citizens by the FBI and the Secret Service reached ominous proportions. The Fourth Amendment to the Constitution became a joke.

But the "incident" in Idaho brought it all home to the American people.

"Greatest government that was ever formed," Darry muttered, heating his coffee over a hat-sized fire. "Now it's no better than the one it fought to free itself from."

Darry had boldly driven right back into the contested area and left his pickup in Chuck's barn. George Eagle Dancer would stay with the old outfitter and take care of the hybrids. Pete and Repeat had taken to Chuck immediately, both sensing that the man was more like them than the two-legged form he had evolved into over the years.

Darry put together a pack and looked at Chuck and George. "I'll be back. I don't know when, but I'll come back."

"All them rogue agents, boy," Chuck told him. "The government thinks they pulled out. But they didn't. They're all within twenty/twenty-five miles of this spot."

"Yes. I sensed that."

"That fine-lookin' female reporter; you figure she'll be back here, too?"

Darry smiled. "Eventually, yes."

"If I was twenty years younger, I'd bed her down. Hell, ten years younger." He looked hard at Darry. "You be careful out there, boy. I don't know exactly what you are, only that you're as different from most as I am."

Darry had worked on his pack and listened to Chuck talk.

''There's gonna be a lot of trouble within this nation, boy. I never thought I'd say that, but now I am. Country's reached a sad-assed state. I read me a book a few months back, 'bout all the rights that has been taken from citizens in America. I knew it was bad, but I didn't realize it was that bad. I made me some phone calls and found out everything that author wrote was true . . . and gettin' worse.''

''The ruling party of any government almost always turns on those who don't support it,'' Darry said. ''But this government is doing so with a savagery that I never expected to see in this nation.''

''You seen lots of big governments, hey, Darry?'' the old man asked with a smile.

''More than my share.''

''Someday we'll speak of that,'' Chuck said.

''Perhaps,'' Darry replied.

Pete and Repeat came to Darry, and he knelt down between them, rubbing them and pressing his face against theirs. He gently bit them on the muzzles, and they very gently bit at his chin. Wolf signs of affection. Darry gazed into their eyes, and instructions flowed silently between them. When he was sure they understood, Darry rose to his boots and shouldered into the heavy pack. He seemed not to notice the weight.

''It will either end here in the wilderness, or it will have its start here. I can't say which one it will be.''

''Only that you will be a part of it,'' George remarked.

''Yes.'' Darry looked at the two men. ''But it won't be the first time for me.'' Darry walked out the door and quickly was gone into the timbered wilderness.

''Something mighty strange about that young feller,'' Chuck observed. ''But I can't quite put my finger on it. Mystical, comes to mind.''

''That's as good a word as any,'' George Eagle Dancer said.

23

The director of the FBI was a party man, and a good friend of the President, but he was also a fair man, believing in the Constitution (as it was originally interpreted; something he kept silent about). But being a political appointee, he knew he had to play the Washington game if he wanted to keep his job . . . however repugnant that game might be. And to his mind, this game was getting dirty. But he, too, knew how to play dirty.

He knew he was being lied to by a few of those around him, and it amused him. But it was such a carefully constructed and practiced lie, he could not break it. Nor did he want to.

He smiled another secret smile, knowing that the President had nothing to do with the out-and-out murders of some obscure families living in the western wilderness. He was equally certain that the attorney general would never go along with cold-blooded murder in the name of . . . what?

Silencing dissidents? He couldn't believe that. Dissent was a basic right for Americans. But just thinking that made the man slightly uneasy. For he was well aware that of late there had been a lot of quiet little dirty work in an effort to silence, or at least mollify, those who were opposed to this administration.

But murder? He couldn't believe it.

Three times he put his hand on the phone to call his old friend in the White House. Three times he pulled his hand back. When the private line to the White House rang in his office, it startled him.

"What the hell is going on out in Idaho?" The President came right to the point.

"I don't know, Mr. President," the director replied. "I've only been back in the States a few hours. This is what I know about it: I got a call from the AG to send some people in there to check out a story about a man who could not die—"

"Wait just a minute," the Pres said. "I didn't authorize that. I asked the CIA to send someone in. I figured that was the way to go since they're always screwing up anyway and if it became public, no one would pay much attention to it."

"Well, the AG told me that she had received a directive from the White House requesting the Bureau look into the matter."

"Was the directive signed?"

"Yes, sir. By you."

"Jumpin' Jesus Christ, man! Do you think I'd sign an order wasting taxpayer money checking out some story that appeared in the *National Loudmouth?*"

Makes about as much sense as midnight basketball for punks, the director thought, but did not vocalize. The director felt the new crime bill was the biggest waste of money since the government's war on poverty began thirty years back and to date had cost the taxpayers about a trillion dollars . . . but being a loyal party man he played the game and kept his opinions to himself. "I did wonder about that, sir."

"How many rogue agents are involved in this?"

"Only a handful."

"Well, I've got damage control trying to figure out some way to blame all this on the Republicans . . ."

The director managed to contain a sigh that was filled

with revulsion. It always comes down to that, he thought. No matter what party is in power, each always tries to blame the other for a fuck-up. Sad. So sad.

". . . this Max Vernon has to be taken care of," the voice on the other end said.

"What the hell are you saying, sir?" That slipped out before the director could stop it.

The Pres sidestepped that. "Did you know that military intelligence—all branches—also had people in that area looking for this man who could not die?"

"I just learned of it, sir."

"Doesn't that give you an idea?"

Of course he knew what the President of the United States was subtly suggesting, but damned if he'd play along with it. "No, sir. It does not."

"You think about it," the Pres said. "And do something about Max Vernon."

The line went dead.

The director leaned back in his chair and thought about the screw-up in Idaho. Somebody had sent the AG a bogus directive from the White House. He was not at all certain it had to have originated from the White House; from someone close to the Man. But whoever it was, for sure, gave Max Vernon carte blanche in dealing with the survivalists and the others in the wilderness area.

But why? Was it someone trying to embarrass the President? Hell, someone was always trying to embarrass a president—no matter what party was in the Oval Office at the time.

Or was the deputy director lying?

If he had to take a bet, that would be where he'd lay his chips down.

He picked up the phone. "Doris? Tell Hank Wallace I want to see him ASAP."

* * *

For three days, Darry slept during the day and prowled at night, covering huge distances as his Other. He was beginning to think that he had misjudged the mercenaries; that they had not returned to this area. Then on the night of the third day, he caught the faint twinkle of a small fire, and his keen nose smelled woodsmoke. Darry flitted through the brush on silent paws until he was just outside the small dancing circle of firelight. There, he bellied down and listened to the two men talk.

"So George is here," one of the men said. "What does that prove? Nothing. That is one crazy Indian, for sure."

"I think he hooked up with this Darry Ransom just after he left us, Joel. And we know for pretty sure this Ransom is the guy we're after."

"Billy, there ain't no man living out here who is seven hundred years old and who can shape-shift into a goddamned wolf. Now I don't mind taking Mr. Roche's money, but that tale of his is pure crap and you know it."

Darry wondered what the reaction of the men would be if he rose up and leaped right between them, and let them see what a one-hundred-and-eighty-pound timber wolf looked like. But he didn't seriously consider doing that. Still, it would have been good fun.

"I don't know about that, but I do know it was stupid for us to come back in this area. How many of those fuckin' feds did we kill, anyway?"

"I don't know. Twenty or thirty, I suppose. Hell, nobody can tie us in to that. We didn't leave any alive to testify against us, and we weren't spotted. So quit worrying about it."

Darry wondered how many of those agents the mercenaries killed were actually involved in the killings and the cover-up, and how many were good, decent men, just doing their jobs.

And as Darry, now in the shape of his Other, lay on the ground listening to the men talk, he again wondered what was the real reason he had returned to this area? George had been right as far as he went: If Darry could contain all the brutality here, there would be no civilian deaths or injuries. If he had run, going to a city, when those after him finally caught up, there could be many innocent people hurt or even killed.

But there was another reason, deeper and darker, that had brought him back to the wilderness: Darry hated big government. All big governments. He had made America his adopted home a few years before the Revolutionary War—although he had left the country many times over the years to roam the world—because he'd felt, at the time, that America was going to be a great and fair nation. And it had been, for many years. Darry was proud to call himself an American.

Now he wasn't so proud.

Darry wanted to expose what had happened out here; wanted all fair-thinking Americans to see what they had allowed their government to become.

But he would need help to do that, and had made up his mind that Stormy was just the person to provide that help.

Then Darry's mind was swiftly returned to the immediate as his eyes caught just the slightest bit of movement on the other side of the camp. Darry's nose caught the scent of something not quite human and not quite animal and knew instantly what it was.

The Unseen.*

Those creatures caught halfway in the evolutionary cycle. Darry knew where half a dozen of their caves were, and they knew he knew. They left him alone, and he left them alone.

Matt Jordan, the retired CIA man who had successfully fought to have the government set aside a chunk of land for them, had moved with most of the half-human creatures to the wilds of Canada after the government reneged on their promise (what else is new?) to allow the Unseen

*Watchers in the Woods—Zebra Books

to evolve naturally; to live in peace without fear of man while scientists studied them.

Darry sensed anger in the breeze, emanating from the big creatures. But why were they angry?

That was answered when Billy Antrim said, "What the hell kind of animal was that you winged this morning, Joel?"

"I don't know. Looked sort of like a bear, didn't it? Funny-lookin' goddamn thing." He laughed. "Maybe it was Big Foot, you reckon?"

Darry slowly turned his head and looked up into the savage eyes of a creature that stood well over six feet tall, with an animal-like head and jaws, but with a nearly perfect human body . . . except for its hands, which were more apelike, with claws for nails. The creature slowly shook its huge head, and Darry understood.

The "animal" the mercenaries had shot that day was one of the tribe called the Unseen who had elected to remain in this area when Matt had taken the others up into Canada.

By shooting one of the Lost Tribe, the mercenaries had screwed up . . . bad.

The creature standing behind and to the right of Darry, who was in the shape of his Other, made no hostile move as Darry rose to his paws, turned away from the firelit circle, and padded back into the brush.

The screaming from Billy Antrim and Joel Bass began a few seconds later. It did not last long.

Rick Battle swung down from the saddle and looked at the dead ashes of the camp fire. He poked at the ashes, but they were cold, holding no spark that might set off a raging forest fire. Rick was on a five-day inspection tour of his area, leaving Alberta at the station to take care of things there.

Rick's eyes found a dark spot several feet away from

the circle of stones that had held the fire. He walked over to look at it. He knew immediately what it was: blood.

His eyes began to pick out faint footprints, and they were footprints, not boot tracks. Members of the Lost Tribe, the Unseen, the Watchers (they were called many things) had, for some reason, struck this tiny camp, silently and savagely. And they had killed those who had camped here.

Rick knew he would never find the bodies. In his years out here, he had known only three other incidents where the Unseen had taken human life, and it was always in revenge for the killing or wounding of one of their own. The bodies were never found, and neither was any of the camping and hunting equipment.

Sheriff Paige knew what had happened in all three cases, and other than sending out the obligatory search parties (which were always unsuccessful) nothing was ever done about it. For Sheriff Paige was also a descendant of the Lost Tribe.

"Hello, Rick," Darry said from the edge of the clearing.

Rick turned and smiled. "I thought I'd see you again, Darry. Do you know what happened here?"

"Yes, and so do you."

"Who were the men?"

"People who will not be missed, and no inquiries will ever be made of them—in all probability. They were among a team of mercenaries, hunting me."

"How many men were here?"

"Two. One named Billy, the other Joel. One of them shot a member of the Unseen."

"Shit!"

"Hello, the camp!" The shout came from a few hundred feet away, in the timber, and Rick turned in that direction.

"Come on in," Rick called. "I wonder who that is?"

he muttered. When he received no reply, he looked around him.

Darry was gone, vanishing without a sound.

"So who sent the directive with the President's name on it?" the DIR/FBI asked Hank Wallace.

"We don't know, and probably never will know."

The director hid a smile. "What does the Secret Service say?"

"Nothing. As usual. If they ever do find out who sent it, we probably won't know about it."

The director grunted. "What about this Darry Ransom person?"

"Now there is a mystery man. His birth certificate is bogus. The name was taken from a tombstone of a person who died shortly after birth back in '64. Everything about the man is bogus."

Carol Murphy smiled. "Except for his fingerprints. There the story gets complicated."

"So uncomplicate it for me."

"They are the identical match with two men, both of whom served in the army, one in the Second World War, the other in Vietnam. Both men served with distinction and honor. Both men won a lot of medals. But their names are as bogus as Darry Ransom. William Shipman died in California in 1922. Dan Gibson was killed in a car wreck in Michigan in 1950."

The DIR/FBI leaned forward, placing both hands palm down on his desk top. "What are you saying, Carol?"

"Oh, there is a lot more, sir. A lot more. Back in the 1830s there was a mountain man who fits Darry's description to a T. In the 1850s there was a scout who also fits the same description; then in the late 1870s and early 1880s, there was a famous gunfighter who also fits the description, right down to the color of his eyes." She looked at Hank.

"We also discovered that a man fitting the same description, right down to the color of his eyes, served in the army during World War One. He went by the name of Billy Wilson." Hank opened his briefcase and laid a worn photo of a company of soldiers on the director's desk. One of the men was circled. "That, sir, is Billy Wilson. He is also William Shipman and Dan Gibson."

The director was stunned; having some difficulty grasping all he was being told and shown. He picked up and quickly scanned several military DD 214s Carol laid on the desk. "Now, wait a minute. Just hold on. Are you telling me that a man who had to be at least seventy-five years old served as an Army Ranger in the Vietnam war?"

Hank tapped the circled man in the faded photo. "That, sir, is Darry Ransom. And he's a lot older than seventy-five."

"Are you certain?" the director finally found his voice.

"That it's the same man? Yes. Both of us are. We were with the man for several days in the wilderness."

"We've also discovered something else, sir," Carol said.

The director sighed. "I'm developing a really bad headache. But go on."

"The billionaire industrialist, Robert Roche, is very interested in finding Darry Ransom. We now have information that it was Roche who hired the mercenaries who killed most of our people in the wilderness. They were hired to find and bring Darry Ransom back alive."

"Why?"

"It might be that Roche believes Darry holds the key to the fountain of youth. He probably wants him for study," Hank said.

"Why did the mercenaries turn on our people? Weren't they aligned with this Sam Parish person?"

"Not at first, according to one of the survivalists we

have in custody. We've been told that federal agents confronted the mercenaries as they were pulling out, probably doing so rather rudely. There is a certain type of person who objects, often quite violently, to that type of behavior.''

"Then . . . this business about the man who could not die. It's . . . ?"

"True. All of it. Darry Ransom is immortal."

"Oh, my God!" the FBI director said in hushed tones. He certainly hadn't planned on anything like this.

24

Rick didn't like the looks of the two men who were walking toward him. They weren't making any threatening gestures; but something kicked off his mental alarms. They both carried tubes, about three and a half feet long. For their fly rods, Rick guessed.

"What happened to your friend, Ranger?" one asked.

"What friend?"

"The man who was standin' right here about thirty seconds ago," the other said.

Rick smiled. "There is no one here except me and my horses. Your eyes must be playing tricks on you." Rick didn't know why he was lying about Darry. He just felt it the right thing to do.

Tom Doolin and Bobcat Blake exchanged glances. Tom said, "We was supposed to meet some friends here and go fishing." He let that statement stand in silence for a few seconds.

"Someone was here," Rick said. "But the camp fire ashes are cold. Whether or not it was your friends, I can't say. Where were you planning on fishing?"

"Over there," Bobcat said, pointing.

Rick picked up on the lie immediately. Not unless you want to walk about ten miles, he thought. "Well, you men have a good time. I hope you find your friends. I'm sure they're close by." Of course, if you really wanted to contact them, you could use those radios you're both carrying in leather on your belts. What the hell is going on around here?

Tom squatted down beside the splotch of blood. "Bobcat? This is blood. Did you see this, Ranger?"

"Yes. Probably animal blood. Someone's been doing some poaching," he added drily.

"Not our friends," Bobcat said. "They weren't armed." He looked at Doolin. "I don't like this one damn bit." He glanced at Rick. "You gonna do something about this?"

"About what? Animal blood? If your friends haven't shown up in a couple of days, contact the ranger station and we'll launch a search party. Did your friends have a compass; were they skilled in back woods country?"

"Oh, yeah. They wouldn't get lost," Tom said.

Rick shrugged his shoulders. "Then don't worry about it." He paused. "You men have licenses to fish?"

"Ah . . . sure we do," Bobcat said, but the slight hesitation gave away the lie.

"Show them to me, please."

The two mercenaries exchanged glances. Then Tom Doolin smiled. "Well, I guess we left them back at camp, Ranger. Sorry about that. We promise to do better."

"Leave your fishing gear with me. You can pick it up at the ranger station by showing a current fishing permit."

"That's a little strong, isn't it, Ranger?" Bobcat asked.

"Put your fishing gear on the ground," Rick said, backing up a few steps. "Right now. And show me some ID. And do that carefully."

"For the want of a nail," Tom Doolin muttered, realizing that Robert Roche had thought of nearly everything . . . except for the men getting fishing licenses.

"What's that?" Rick asked.

"Oh, nothing. Just a bit of verse from long ago."

The mercenaries were in a bind. If they opened the

tubes, the ranger would see the tranquilizer guns, and they would really be in trouble.

"Well," Bobcat said, "I don't reckon we have much choice in the matter, Tom."

"None at all," Tom said. "I am sorry, Ranger. You just happened along at the wrong time."

"What the hell are you talking about?" Rick demanded.

"Killing you." Darry spoke from the edge of the small clearing.

Tom Doolin grabbed for the weapon he carried in a shoulder holster. Darry crossed the clearing with amazing swiftness and hit Doolin with a shoulder running at full speed. The charge knocked the man into his partner, and they both went down, pistols flying from their hands.

"Grab the guns, Rick!" Darry said, bouncing to his feet.

Rick kicked the pistols away and spun around, hands balled into fists. "I was a pretty good boxer in college, Darry."

"Not here," Darry said. "This isn't going to be boxing."

Bobcat and Doolin were on their feet, both of them smiling, standing with their hands open, held in front of them.

Rick jerked out his side arm. "I can stop this right now."

"No," Darry said. "Let them show me what they've got. I think I've picked up a few tricks of my own over the years."

"You're a fool, Ransom," Bobcat said, as both mercs dropped their backpacks and tubes. "I can take you apart by myself."

Darry's foot lashed out and impacted with the side of Bobcat's face. As graceful as a ballet dancer, Darry spun around and kicked Doolin in the stomach . . . showing the pair a simple exercise in savate. Both men went down and got right back up.

"He ain't no pussy," Bobcat remarked, blood leaking from one corner of his mouth.

Darry stepped in and slapped the man hard, open-handed, rocking Bobcat's head back and momentarily glazing his eyes. Darry turned as fast as a snake and jabbed stiffened fingers into Doolin's eyes. Doolin backed up, his hands flying to his eyes and his head shaking. Darry drove a balled right fist into Bobcat's chest, directly over the man's heart. He hit him three times on the chest, blows delivered so fast they were a blur to Rick's eyes. Bobcat paled as his heart skipped a couple of beats, faltered, and he struggled for breath. He sat down hard on the ground, both hands going to his chest. Darry spun and kicked Doolin in the mouth, pulping the man's lips and knocking him down. Darry then stepped in close and brought both hands in hard and fast, palms open, over the man's ears. Doolin's world went silent for a few moments, and he rolled on the ground, his head exploding in pain.

"You want to cuff them now?" Darry asked, stepping back. Rick noticed that the man was not even breathing hard, and he had not worked up a sweat.

Rick handcuffed the men, hands behind their backs, using the cuffs he carried on his belt and cuffs he carried in his saddlebags.

"Now let's see what's in those tubes," Darry said, although he already knew, from George Eagle Dancer's own lips.

"Well, I'll be damned," Rick said, hefting a tranquilizer rifle.

"What the hell are you charging us with?" Tom Doolin asked, shaking his head. His hearing still wasn't right.

"We'll start with assault with a deadly weapon against a federal officer," Rick said. "And work down from there."

"Shit!" Bobcat said.

* * *

"Mr. President," the White House legal counsel advised him. "It is not against the law to live to be seven hundred years old. We have no right to send agents in to capture this . . . Darry Ransom or whatever his name is. He has broken no laws . . . well, not really. We've got more important matters confronting us than a man purportedly seven hundred years old."

The President looked at him. "Such as . . . ?"

"The Collier family."

"Who?"

"The doctor and lawyer who were roughed up in the Idaho wilderness area. While protecting his mother, their son shot and killed a federal agent."

"What about them?"

"Agents from the Justice Department visited them in their home in Los Angeles, making veiled threats about what will happen to their son in prison . . . among other things."

"Son of a bitch!" the Pres said.

"Then, when they refused to deal, the IRS froze their assets and put them under audit."

The Pres sighed. "Go on," he said wearily.

His chief of staff said, "Sir, it is common knowledge among the people, albeit unproven, that the government uses the IRS for punitive measures against citizens they want to silence or whip into line."

"That's a damn lie!" the Pres said.

"No, it isn't," the DIR/FBI spoke up. "But it sure needs to be stopped. This nation is borderlining on become a dictatorship."

"Horseshit!" the Pres flared.

"You can shit your horse as much as you like," the director told his long-time friend. "But you can't deny the truth. And you just heard the truth."

The attorney general, who had finally been found

plucking wildflowers and running barefoot through meadows in the Smoky Mountains National Park, stirred uneasily. She knew without a doubt that many (if not all) federal enforcement agencies were in bed with the IRS and had been for years.

"I don't want to hear this," the Pres said.

"Mr. President," the legal counsel said. "Your approval ratings are very low. To be brutally honest, I have to say that the odds of your having a second term are slim to none. This is a golden moment for you to rise in the polls. Denounce the practice of using the IRS in a punitive manner. Hell, you don't have to stop it, just say you're going to."

(Isn't politics wonderful?)

"We are investigating more private citizens than ever before in the history of this country," Hank Wallace said. "We're investigating a writer of popular fiction because—"

The Pres waved a hand. "I don't want to hear about it. If this writer is being investigated, there must be a good reason for the investigation."

"He makes fun of liberal Democrats," Hank said. He looked over at the AG, who was fully aware of the order putting a full field investigation of the man into effect.

The AG chose not to return the gaze or comment on the statement.

The Pres answered his intercom. "An urgent call for Mr. Wallace."

"You can take it over there, Hank," the Pres said.

Hank spoke for only a few seconds and then returned to stand behind his chair. "A few hours ago, Ranger Rick Battle brought in two of the mercenaries who were in the area during the, ah, incident. They've been positively identified by captured CDL members as being part of the group who killed several federal officers." He looked at the director. "I'd like to talk to those people, sir."

The director looked at the Pres and received a slight nod. "Go."

Hank and Carol left the Oval Office.

Stormy took the video tape from the Colliers' camcorder and showed it to the network's legal department in Los Angeles . . . after making two dubs of the tape just in case the original tape might mysteriously disappear, and she felt sure it would if the federal government ever got its hands on it.

Politically, Stormy was a changed woman.

"We don't want it," was the legal opinion the next day, after the lawyers spoke with the CEO of the network.

"I didn't think any of you lace-pants liberal bastards and bitches would have the courage to show it," Stormy said. "So I quit!"

"Me, too," Ki added.

"That makes three of us," Craig said.

The news chief in New York, upon hearing that two of his top reporters and an award-winning camera-person had quit, told the head honcho of the network, "There is a fourth network out there who has been trying to assemble a good news team for several years. And as of right now, they've got a damn good nucleus of one. Fuck you! I quit!"

"Harold, goddammit, listen to me!" the head honcho said. "Sit down, please, and listen to me."

Harold Rushing sat. "So talk to me."

"What do you want, Hal? For the government to yank our license?"

"Oh, bullshit! It's time to take a stand. The government is fucking people over. Get off your liberal ass and stand up for the people, goddammit!"

"Are you forgetting who you're talking to, Hal? I run this network. Not you."

"No, I'm not forgetting who you are. I know who you

are. You and every anchor and the majority of the reporters on the Big Three. You've all got your noses jammed so far up the asses of cry-baby liberals, every time they fart you all have to put on a gas mask.''

"You're *fired!*"

"You can't fire me, I already quit!"

"You're through in this business! All of you. You'll never work again."

Harold Rushing tossed him the Rigid Digit and walked out of the office. He passed Don Weather, the co-anchor of the evening news, in the hall.

"Hi, Hal!" Don said, putting on his best "I like everybody, don't you like me" tone.

"Fuck you, too!" Hal said, and kept right on walking.

"He must have really had a bad day," Don said to a copy editor.

She rolled her eyes.

Just as Hal was approaching the door to his office, the other co-anchor of the evening news, Bonnie Fang, came strolling up the hall. "Hi, Hal!" she called.

Hal really didn't have anything against Bonnie. She was an okay sort of person. "Take a stand, Bonnie," he told her. "Speak up for what you know is right." Then he walked into his office and closed the door.

Bonnie stood in the hall for a moment, looking rather confused. She blinked a couple of times and finally said, "What?" Bonnie opened the door to Hal's office and found his secretary all red-eyed and opening a box of tissues. "What's up, Sally?"

Ten minutes later, Bonnie stormed into Don's office and exploded all over the place.

"I know all about it." Don finally got her quieted down. "I just heard. I'm just sick about it. It's regrettable, but I have to side with network policy. We simply can't support a right wing radical movement."

"What the hell are you talking about, Don? This is an issue about basic human rights being violated. The government using its enforcement agencies in a punitive manner against good, decent citizens.''

''I won't support anarchy, Bonnie.''

''Don,'' she said softly. ''You're a real prick, you know that?''

''I really, really resent that, Bonnie. That remark is so uncalled for.''

She stood for a moment, glaring at him. Then, for the second time in less than twenty minutes, Don was told to go commit an impossible act on his person.

''My word!'' Don said, after Bonnie had exited his office, slamming the door so hard it almost came off its hinges.

Before the sun set that day on the concrete canyons of New York City, dozens more resignations from employees who worked for the big three networks landed on various desks and twenty-two faxes announcing resignation came in from around the world. By late afternoon, seventy-two people, representing top reporters, news chiefs, producers, directors, award-winning camera-persons, and other experienced people in all aspects of news gathering grouped in the lobby of the offices of the Coyote Network, a maverick network that was fast becoming a major player in entertainment, sports, and investigative reporting. The owner of the Coyote Network, a free-wheeling, do-anything, hell-for-leather individualist who was Scotland-born, smiled at the group. As soon as he had heard word of the mass resignations, he had begun contacting TV and radio stations around the nation. The response had been so overwhelming it had staggered the man. Ian MacVay had sensed some time back that the American public wanted real news about America and Americans, not the same old tired bullshit that filled the TV screens every evening; not the same old time-worn liberal sobbing and hanky twisting; but real news about real working, law-abiding, over-tax-burdened Americans struggling to survive while it appeared the very government that was supposed to represent them was doing everything possible to grind them under the heel of socialism.

Tables were set up all around the huge lobby. Coyote personnel were ready to start hiring. Ian raised his arms for silence. He said, "We're going to go on the air in seventy-two hours, people. It might be rough and ragged for a time, but we're going to do it. We're going to give the American people news about America; news about big and small government waste and excesses; news about government sticking their noses into the private lives of the citizens; news about lost rights and personal liberties of American citizens. The bulk of our news will be for *Americans* and about *Americans*. Coyote affiliates have agreed, unanimously, for an hour's news each evening. We're going to go in-depth; we're going to bulldog stories from beginning to end. We're going to start a news revolution in this country. We're going to go after big government with a vengeance. Now, Washington will do its best to silence us. Be ready. They'll be sending their secret police in to snoop and pry and try to discredit us. It's going to get dirty, people, for Washington doesn't like its lid to be lifted up, exposing all the slime underneath. But we're going to do it. And we're going to have unlimited resources behind us. As you all know, I am a wealthy man, but just moments ago, the richest man in the world called me and agreed to throw his wealth behind our new endeavor. Mr. Robert Roche, of Roche Industries, is now officially on board."

Ian waited until the applause died down. He then waved toward the tables situated around the lobby. "Step up and sign on, people. The news revolution has begun."

Darry, listening to a small, battery-operated radio, leaned back against a tree and sipped his coffee, his face a study in concentration. "Well, now," he murmured. "Isn't that interesting. I wonder why the great billionaire capitalist, Robert Roche, would suddenly turn philanthropist and be so concerned about truth in government and so very distressed about the lives of ordinary American citizens?'' He laughed. Of course he knew why: to get at him.

Not far away, a wolf sang its lonely, lovely song to the fading afternoon skies. Darry smiled as the plaintive call was answered. Darry threw back his own head and howled. Then the twilight was filled with returning calls of the wild.

''You want me, Robert Roche?'' Darry muttered. ''Come get me.''

25

"Shit, shit shit!" the President said, using the remote to click off the TV after Ian MacVay had concluded his press conference. He looked at an aide. "Get me the commissioner at the FCC."

"Don't do it," his chief of staff cautioned. "You'll be playing right into their hands. That's the first move they'll expect, and they'll be ready for it."

"You expect me to stand by and let that pack of right-wing radicals get this network off the ground. No way will I allow that to happen."

"You can't stop it, sir," the chief legal counsel said. "I've already spoken with the FCC. Coyote submitted all the proper papers for a news department some time back, and it was approved. All we can do is ride it out."

"You mean ride this administration right out of office," the attorney general said. "Because that's what they plan on doing. Let me approve a full field investigation by the Bureau against everyone involved in this crazy scheme. We'll discredit them. We'll—"

"Good God, no!" the White House counsel said, considerable heat behind his words. "That would backfire on us before the ink was dry."

The President looked at the sheets of paper spread out on his desk. On the sheets of paper were the names of all who had resigned from the big three networks. "Hard-line conservatives," the Pres said. "Every one of them. Men and women who have, up until this moment, had to conceal their political leanings in order to keep their jobs. God, just look at this list. These people *hate* me. They hate *all* liberals. One can only shudder at the type of reporting that will be coming from the Coyote Network."

"Considering all the drivel that's been coming from the networks for the past several decades," the DIR/FBI remarked off-handedly, "I'm looking forward to it."

The Pres sighed. He knew very well his friend was far more conservative than liberal, and he also knew that the director of the Bureau was a very moral man. Many had considered that to be a liability when the Pres suggested him for the job.

The intercom buzzed, and the call was for the Bureau director. "Wonderful," the DIR/FBI said after listening for a moment. His voice was filled with sarcasm. "That is just wonderful." He hung up. He looked at the President. "The Collier family has filed papers to sue the federal government for half a billion dollars. The charges are attempted murder by a federal officer, three counts of assault and battery by a federal agent, ordering the Internal Revenue Service to engage in punitive measures against a citizen—or words to that effect—harassment, invasion of privacy, threats of bodily harm by agents of the Justice Department . . . and about fifteen other charges, pertaining to that family alone. In addition, the law firm of Bennett, Duran, Collier, and Williams is now representing the families of Carmouche, Clayderman, and Noble. They are suing the government for half a billion dollars. Do you want to hear the charges, Mr. President?"

"No," the Pres said with a sigh. "ShitShitShitShit!" he shouted.

Ian MacVay spent several million dollars in advertising during the three days prior to the Coyote Network kicking off their evening news. MacVay never even thought about making a profit; he didn't even consider breaking even. But when people began to understand that his news would be a total departure from what the public had been force-fed over the years, the sponsors began flooding his studios with calls wanting to buy time.

MacVay's people had not even worked up a rate card for the news; but someone had copies of the rates charged by the Big Three, so that's what MacVay's people went by.

Within six hours, the Coyote Network's evening news program was sold out for the rest of the month.

The six mercenaries who remained active in the wilderness were ordered to lay low . . . among other orders received from Robert Roche. Robert Roche had gotten word from Ian MacVay that the first segment of the Coyote Network's news was to come from that area: Stormy standing in front of the shot-up cabins of Kevin, Vince, and Todd. Darry was sure to make an appearance either before or after the taping.

Mike Tuttle had also made contact with Max Vernon. The now disgraced Bureau man and a few of the agents who had willingly gone along with the failed cover-up were living a rather miserable existence in a cave, poaching game and fishing to eat.

"Here's the deal," Mike told the man.

"Who are you working for?" Max interrupted.

"You don't have a need to know," the mercenary told him. "Are you in or out?"

"Do I have a choice?"

"No."

Max nodded his head. He was in bad need of a hot bath and a shave. "All right. We're in."

"We want Darry Ransom, and we want him alive.

Dead is no good. If he's dead, the deal is off. You understand?''

"Right.''

"Pull this off, and you and your boys go to work in South America. New names, new passports, new everything. You'll be paid well and you won't go to prison.''

"What about our wives and kids?'' another rogue agent asked.

"Forget them. Take it or leave it.''

"We'll take it,'' Max said, after conferring with the men.

Mike laid out the plan, ending with, "After you kill his dogs, Ransom will be so pissed off he'll throw caution to the wind and come after you. Me and my boys will be waiting. It's a simple plan and you know why . . .''

The more complex a plan the more likely it is to screw up.

"Transportation will be standing by to take us out of here. In seventy-two hours, you'll be in South America. Now, what about this location? What about the men who left you and got out?''

"We shifted locations as soon as the others decided to leave and try it outside on their own. They'll eventually be caught. But no one except you knows of this cave.''

Max was sure wrong about that. Chuck knew where the rogue agents were hiding out. Buckshot Jennings knew where the rogue agents were hiding. Darry knew where they were hiding. And the Unseen knew where they were hiding.

Max was not a totally stupid man. For a long time he had been a loyal agent of the Bureau. He had carefully kissed enough ass and made enough friends with power to enable him to reach a supervisory position, and he'd been very careful to always have men under him who would blindly follow orders and not make waves. Men who were assigned to him who had a lot of initiative didn't last long with Max. Max had always found a way to either have them transferred or run completely out of the Bureau. This operation was to have been his crowning glory; the pinnacle of success.

Max blamed his failure on Darry Ransom.

"Stormy is due in the area later today. They'll be setting up satellite equipment and all that other shit that reporters do. She'll be visiting Kevin Carmouche and the others tomorrow. Darry will be close by, bet on it. That's when she's going to get the news that a raid was done on that old outfitter's place and Darry's dogs are dead. Darry will surface then, and we'll get him and we're out of here. Understood?"

"Understood."

"Start getting your boys in place. But be careful. George Eagle Dancer is staying at Chuck's place. And that Indian will eat your boys alive if they're spotted. Don't underestimate George."

Max didn't immediately comment on that remark, but he didn't take it seriously, either. No damned mercenary was better than a trained Bureau man. That just wasn't possible.

"Do you understand about George?" Mike pressed.

"I understand."

"You better," Mike said very grimly. "George is almost the best there is."

"Who is better?" Max questioned. "You?"

Mike smiled and shook his head. "No. Darry Ransom."

Bobcat Blake and Tom Doolin were being held under heavy guard at the county jail. Hank Wallace didn't really trust Sheriff Paige, so he'd arranged to have federal marshals throw a ring around the jail just in case. It wasn't that Sheriff Paige was not a good man, for Hank knew he was. A damn good man. But a damn good man whose opinion of the federal government borderlined on open, undisguised hate.

One among hundreds of thousands, possibly millions, and steadily growing, Hank thought, as he and Carol drove back to the ranger station. And why not? Why should any observant, thinking citizen have much faith in their government? We spy on the people, we snoop into every aspect of their private lives, we investigate any who openly and loudly criticize the administration—no matter what party is in office—we position the IRS over Americans' heads like a spiked club. We can and do seize property, throw citizens out of their homes, freeze their assets, put them in jail, and in some cases, kill Americans if they resist.

"A penny for your thoughts, Hank," Carol said.

"To paraphrase my son: 'Government sucks!' "

"With a capital 'S,' Hank."

Steve Kelly, who used to cover Southern California for another network, was standing by at the Collier home in L.A. Debbie Howard, another top-flight reporter recently defected from one of the big three networks, was standing by at the home of the Kansas schoolteacher, Beverly Stevens. Mark Cole, one of the brightest and fastest rising stars in broadcast journalism (and an avowed conservative and anti-big government, which had not set well with his liberal bosses at the network he'd worked for until a few days ago) was standing by at what was left of the home of a man who had suffered through an early morning raid by agents of the Bureau of Alcohol, Tobacco, and Firearms—BATF. The man belonged to a group of hardworking, law-abiding, tax-paying American citizens who believed that government was out of control and were not afraid to say so, often and loudly. Naturally, the government couldn't allow people to group together and get organized and say bad things about their government. So acting under an "anonymous tip," federal agents, legally armed with a search warrant, raided the home at one o'-clock in the morning, looking for illegal weapons (assault rifles, naturally). Of course, none were found, but the man's wife was now in a local hospital, having suffered several broken ribs and a broken arm while resisting the ninja-suited and ski-masked goons who broke into her home. Trying to protect his mother, a ten-year-old boy was butt-stroked unconscious by an agent carrying an assault rifle (what else?). The child was now in the same hospital as his mother, with a broken jaw. Inside, the home was a wreck. Mattresses had been cut open, the floor ripped up, sofas torn apart, wall paneling pulled down, commodes and sinks ripped out. The agents had used metal detectors, scouring the backyard, looking for underground caches of weapons. Thousands and thousands of dollars worth of damage had been done to the home, and the only weapons found were a .22 caliber rifle, a .38 pistol that the man had bought at a gun show and was not registered, and one twelve gauge shotgun the man used for duck hunting. The man was placed under arrest and tossed in jail for having an unregistered pistol.

Your government at work, friends.

The local sheriff promptly released the man on his own recognizance and was standing by, with the homeowner, to give his opinion of the raid—which was not going to be very complimentary toward the government.

In New York State, another reporter from the Coyote Network was standing by with a man who had stopped a mugging in his town. He had broken the mugger's arm in doing so, and now the mugger was suing the citizen for zillions of dollars, claiming his civil rights had been violated because the citizen had called him an uncomplimentary racial name while he was preventing the mugger from using a knife on the woman he had attacked.

Six other reporters from the Coyote Network were standing by in other parts of the country, with similar stories to air. Naturally, the government knew where all the reporters were (having sent federal agents out to spy on them), and naturally, the agents reported back as to the content and substance of the stories, and naturally, the government was highly distressed about it. The AG's office concluded that these stories were going to agitate an already irritated American public and further exacerbate the situation. In other words, the average citizen was going to get pissed off.

The President looked at the field reports from around the nation and said, ''Oh, shit!''

''You've got more balls than Dick Tracy,'' Craig Hamilton said to Darry. ''There must be two hundred and fifty federal agents looking for you, and here you sit, calm as can be, drinking coffee and eating doughnuts.''

Darry had slipped into the home of Chuck, the outfitter, just before dawn on the day Max Vernon and team were due to arrive at the remote ranch to kill his dogs. One of Chuck's distant ''cousins'' had told the man what was going to happen. The cave in which Max and his cohorts were hiding ran for miles underground and was a natural amphitheater, a whispered word carrying for hundreds of feet.

Darry smiled at the reporter. ''Do you have the capability to go live from here?''

''Anytime I choose. Why?''

''Max Vernon and his boys will be here in about an hour. They're about two miles away right now. They've got some silly plan to try and flush me out.''

''How do you know they're two miles away at this moment?'' Craig asked.

''Signals,'' Chuck told him, sitting by a window. ''They're moving again, Darry.''

''Time to get into position. We—''

''Car pulling into the driveway,'' George called from

the front porch. "It's those two feds; Hank Wallace and Carol whatever-her-name-is."

"Just keeps getting more and more interesting," Darry said.

The satellite truck had been hidden in the barn, the technicians standing by, ready to relay. Stormy and Ki were at the remote cabins of the three families who were attacked by federal agents, ready to roll tape.

Hank and Carol stopped short at the sight of George Eagle Dancer, sitting on the porch, Pete and Repeat on either side of him, but recovered quickly. "You're just in time for the show," George told the pair from IAD. "Go right on in. If you don't mind, I'll pull your car around to the barn. We don't want our unexpected guests to be tipped off."

Hank looked at the mercenary with the hard eyes, taking in the face with the map of the world written on it. He shrugged and tossed him the keys. "All right. I'm not too old to enjoy a surprise."

"Go in the house," George told the hybrids. Pete and Repeat rose as one and padded into the house, through the door held open by Carol.

"Jesus!" Carol said, stepping into the den and spotting Darry.

"There are a lot of people looking for you, Mr. Ransom," Hank told him.

"So I've been told. I believe you know Chuck and Craig. Get yourselves a cup of coffee and relax for a few minutes. The show will start in about fifty minutes."

"What show?" Carol asked.

"One I'm sure you'll enjoy," Darry said.

Hank poured two cups of coffee and turned to Darry. "We got a tip that something big was going to take place here. The call came to us, through the sheriff's office, about two hours ago. The sheriff didn't seem all that interested in it."

Chuck smiled. "Greg don't have much use for you federal people."

"We gathered that much," Carol said drily.

"Would either of you care to make a statement for the press?" Craig asked innocently.

"I think not," Hank said. He looked at Darry. "It is my duty to inform you, Mr. Ransom, that you—"

Darry waved him silent. "Save it for later."

Hank sighed and sat down. He looked at his partner. "Why not?" he said.

Max Vernon really wasn't very intelligent. But he was prodding and thorough, and given enough time, he could figure things out. Now, squatting on a ridge about half a mile from the outfitter's house, he finally put it all together.

"It's a set-up," he told his men. "That goddamn mercenary set us up."

"How do you figure?" a young agent named Pat Lewis asked.

"Call it a gut feeling," Max answered sourly. Like the others, he was physically tired, mentally exhausted from being on the run, and his clothes were stiff with dirt and sweat. "Among other things."

"What other things?"

Richard Adams said, "I'm with you, Max. That ranch down there is just too goddamn peaceful-looking to suit me."

"Max?" called Marty Stewart, who had been bringing up the drag. "We got . . . *things* behind us and to the left and right of us."

"Things?" Max said, twisting around. "What the hell do you mean, *things?*"

"Just what I said, Max. Things. They walk upright, but they're not human. They're things."

Max smiled and then chuckled. "You've got a vivid imagination, Marty."

A series of low growls came from the brush all around the knot of maverick agents. The men moved closer together and tightened the grip on their weapons.

"Remember those footprints we saw back in the cave, Max?" Pete Elkins reminded him, nervously looking all around him. "I think those things out there made them."

"I hate this goddamn place," Sonny Martin said. "It's spooky out here."

Max glanced at his watch. It had stopped. He sighed. "What time is it?" he asked.

"We're supposed to hit the ranch in fifteen minutes," Pete said.

"Then let's do it," Max said, standing up.

From out of the brush and the timber and the rocks there came a strange sort of laughter. It was not human, but yet, oddly, it was. The sound rattled the nerves of the rogue agents.

"I hate this goddamn place," Sonny repeated.

"If we go down there, we're gonna die, Max," Richard said. "I feel it."

"Would you rather go to prison for the rest of your life?" Max countered.

That was met by stony looks.

"That's what I figured. Move out. We got a couple of goddamn dogs to kill."

26

In the loft of the barn, Craig's cameraman was filming the advance of the rogue agents. In the house, Hank lowered his borrowed binoculars.

"What in the world is the fool thinking?" Hank said softly.

"Oh, he's coming here to kill my dogs," Darry said. "He's now working with the mercenaries—he thinks. But they set him up. They called you and told you about the 'something big' going to take place here."

Hank and Carol both pulled their S&W stainless steel 10mm autoloaders from the high-rise regulation holsters.

Chuck snorted and tossed Darry the .375 Winchester. Darry levered a round into the chamber.

"You stay out of this, Ransom!" Hank said sharply.

"They came here to kill my dogs," Darry said. "That makes me a part of it."

"I am ordering you to . . . oh, to hell with it!" Hank said.

Carol turned her head for a moment so Hank could not see her smile.

"Call in!" Hank told Carol. "Tell base to . . ." He fell silent. "Sure we will. How are we going to do that when the damn car's in the barn?" Hank looked over at Chuck. The man was standing by a window, a rifle in his hands. The IAD man looked over to his right. George Eagle

Dancer stood by a window, a heavy caliber rifle held in his hands.

"Hank," Carol said. "Max and his people are armed with automatic weapons. These pistols aren't going to do us a lot of good."

"Rifle rack's over there," Chuck called. "Hep yourselves."

Carol chose a .308, Hank picked up a 7mm mag, and both loaded up, dropping a few extra rounds in their jacket pockets. By now, Max and his people were well within range. Before anyone could stop him, Hank stepped out onto the back porch.

"Damn fool!" Chuck said.

"By the book," Carol said. "That's the Bureau way. We're both wearing vests."

"Not over your heads, you ain't," Chuck replied.

"Hold it, Max!" Hank called. "FBI. It's Hank Wallace. It's over, Max. Give it up. You men, lay your weapons on the ground and advance toward me, hands where I can see them."

Max cut loose with a burst of .223 rounds, and Hank just managed to drop to the porch floor, safe behind a stack of firewood. The rogue agents scattered, two of them heading for the barn. Craig had left the house just after Hank and Carol had arrived and was in the loft. When the agents ran into the barn, Craig tipped over a tall stack of baled hay and flattened the two men, breaking the arm of one and knocking the wind out of the other. He jumped down and retrieved their weapons, then used their own handcuffs to secure the men.

"I got all of that, Craig!" his cameraman called.

"All right!"

Carol drilled one of the rogue agents in the belly with her .308, and Chuck doubled one over with a round from his old .30-30. Max, Marty Stewart, Peter Elkins, Richard Adams, and Sonny Martin headed for the road and crossed it, making the timber. Young Pat Lewis and the rest threw down their weapons and stepped out, hands in the air.

"We were just taking orders from the team leader, Mr. Wallace!" Pat hollered. "We were just following orders, that's all! I swear it."

Carol looked over at Darry and was shocked. The man's expression was one of sheer savagery. His pale eyes were glowing with an eerie light.

"Just following orders," Darry said, his face losing its barbaric look and the glow fading in his eyes. "Just following orders."

"There's been more innocent people killed by assholes just following orders than fleas on a bear," Chuck remarked.

Carol said nothing. But silently, she agreed with the outfitter.

The satellite truck was driven out of the barn and equipment made ready for broadcast.

No one noticed that Darry had slipped away as silent as the breeze . . . until the sounds of a fast-galloping horse reached them. But there was nothing anyone could do to stop him, for first off there was the business of arresting people to attend to.

"Don't say a word," Carol advised Pat Lewis. "It can and will be used against you in a court of law."

"Yes, ma'am," the young agent said.

She advised him of the rest of his rights as Hank was reading the rights to the others.

"Why?" an older agent now in handcuffs asked. "Just answer me that, Inspector. Why?"

"Why what, Dickerson?" The two men had known each other for over ten years.

"Why send us against people who haven't done anything wrong, that's what?"

"That's the very question a lot of American people are going to be asking," Craig Hamilton said, walking up, a microphone in his hand and his cameraman filming.

"There will be an official statement later on," Hank said. "Until then, no one here has anything to say."

"I do!" Dickerson shouted. "By God, I do!"

"Shut up, Dickerson!" Hank warned him.

"Max Vernon knew all along those hippies were clean," Dickerson plunged ahead. "And so did some of the other people in the various agencies involved in this screw-up."

"Goddammit, Dickerson!" Hank roared, trying to wrestle the man away from the damning microphone and the camera. "Will you be quiet?"

But Dickerson wasn't having any of it. "It's political. That's all it is. The orders come from higher up. We just take them and follow them. If we don't, we lose our jobs. And that's the God's truth."

"He's right, Mr. Hamilton!" young Pat Lewis shouted, jerking away from Carol. The mike and camera swung around. "It's political. Waco didn't have to happen. Neither did those killings up north of here. All that could have been handled without bloodshed. The government is out to get anyone who opposes it. And I mean anyone." The young man stared at the logo on the microphone and then shifted his eyes to the big van. "Coyote Network. But I thought you were with . . ." He trailed off. "Well, it doesn't make any difference. News is news."

"It is now," Craig said. "Now it's from the side of the people."

Hank and Carol could see their long careers with the Bureau slowly fading into the sunset with each damning word from the mouths of the captured agents. The men were in their custody; it was up to them to put a lid on comments from them.

Hank looked at Carol, and she smiled. Both could retire whenever they wanted. They had their years in. Both were lawyers and both wanted to practice.

"Well," Carol said. "Fuck it!"

"Yes," Hank said. "That sums it up rather well. Just . . . fuck it!"

They backed away and let the rogue agents talk. And talk they did.

In Washington, D.C., the President of the United States put his head down on his desk. He felt like weeping. He could practically hear the flapping wings of the circling buzzards, coming to pick the bones of his career clean.

Over in Justice, the AG wondered if it was time to start desk cleaning.

At the Hoover Building, the DIR/FBI leaned back in his chair, a strange smile of satisfaction on his face. No one else would ever know exactly what that smile meant. But then, the press had missed one important fact of his college days: the student had almost not gone on to law school. He had come very close to choosing another vocation, for his drama coach thought he would be a really terrific actor. And not only was the man ambidextrous, but the director had another talent besides the ability to play a part so well he almost believed it himself, and did, in fact, sometimes get so immersed in a part he actually played devil's advocate in his own mind: he would have also made an excellent forger, for he could copy anyone's signature well enough to fool most experts. He used to practice doing so with the signatures of his close friends.

"Is this what the government's coming to?" The man whose home had been ransacked and whose wife and ten-year-old child were now in the hospital spoke into the camera. He was angry but keeping that anger under control . . . with a visible effort. "Neither my wife nor I, and certainly not our ten-year-old son, committed any crime. Neither my wife nor I have ever received so much as a traffic ticket. We belong to a group of citizens who think that government has grown too large and is out of control. And we speak up about it. We send out literature detailing government excesses. We are not racist; we have people of all creeds and colors in our group. What happened here''—he held out a hand to the destroyed living room of the home—''is nothing more than a move by the government to attempt to silence us. Well, it won't work, Mr. President . . .''

''I didn't have anything to do with it,'' the Pres muttered, his eyes fixed on the TV screen in his office. ''You think I know every damn thing that goes on in every agency? How the hell can you blame me?''

Because you make the policy, stupid.

''This tragedy just strengthened our resolve,'' the man said. They had moved into the bedroom, which was a shambles. The camera panned to the bathroom, where the sink had been torn from the wall and the commode ripped from the floor. The man pointed a trembling finger at the camera. ''Now you hear me well, Mr. President. You're going to have to kill me to silence me. But when you kill me, there will be someone else to take my place. And yet another person ready to take their place . . .''

''It's not my fault!'' the Pres yelled, startling his chief of staff and others in the room.

Oh, but it is, Pres. You're the Man with the power. You could stop it with one phone call.

Mark Cole, the reporter for the Coyote Network, said, ''The phones in the small offices of the Citizens Against Big Government have been ringing nonstop all day. People from all over America calling in to sign up, to pledge money, asking what they can do to prevent another tragedy like this from occurring. And the answer is always the same: get organized. The number to call is . . .''

''Jesus Christ!'' the Pres hollered. ''News programs don't do things like that.''

''Relax,'' the President's legal counsel told his boss. ''Those captured Bureau agents are just babbling. Nothing they have said or will say can be proven. You certainly didn't order that tragedy at Waco, and you weren't in office when the killings took place in Northern Idaho.''

"I'm in office now," the Pres mumbled.

Most senators and representatives were in their Washington offices, watching the special reports from the Coyote Network on TV. Their phones had been ringing incessantly, fax machines dinging and donging; telegrams were pouring in.

"I think," the recently elected Speaker of the House whispered in awe at the events unfolding, "the revolution has begun.''

"No sign of Ransom," Ike Dover reported in by walkie-talkie. "But I thought I heard shooting over at the outfitter's ranch.''

"Stay loose," Mike ordered. "He'll be along. Out.''

That was the last report Ike would make on this day.

"Phsstt!" the sound came from behind Ike.

The mercenary turned around. "Oh, shit!" he managed to say, a micro-second before Darry hit him on the side of the jaw with the butt of the Winchester .375. Dover's world turned dark as he kissed the ground.

Darry trussed him up, threw his weapons into the brush, and moved on.

The mercenaries had formed a loose semicircle around the cabins of the families Stormy was about ready to interview, laying back about a half mile from the shot-up homes.

Miles Burrell felt a stinging in his butt and twisted around. He saw the feathered syringe sticking out of his left buttock and cussed as the powerful drug began to freeze his muscles, preventing him from moving. Within seconds he was fast asleep. Darry gathered up the man's weapons, reloaded his tranquilizer gun, and moved on.

John Webb thought a bee had stung him in the butt.

Then the knock-out drug began working on him, and he realized what had happened. But he could not move. He sighed, drifted off, and Darry moved on.

A few moments later, when none of his men would answer his radio calls, Mike Tuttle smiled grimly. ''Damn, but you are good, Ransom. Just about the best I have ever seen.'' A feathered syringe buried itself in Mike's butt, and Mike grunted as he went to his knees. ''Another day, Ransom. We shall meet again. Bet on that.''

Mike Tuttle collapsed on the ground and didn't fight the drug. He knew that to fight it was useless. He drifted off to sleep and would remain that way for several hours.

A federal judge, after sensing the political winds were very rapidly changing directions, had ordered the immediate release from jail of Kevin Carmouche, Vince Clayderman, and Todd Noble. In his decree, he wrote, ''Law-abiding citizens of the United States have the constitutional right to protect themselves against armed aggression, even when that aggression comes in the form of duly constituted officers of the law who have clearly made a mistake.''

The ruling was landmark, and the attorney general of the United States went ballistic.

''Don't say a goddamn word,'' the chief legal counsel to the President warned the AG. ''The attention span of the American people is too short to sustain it. The Coyote Network is a fluke. It will pass.''

He was sure wrong about that.

Darry Ransom slipped back into the deep timber of the wilderness, stretched out under the shade of a tree, and took a nap. He went to sleep with a very satisfied smile on his face. This was not the first time he'd helped fan the flames of revolution.

* * *

The American people had never seen news such as the reports airing on the Coyote Network. Those with any astuteness about them at all were mesmerized. Work in many factories and businesses around the nation slowed to a snail's pace that day, as the special reports kept coming in. The workers, whenever possible, were glued to TV sets.

When the hour-long evening news came on, the anchors from the Big Three felt like they'd been raped. They were airing reports about events in countries ten thousand miles away (most of which the average American had very little interest in, if any interest at all) while the Coyote Network was airing stories about America and Americans, events and happenings that touched a raw, exposed nerve in TV viewers.

"By God, the press is finally doing something right," was the general reaction from people who had stopped watching the evening news years back . . . since the content was always so boringly predictable.

Neighbor called neighbor that evening; friend called friend, all over America.

Ian MacVay took the last sixty seconds of air time that evening, proclaiming, "The Coyote Network will always put events about Americans and America first. If situations arise that might touch the lives of all Americans, we realize that residents of Binghamton, New York, want to know about those events, even if they are taking place in Valdosta, Georgia, or Santa Paula, California, or Kennett, Missouri. We are all a part of the whole. What takes place in one part of the nation directly affects those living in other areas of the United States. This is my adopted home, and just like all of you, I want to know what is happening in *my* country. And I want to know it immediately. And you will know about it when it happens, and that is the Coyote Network's pledge to you."

"Crap!" said the Pres, clicking off the TV. "I would very much like to get drunk tonight."

266 William W. Johnstone

"You can't," his chief of staff told him. "You're having dinner with selected members of CLAPCAA."

"What the hell is CLAPCAA?"

"Citizens for the Legislative Advancement of Political Correctness for All Americans."

"Shit!" said the Pres.

"You got that right," the chief of staff muttered, as he closed the door behind him.

27

Mike Tuttle awakened in the chill of early evening. He was stiff, sore, and the heavy drug had left him addle-headed. He reached for his pistol. It was gone. "Naturally," he mumbled, his tongue thick. He sat up with a groan and fumbled for his canteen. He rinsed out his mouth and then washed his face with the water. "This is getting real personal, Ransom. I think I'm going to make you my own private little war."

One by one, his team of mercs began reporting in, all of them thick-tongued and mad as hornets at being taken so easily. Mike acknowledged their check-ins and told them to make it to the rendezvous point. They had cached supplies there.

At the jump-off point, Mike said, "Ransom's gone. Don't ask me how I know, I just know." He paused, deep in thought. "This was a warning, boys. I think Darry just told us that he could have easily killed us all, and that the next time we meet, he will do just that."

Ike Dover said, "This Ransom person spooks me, Mike. He's the best I've ever seen. We need some more men."

"Yeah," Mike slowly agreed. "Roche said he wanted this prick alive, but he didn't say anything about crippled. We'll get a long-distance shooter and knock a leg out from under the bastard."

"Dale Williams," Nick Sharp suggested.

"That's who I was thinking of." He smiled. "And Dale don't like dogs."

Dennis Tipton gave him a hard glance. "Mike, I told you before, now I'm tellin' you again: you hurt those dogs of his, Ransom will kill you slow and hard. Not only you, but everybody connected with this operation."

"For Christ's sake, Dennis. They're *dogs,* goddammit. Just a couple of mutts."

"I don't like it," Dennis muttered. "I just don't like it."

The others laughed him silent.

None of them were aware of being watched from the edge of the clearing.

"Goddamn a person who would kill a man's dogs to get at him!" Chuck raged, after his midnight visitor had left. "Takes one sorry son of a bitch to do that."

"I know Dale Williams," George said. "He was thrown out of the army. Dishonorably discharged. He's a killer. He's a good shot, but he enjoys killing. It's almost a . . ." He grimaced. "A sexual thing with him."

Chuck spat in the cold fireplace, as if suddenly he had a very bad taste in his mouth. "How good is he?"

"Up to three, maybe four hundred meters, none better. Beyond that, I've seen others out-shoot him."

"That's a good shot, four hundred meters."

"Not bad," George said with a smile. "You're sure Mike and his people have left?"

"Yes. They packed up and pulled out."

"Darry?"

"He's over at his cabin with that female reporter." Chuck grinned mischievously. "I 'spect they both all worn down to a frazzle now and just talkin' low to one another."

"You're a dirty old man, Chuck."

Chuck laughed and slapped his knee. "Ain't it the truth?"

Network executives from the Big Three and two all-news networks had met in their conference rooms until late that night. Phone surveys had been done, and the Coyote Network evening news had blown them all out of the water. None of them had ever seen their ratings fall to such a dismal low.

News ratings were never great . . . but this was just *awful*. The talk in the various conference rooms went something like this:

"But they didn't even talk about the civil strife in Africa," one harried-looking executive said.

"Or the problems in the Mideast," another pointed out.

"Or the situation in the Balkans," another said.

"Or that terribly important conference in Pakistan concerning proper diet for Tibetan monks."

"*Nobody* watched the segment by Dr. Farnot on the heartbreak of facial hair on teenage girls. I thought that piece was exceptionally well done."

"I was enthralled by our piece placing the blame of the upswing in gang violence on either the lack of vitamin C or the Republican party. I thought it was very timely."

"I just don't understand it," another executive said, waving a handkerchief. "They didn't even run my favorite piece about the success of midnight basketball for disadvantaged youth."

"They didn't run it because while the game was going on there were two stabbings on the court and a thirteen-year-old girl got gang-raped in the locker room," it was pointed out.

"That doesn't mean the program isn't working," the hanky-waver rebutted.

A woman stood up and closed her briefcase. "You just

don't get it," she said. "None of you. And I doubt you ever will. We, and the other networks, are perceived by a large percentage of the population as antigun, liberal to the core, soft on crime, and pandering to punks. We're losing viewers because we don't run stories that a vast number of Americans want to see. Americans are overtaxed, overlegislated, drowning in federally mandated paperwork, distrust and in many cases openly hate their own government. They think the majority of senators and representatives are a bunch of crooks, live in fear behind barred windows and locked doors in their own homes . . . while we run stories about ingrown toenails, facial hair on teenage girls, carp every goddamn night about the Mideast—when only about five percent, or less, of the American public actually gives a big rat's ass what happens over there—we've all stopped editorializing because our editorials were so damned liberal it made the average American want to puke . . . and you people can't understand why the Coyote Network News just kicked our asses right off the ratings scale. Me? I'm going home. Providing, of course, I can get there without being mugged, or raped, caught up in a drive-by shooting, don't get run over by a drunk driver who already has been ticketed for DWI fourteen times and is still driving . . . or any number of equally depressing scenarios, while you people are sitting around here discussing tomorrow's news, contemplating about whether to run a piece on Mongolian yak drivers or the lack of political correctness in America. Personally, I'd opt for the yak drivers. Americans are much more likely to watch that. It has some human interest value. Animals, you know? Good night."

The morning was cool, and Stormy lingered for a time under the covers. She had told herself a hundred times that she was not going to make love to Darry Ransom. But she had, and now her story about him, if she did one, no matter how hard she tried to be objective, was going to be tainted.

Darry was up, had been for some time. She could smell the coffee. She smiled. Before coming out to Darry's cabin late yesterday afternoon, she'd called in to Coyote headquarters and heard some beautiful words: Coyote Evening News had kicked some butt. They'd earned the highest shares in television news history. The White House and everybody associated with it was furious; the IRS was vehemently denying it ever went after anybody for punitive reasons, certainly not at the suggestion of the White House, or any federal enforcement agency. Senators and representatives were being inundated with faxes, phone calls, and telegrams from hundreds of thousands of pissed-off Americans, demanding that big government be cut back and rigidly controlled. The FBI, DEA, BATF, Federal Marshals Service, and others were maintaining a tight-lipped, no-comment policy about anything and everything, and sponsors were literally hammering at the doors of Coyote headquarters wanting to buy time.

Life was good.

She closed her eyes, stretched under the warmth of blankets, and sobered. But now, what the hell was she going to do about Darry?

"You can start by having a cup of coffee," Darry spoke from the doorway.

Stormy jerked under the blankets. "Will you please stop doing that?" she said. "How the hell can you get inside a person's head like that?"

"My mother was a gypsy." Darry sat down on the edge of the bed and held out a mug of coffee.

"Sure she was," Stormy said drily, sitting up and taking the mug. Despite the coolness of the morning, Darry was shirtless, and her eyes took in the scars on his chest. "You can be hurt," she said softly.

"Oh, yes. But I heal very quickly." How quickly would have boggled her mind and mystified medical science. "You'd better make plans to get out of here, Stormy. This area is about to get very dangerous."

Her eyes widened, and the blanket and sheet fell from her shoulders to her waist. She paid no attention to that, but Darry sure did, enjoying every second of it. *"About* to get dangerous? What the hell has it been for the past couple of weeks?" She realized she was naked from the waist up and grabbed at the sheet while Darry laughed at her antics and took the coffee cup from her hand before she spilled it all over herself, and him.

"My parents really were gypsies," Darry said.

"Fine. Now tell me why this area is going to get more dangerous now than it has been?"

"Because the war between the mercenaries and me is about to get personal, that's why. They plan to kill my dogs in an attempt to anger me and cause me to slip up, get careless. But that will not happen."

"Kill Pete and Repeat? That's horrible!" She bit at her lower lip. "But how do you know this?"

"A friend told me last night."

A friend about six and half feet tall, weighing about three hundred pounds, with a head like a prehistoric bear and paws and claws for hands.

"Where was I?"

"Asleep." The press had never really believed the stories about the Unseen and, for the most part, paid no attention to the rumors. "Get dressed. I'll walk you back down to the ranger station."

"Maybe I don't want to go."

"You have to. You and the others have to keep hammering away at the government. You have to make the people so angry they'll approach an open revolt stage. Only that will make the government take notice and start heeding the wishes of the majority. You can't ever let up; never stop the momentum. Start asking hard and rude questions about third generation welfare recipients. Start questioning the reasons why the taxpayers should foot the bills allowing young, able-bodied people to live in public housing. Hammer at government waste in all areas. Get on the backs of elected officials and demand to know why an across the board flat tax rate—which the majority of Americans want—is never even brought to committee. Demand to know why we allow our elderly to die from the heat in the summer and the cold in the winter while the government spends billions of dollars in wasteful social programs that don't work. Question why our seat of government, Washington, D.C., is the crime capital of America.''

''Some of those things will make a lot of blacks and minorities very angry, Darry.''

''Good. They need to get angry. That's the only way they're going to solve the problems facing them. But they need to get angry at a small percentage of their own people who are causing the problems, and stop putting the blame on somebody else—stop blaming all their woes on society and whitey.''

''Oh, boy!'' Stormy said with a sigh.

''Start asking hard questions of the thousands of immigrants flooding into this country. Ask them how in the hell they expect to survive. Do they think it's fair and right for them to expect the American taxpayers to support them while some of our own long-suffering citizens are homeless and jobless and hungry? The press has got to stop ducking the issues and get down and dirty and take a stand.''

She smiled at him. ''You want a revolution in this nation, don't you, Darry?''

''I've started or helped start more than one in my time, Stormy. I hate big government. I've seen too many times what it inevitably turns into. The pen is mightier than the sword, Stormy. I've been a writer; I know.''

Stormy was silent for a moment, sipping her coffee. ''You know something, Darry,'' she said, almost wistfully. ''I felt good yesterday interviewing Kevin Carmouche and his friends. I felt like for the first time in my career I was really accomplishing something.''

''You were. Sticking it to big government.''

She laughed. ''You really do hate big government, don't you?''

''Passionately.'' He stood up. ''Get dressed. You've got to get out of here.''

''I told you, I don't want to go. And neither does Ki. She thinks this is where the big story is going to be, and so do I. And, I think, so do you, or you wouldn't be trying so hard to get rid of me.''

Darry slowly nodded his head. ''Yeah. Well, if I can't convince you to leave, you could stay with Chuck and George, I suppose. Both of you would be safe there. That's a fierce old man, and George is tough as a boot and as fast and dangerous as a rattlesnake.''

''I like both of those men.''

''Then you and Ki will stay with them; follow their instructions?''

She cut her eyes to him. ''You worried about me, Darry?''

''Well, yes.''

As their eyes met, something warm and pleasant stirred deep in Darry's soul, and something soft and gentle moved around Stormy's heart.

Don't be a fool! Darry thought. It never works, you know that.

You'll never do that story on Darry now, Stormy thought with absolutely no pangs of regret.

End it right now, Darry thought. Take her to the ranger station, leave her, and walk away and don't look back. You know that's the smart thing to do.

My God, Stormy thought. What kind of life are you expecting with this man? Your future together is hopeless. Don't let this happen.

It's unfair to her, Darry thought. You know it is. Don't let this happen.

Darry is news and I am a reporter! Stormy fought a silent battle she knew she would lose. He is news, dammit.
And the people have a right to know.

What kind of a life can you offer her, you damn
dreamer! Darry thought. After seven hundred years, isn't
it about time you accepted what you are?

Stormy slowly put out her hand and touched Darry's
bare chest, her fingers lingering on a scar that she was
sure had been made by a knife, or, she thought, more
likely a sword. "Do we have to leave this very second?"
she asked, her voice husky.

Darry touched her face with gentle fingertips. "No."
His eyes twinkled. "You have something in mind?"

She smiled.

Book Three

Book Three

28

A statement made by Pastor Martin Niemoller at the time of his arrest by the Nazi Gestapo in the late 1930s: "In Germany, they came for the communists, and I didn't speak up because I wasn't a communist. Then, they came for the Jews, and I didn't speak up because I wasn't a Jew. Then, they came for the trade unionists, and I didn't speak up because I wasn't a trade unionist. Then, they came for the Catholics, and I didn't speak up because I was a Protestant. Then, they came for me, and by that time, there was no one left to speak up."

The United States of America, in the mid-1990s: "In America, government agents came first for the machine guns, and I didn't speak up because I wasn't a machine gunner. Then, government agents came for the handguns, and I didn't speak up because I wasn't a handgunner. Then, government agents came for the semiautos, and I didn't speak up because I wasn't a semiauto owner. Then, government agents came for the antique gun collector, and I didn't speak up because I was a hunter. Then, government agents came for me, and by that time, no one was left to speak up."

* * *

"If this continues, Mr. President," a top aide said, "we will have a full-fledged revolt on our hands. And it will be unstoppable."

The Pres said nothing.

"I don't think it's quite that serious," a senior senator said. "Not yet. But I agree that the seeds of revolt have been planted."

"We could start deportation procedures against Ian MacVay."

"Don't be stupid. The man hasn't broken any laws."

The Pres remained silent, staring at his coffee cup on the conference table.

"We're all shooting at phantoms," another senior senator said. "Somebody is behind this movement. One person started this. But who?"

"I think it's that damn rabble-rousing writer from Louisiana," a representative from a NY district said. "We should have done something about him last year."

"What would you suggest?" a senator asked.

"We could have the IRS investigate him."

"We did," another representative said. "He's clean. And the FBI report stated that the man has never even received so much as a traffic ticket."

"He's preaching sedition!"

"Let's drop this. He writes fiction books," a more moderate Democrat said. "I don't even want to talk about tampering with the First Amendment."

"Why not?" the question was tossed out. "We've already violated the second, the fourth, the fifth, the tenth, and God only knows what others. Probably most of them, one way or the other."

Still, the Pres said nothing.

"We've got to disarm the people," the AG said. "A weaponless society cannot revolt."

A senior senator looked up, his eyes blazing. "You try to forcibly disarm the American public and there will be open warfare and blood in the streets.'' That statement was poo-pooed by the others at the conference table.

''Darry Ransom,'' the Pres blurted out.

''What?'' the VP asked.

''Who is Darry Ransom?'' a senator asked.

''What about him?'' the AG asked.

''He's behind all this. Bet on it.''

''Who the hell is Darry Ransom?'' the VP pressed.

''That's what I'd like to know,'' the rep from Brooklyn said.

The Pres sighed. ''Not one word of this leaves this office. I mean that. It could make us look like total idiots.''

''Seems to me the Coyote Network is doing a pretty good job of that, and their news department is only a few days old!'' another senator spoke up.

The Pres ignored that. How does one deny the truth? When the men and women in the room were settled down, the Pres began explaining about Darry Ransom. At first they exchanged dubious glances, but that quickly changed to astonishment as the President's words sank in.

When the Pres had finished speaking, the men and women were at first silent; then the room erupted into a babble of voices, all of them stating opinions about Darry Ransom, the man who could not die.

It would have been so easy to rectify the situation confronting the government of the United States. But the men and women who ruled governments never seemed to want to take the easy path. They inevitably chose a rough and rocky road in a vain attempt to please everybody . . . and that is impossible.

All the President had to do to defuse the situation was to go on national television and admit that government enforcement agencies were a bit out of control, and promise to put them on a shorter and stronger leash. All the Pres had to do was admit to the existence of the Bureau's ''secret files'': a massive and totally illegal file kept on citizens who had broken no laws. All he had to do was promise the files would be destroyed, and those investigations stopped. But of course, he didn't.

All the Pres had to do was promise to the American public that he would personally steer through congress a flat-rate tax bill, thereby easing the terrible burden on taxpayers and making the system much simpler and fair to all. He could have said that the dictatorial powers of the IRS would be put on a short rein. But of course, he didn't.

All the Pres had to do was promise that the hated (by many) gun grab bill was history. He could have let the current assault rifle ban stand and promise that no further legislation to disarm the American public would be forthcoming, and that would have satisfied any reasonable-thinking gun owner. But he didn't.

There were a lot of things the Pres could have done to defuse a bad situation. But of course, he did none of them.

When the Pres had outlined his plan, a liberal loudmouth from the upper Midwest bellered, "Right on! We'll get tough!"

There were dissenters, but they were few, the older and wiser among the bunch; and they were shouted down.

Out in the hall, one older senator, with years of politics behind him, said to another senator, also with years of Washington experience behind him, "What do you think?"

"I think," the senator said, a grim note behind his words, "that we'd better find us some helmets and flak jackets. The goddamn revolution is about to start."

That evening, reporters from the Coyote Evening News spent half an hour interviewing men and women whose lives had been shattered and careers ruined by the IRS. The reporters went in-depth and personal with the stories. When they finished, the IRS came out looking like the monster that elected officials had allowed it to become—

going directly against the wishes of the majority of American citizens.

The next half hour of the Coyote Evening News was devoted to victims of violent crime. Residents of Small Town, Illinois, were not surprised to learn that residents of Small Town, Florida, and Small Town, Texas, and Small Town, California, and Small Town, New York, were all related in that they had experienced mindless incidents of violent crime and the slap-on-the-hand punishment many of the offenders received . . . and what the risks were when a citizen decided to defend himself or herself against violent criminals.

"The son of a (beep) was raping my twelve-year-old daughter in the shed behind the house, and I shot the (beep). The (beep) cops came and arrested *me!* Can you believe that? The (beepbeepbeep) cops arrested *me!* Then the parents of the sorry (mother-beep) sued me in a civil action. They lost in court, but it still cost me thousands of dollars for lawyers. It wiped out our savings. That's not right. It's just not right."

"This sorry little (beep) stole my brand-new car and totaled it. You know what the judge gave him? Probation! My insurance rates went up because my car was stolen and wrecked through no fault of my own, and that little (beep) gets a slap on the wrist. He's out walking the streets, and I'm paying higher insurance premiums for the rest of my life. Do you find something wrong in that?"

Listening to the Coyote News on a radio, Darry smiled. He'd helped sow the seeds of revolution back in America's infancy, and now he had the chance to do it all over again.

It was a very satisfying feeling.

He turned up the volume.

"This (beep) smashes my wife in the head with a tire iron, fracturing her skull and blinding her in one eye. He grabs her purse and takes off. My son jumps in the car and goes after the (beep). The alley is dead-end, and my son pins the (beep) against a brick wall, breaking both his legs. The (beepbeep) punk sues us and *wins!* Can you believe that? You're (beepbeep) right I think it was racial. I'm white, the (beep) is black, and the jury was eight-to-four black. What do you think? This nation is all (beeped)-up.''

Darry heard the slight noise behind him and tensed. Then his acute olfactory senses told him the man was George Eagle Dancer. He relaxed. George was one of the very best men in the brush Darry had ever seen. The half-breed could move like a ghost.

George squatted down beside him, a smile on his lips. ''I almost got up on you, didn't I?''

''Almost, George. But close only counts in horseshoes and hand grenades. What's going on?''

''You've been formally charged with sedition against the government of the United States. Among other charges.''

''Name some of the other charges . . . as if I didn't know.''

''Evading income tax for the purpose of defrauding the government, living under an assumed name, taking a false social security number, aiding and abetting federal fugitives . . . the list is pretty long.''

''How are my dogs?''

''Fat and happy. They're safe. What about these charges, Darry?''

''They're just about what I was charged with in Europe several centuries ago. Wording is different.''

''What did you do?''

Darry smiled. ''I killed a king. Now bring Stormy out here.''

George chuckled. ''How did you know? I left her a hundred yards back.''

''I smelled her scent.''

George discreetly vanished into the brush and gave Darry and Stormy some time alone. ''You've got to let me broadcast your story, Darry,'' she said, pressing against him, her arms around his neck. ''I don't want to, but it's the only way to expose the government for what they are.''

''No. That's what the government wants.''

She pulled back and looked at him. ''What?''

''The Ottoman Turks tried the same thing. In a manner of speaking. The government wants to deal, Stormy. I turn myself in to them for study, and they drop the charges against me. All a big mistake, they'll say. No. I won't do that. But it's going to get rough. You don't know big government the way I do. Everybody who was involved in this 'incident' in the wilderness is going to get dirtied. The government will very carefully manufacture charges to bring against everyone involved. Those charges might not stick in court . . . probably won't. But the government has batteries of lawyers, and it'll be expensive.''

''A month ago I would have called you a liar, Darry.''

''I know.''

''Now what?''

''I always say I am never going to get involved with big government again.'' He smiled. ''But I always end up doing exactly that. Keep hammering and chipping away at government excesses, Stormy. Do as much as you can in the time the government allows you.''

''Darry, they *can't* stop us. For all its faults, this is still the United States of America. And there is such a thing as the Constitution. We have rights—all of us.''

Darry's smile was sad. ''I hope all the reporters now working for Coyote are clean. For if there is a blemish in the past of any of you, you can bet the hundreds of government agents now investigating each and every one of you will find it and use it against you. You can bet a year's salary there is a full field investigation going on right now.''

''We're being investigated by the FBI?''

"You better believe you are. And it's being done by men and women who are very, very good at what they do."

"But we haven't done anything wrong."

"That doesn't make any difference, Stormy. The government has extensive files on Americans who have broken no laws. Now come on! Surely you knew that?"

"I . . . suspected it."

Darry studied her face for a moment as they sat in the shade of a clump of trees, the Salmon River, the River Of No Return, miles to the south of them. "You really didn't know about the secret files, did you?"

She shook her head. "No. I didn't. But that's against the law, Darry."

He laughed bitterly. "Whose law, Stormy? What law? The same laws that apply to American citizens don't apply to big government. You think you can gain access to them through the Freedom of Information Act? Forget it. Think again. All the investigating agency has to do is run behind the National Security Act, and they don't have to tell you a damn thing. Ever. Or more than likely, if you confront the agency that is investigating you, they'll just say: 'Files? What files? We don't have any files on you. Who are you?' "

"You make our government sound . . . so evil."

"It is, Stormy. It's also profane."

"Riders coming, Darry!" George Eagle Dancer called out softly.

Stormy had one arm around Darry's neck. A second later she had her arm around the neck of an enormous gray wolf with jaws so powerful they could crush the spine of a buffalo with one snap. She was so startled she could not utter a sound.

The big wolf licked the side of her face and was gone into the brush with one bound.

Stormy came very close to peeing her panties.

29

That Sam Parish and many of his followers in the Citizen's Defense League could vanish so completely and stay hidden was a tribute to the burgeoning survivalist movement in America. While many, if not most, of the survivalist groups in the nation were not racist (although why that should be any business of big government was a mystery to many, unless the government was now attempting to monitor and control individual thoughts), and did not present any threat to the government of the United States, there were quite a few who did—at least in the minds of many government officials—and those groups networked with each other. With the government's ability to listen to anybody's phone calls (which many believed they did with an alarming frequency), government enforcement agencies able to intercept private mail and duplicate envelopes in a matter of seconds (which they did), citizens who wished to engage in private conversations had learned to be very inventive in communications.

It drove the government crazy.

Any coded message was a threat on the life of a senator or representative or some other elected or appointed bureaucratic and officious little dipshit. Scrambled or coded communications between private citizens were a plot to overthrow the government to the paranoid, sneaky, and devious little minds of many government officials, whose sole purpose for existence (or so it appeared to many) was to foul up the lives of as many law-abiding, tax-paying American citizens as possible . . . especially if they were ultraconservative (liberals referred to them as right wing and fascist) in politics and had the courage to speak out against America's steady advance toward socialism.

Sam and his group went underground and kept their heads down.

Three weeks had passed since the fiasco in Idaho ended and the Coyote Network had gone on the air. The so-called "fluke" of news reporting and broadcasting had turned out to be anything but. The Coyote Network's evening news and special reports consistently, night after night, garnered the highest ratings in TV news history as they stubbornly hammered away at government excesses and Big Brother's insidious invasion into the lives of private citizens. Elected officials were warned, quite bluntly, by their constituents, that there had better be a flat tax rate brought to the floor for a vote, and it better be done damn quickly or a lot of elected officials were going to be out on their asses looking for work.

The Coyote Network reminded viewers that when the tax code was first written, it was about fourteen pages long. Now it was over ten thousand pages long.

"As usual, the ultraright-wingers are misinformed," one ultraliberal U.S. senator solemnly intoned, looking and sounding as if he were delivering the eulogy at a funeral. "It is only nine thousand seven hundred and fifty-three pages long."

Someone in the group of reporters gave him a loud, wet raspberry.

"It is no laughing matter," the senator mumbled on. "Every word in those tax codes is vital to this nation's very existence and to the welfare of its citizens. The voluntary compliance to the gathering of taxes is the very rock this nation stands on."

"I thought that was Plymouth Rock," a reporter called. The senator gave her a very dark look.

"What do you mean, voluntary?" the reporter from the Coyote Network called. "There is nothing voluntary about it. The government collects taxes at the point of a gun."

"That's a vicious lie!" The senator lost his cool.

The Pres, watching the news conference from the Oval Office, said, "Oh, shit!"

Darry's wait for the return of the mercenaries ended one rainy morning in early June. He had been alerted the day before that all federal agents who had been in the area looking for him had suddenly pulled out.

"So Mr. Roche has some considerable stroke with the government," Darry muttered. "That is very interesting. Sometimes, Mr. Roche, when you play both ends against the middle, you can get hurt."

But he knew getting to Roche would be next to impossible.

"Are the dogs safe?" he had asked Chuck.

"Yes. Don't worry about them. Darry? My . . . ah . . . relatives could take these men out and there would be no trace ever found of them. These ol' boys plan to hurt you, Darry. Cripple you."

Darry shook his head. "No. This is my fight. It's personal now. Tell the Unseen to lay low until this is over. Chuck, thanks. You better get back now."

The outfitter nodded his head and turned to leave. He looked back. "Stormy said to tell you she'd see you when this mess is all over."

"She didn't file a story about me, did she?"

"No, and she never will, neither. She's in love with you, Darry."

Darry offered no reply to that. He sat under the low overhang of branches until Chuck had disappeared from sight. "I warned you men," Darry muttered. "I gave you ample opportunity to leave here with your lives. Now you've returned to harm me. So be it. You have no one to blame but yourselves."

Darry rose and began moving through the brush and timber, never exposing himself on any clearing. An hour later, he heard a shot, followed by a howl of pain. He recognized the cries as coming from a two-year-old member of a pack. A young male. There would be mourning in the pack over the loss. The cries died away as life left the young wolf. A mercenary had shot the animal thinking it was Darry; and had it been, it would not have died, and their capture would have been successful.

"Bastards!" Darry muttered.

A half mile away, Miles Burrell looked down at the dead wolf and shrugged. "I guess that ain't him," he said to Ike Dover.

Ike gave the still-warm body a vicious kick. "We'll shoot every goddamn wolf we see."

"What if the rangers show up?" one of the three new additions to the group asked.

Mike Tuttle looked at Roy Craft. "We shoot them, too. But don't kill that foxy little ranger. I want to pack that little pussy of hers full of meat." He smiled. "Then we kill her."

Standing a few yards away, Dennis Tipton made up his mind. He was out of this. All the way out. He'd warned the men time and again they were making a mistake coming back into the wilderness for Darry, and making a terrible mistake by killing dogs and wolves in order to get to Ransom. War was one thing, this was something else entirely. But how to get out was the question. Mike and the others had crossed that invisible line. They had turned from soldiers into killers.

"I thought I saw tracks back yonder a ways, Mike," Dennis said, his mind made up. "I'll see where they go and bump you."

"All right. Stay in touch."

Oh, you bet I will, Dennis thought. I'll send you a tele-gram from my farm back in South Carolina. Providing Darry lets me get out of here alive.

Dennis walked away into the mist that hung close to the land. A few minutes later, Darry watched the man throw his rifle and tranquilizer gun into some brush, then re-move his holstered pistol and toss that into the brush.

"Keep your knife," Darry said, stepping out of the thicket and almost causing Dennis to shit his underwear. "You might need that."

"I'm out of this foolishness," Dennis said. "I warned Mike and the others not to come back. Told them it was wrong. Now I'm through."

"Go on back to the ranger station. Tell Rick and Al-berta what's happening out here. And tell them I said to stay put this day. Don't come out into this sector." Darry took a stub of pencil and wrote a few words on the back of an envelope. "Give this to Rick. That will convince him you are being truthful. Don't return here, mercenary." Then Darry threw back his head and howled, the waver-ing notes sending shivers up and down Dennis' spine. Darry howled and howled, each chilling call a bit differ-ent from the other.

"What in the name of all that's Holy was that about?" Dennis blurted.

"I just assured you safe passage, mercenary. You, alone. Now go."

Dennis needed no further urging. He set out for the ranger station at a fast walk. He did not look back.

It was nine o'clock on the morning that America's sec-ond revolution was beginning.

"We've got a situation out in Texas, Mr. President," a very nervous aide informed the Pres.

"Oh, shit! Not another Waco?"

"Worse."

"What the hell could be worse than Waco?"

Before he could reply, another aide came up, his face shiny with nervous sweat. "We've got a situation in upstate New York, sir."

"My mother warned me not to go into politics," the Pres said. "She wanted me to take over the ranch instead. But I ran for senator and to my surprise I got elected the first time out of the gate. Worse goddamn decision I ever made. I could have been very happy as a cowboy." He sighed. "What's going on in Texas and New York?"

"You want the condensed version or the whole picture?"

"Just turn on the damned television set," the Pres said sourly. "I'm sure the Coyote Network is already on the scene and playing it for all it's worth."

At the urging of all concerned, Stormy and Ki had left the wilderness area to step back into the modern world. As soon as they heard what was happening in Texas, they had taken a private jet into Lubbock and rented a car for the short drive north. Another Coyote Network news team had jetted into the closest airport in upstate New York and rented a car for the drive west and slightly north. Both news teams were as close to the trouble spot as the police would allow them to get and were set up and broadcasting.

"From what we have learned so far," Stormy said, "it seems that a Mr. Roy Linwood had several hard choices to make. None of those choices easy ones. Faced with years of enormous medical bills that his insurance did not cover, Mr. Linwood decided to pay what he could on his medical bills and house notes rather than pay income tax. Over a period of three years, the man has struggled to keep his wife and son alive, and also to pay what he could on his mounting income tax bill. Early this morning, agents from the IRS moved in to seize Mr. Linwood's property . . ."

"Oh, Jesus Christ!" the Pres said, putting his face into his hands. "Not this, not now!"

In upstate New York, Mark Cole was broadcasting. Coyote cut away from Texas and switched to his location. "Barricaded inside this modest frame home is Mrs. Georgia Hill and her three children, ages nineteen, sixteen, and thirteen. The youngest is a girl, Sally. Since her husband's suicide five years ago, Mrs. Hill has worked as a waitress at a local restaurant. Prior to her husband's suicide, Mr. and Mrs. Hill operated a small but profitable business in this small community. Like nearly all middle-class Americans, they struggled to pay their taxes and, at the same time, tried to maintain a decent lifestyle . . ."

It was a horror story, and the President was the most horrified, but much of it for strictly political reasons. He grabbed up the phone. "Get me the director of the IRS—now!" he shouted. A moment later: "Get those goddamn agents out of there!" he screamed. Then his face went chalk white. "What in God's name do you mean 'what agents?' Don't you know what the hell is going on in your own fucking agency?"

Then the President heard shots coming from the TV speakers. "Oh, Christ!" he yelled. "Good God, no!"

"The people inside the house fired on the agents first!" a very excited aide said.

"I don't give a damn who fired first!" the Pres yelled. "Tell your people to stand down and back off," he shouted into the phone.

"Shots have been fired in Texas, sir."

"Shit!" the Pres yelled. "Stop the shooting! Stop the shooting!"

*   *   *

Close, Darry thought, as the slug from the high-powered rifle slammed into a tree just inches from his right leg. Darry bellied down on the ground, cradling his .375 Winchester, and crawled into a thicket, then rolled down into a ravine and began circling. Darry knew every foot of this terrain; knew where all the hidden depressions were, all the places that afforded even the smallest bit of cover.

"I think Dale winged him!" The shout came from only a few yards away from the ravine.

Darry stood up, cocking back the hammer as he did. He let the Winchester boom. Ike Dover never realized what hit him as the big slug exploded his heart.

"Did you get him, Ike?" Miles shouted.

Darry had already spotted Miles and fired. The mercenary raised up and dropped his rifle. He toppled to the ground and died looking up at the sullen sky, the fat rain drops splattering wetly on sightless eyes.

Darry ran on through the ravine, exited the twisting corridor at a stand of timber and zigzagged through the trees and brush up a long slope. No shots were fired, so he guessed he had not been seen. Darry thumbed two more rounds into the Winchester and stretched out in a prone position. The mercenaries could not approach him from the rear, for that was a sheer climb of about a hundred feet. To his left lay an open field, and to his right was a burn area caused by lightning hitting a tree a few months back. They had to come at him from the front.

Darry took a sip of water from his canteen and waited.

Horrified Americans watched as Georgia Hill staggered out of the house, her chest bloody. She lifted a rifle, and the federal assault team fired as one, a dozen rounds slamming into her body. Screaming their rage at the death of their mother, the three kids opened up with a shotgun and two .22 rifles from the windows of the house. The federal agents returned the fire. All America watched the tragedy on television, and many, male and female alike, wept as thirteen-year-old Sally Hill tumbled out of a window, half her head blown off. Her brothers, nineteen and sixteen years old, solemnly shook hands and charged out the back door, firing as they ran. They were chopped down by automatic weapons fire and died in a sprawl. Mark Cole noticed that both soles of the shoes the sixteen-year-old was wearing had holes in them.

Mark was so angry, so shaken by what he had just witnessed, he lifted his microphone and said, in a voice choked with emotion, "The America our forefathers envisioned has turned into a bloody nightmare."

In Texas, Stormy watched as federal agents, wearing gas masks, assaulted the home of Roy Linwood, running through clouds of choking gas. From inside the house, three carefully spaced shots boomed. Roy Linwood had killed first his paralyzed son, then his wife, and then himself.

"Everybody's 10-7 in here," a federal agent called from the porch of the house. Law enforcement ten-code numbers for "out of service."

"Get out of here," a local radio newscaster said to Stormy and Ki, his voice shaky. "Right now. All hell is about to break loose."

The women turned. The street in front of the Linwood home and the lawns on both sides and to the rear was filling with grim-faced Texans, men and women, all of them carrying rifles or shotguns. It got very quiet. The sounds of bolts and levers and slides working, jacking rounds into chambers, was loud in the sudden stillness. Stormy and Ki had backed up, Ki filming as she went.

"We are witnessing the beginning of a revolution," Stormy reported.

"You people are going to be in serious trouble if you don't put those weapons away!" the team leader said through a bullhorn. "You are interfering with federal officers."

''Don't film any of the citizens' faces,'' Stormy said to Ki.

A deputy sheriff standing close by smiled at that. ''Finally, the press is on the side of the people,'' he said.

The team leader of the federal agents turned to the county sheriff, standing off to one side, and lifted his bullhorn. ''These are your people, Sheriff. You'd better do something.''

The sheriff folded his arms across his chest and smiled.

31

The standoff in the small town in Northern Texas ended without further bloodshed, but it left some very badly shaken federal agents, who all knew they had come within a heartbeat of dying at the hands of very pissed-off citizens. And they all knew, too, that their power would never again be the same—anywhere in the United States—unless Big Brother came back to this town and came down hard on the citizens who had taken part in the . . . well, call it another "incident."

"Take the film from all the reporters," Stormy whispered to the deputy who had smiled at her.

"Right good idea, little lady," he said. "But you can keep yours. You people from Coyote are all right."

The FBI was in town less than an hour later, meeting with the sheriff.

"What happened to all that film of the incident, Sheriff?"

The sheriff shrugged. "What film?"

"Don't play games with us, Sheriff. The citizens of this town are in a lot of trouble."

Wrong words to say to a tough ol' Texas sheriff who grew up on a working ranch and won a chestful of medals in Korea with a regimental combat team. The sheriff pointed a finger at the special agent. "Let me tell you something, you goddamn blow-dried federal fart. Agents from the IRS came into this town prepared to put a sick man, his dying wife, and their paraplegic son out into the goddamned street with just the clothes on their backs, because they couldn't pay their fucking federal income tax—''

"Now you listen to me, Sheriff!" The Bureau man got his dander up. He wasn't accustomed to being spoken to in such a manner. "Nobody, *nobody,* points guns at federal agents and gets away with it. I want that film."

"Good luck in getting it," the sheriff said with a smile, leaning back in his chair. "I heard, through the grapevine, of course, all that film was burned up. However, I disremember exactly where I heard it."

"Sheriff, we both wear badges. We both enforce the law. We're on the same side."

"Are we?" the sheriff questioned softly. "Maybe it started out that way. But no more. I think most of the time now we're on opposite sides of the fence."

"You can't mean that, Sheriff."

"The hell I don't! What about all that mess that happened last month up in Idaho? What about that uncalled for, god-awful, government fuck-up over in Waco? What about that mess up in Idaho two/three years back where that young woman and her son was killed? I work for the people, sonny. I don't spy on them. We don't keep secret files on hard-workin', decent people. Roy Linwood was a good, decent man who fell on hard times. He had a series of terrible choices to make, and he made the right ones, I think. He chose family ahead of all else. And if you wouldn't have done the same, then you're a damn sorry excuse for a man. Now get the hell out of my office. I want to listen to the Coyote News special report comin' up shortly. They tell it like it is."

* * *

Darry held high, and the slug took the mercenary just under the throat and blew out part of his spinal cord. John Webb was dead before he hit the ground.

"Jesus Christ, Dale!" Mike shouted into his radio. "Will you get some lead in that son of a bitch!"

"He's behind good cover, Mike," Dale radioed. "I can't get a clear shot at him. And that is no off-the-rack rifle he's using, either, and that ammo is hand-loaded."

Right on both counts.

"And he's got the high ground," added Roy Craft, one of the three new mercs hired, just as the third new mercenary jumped from his position and tried to make it up the burn area.

Darry dusted him, the round going in one side and blowing out the other. The man rolled slowly down the hill, coming to a stop only after getting wedged between two burned-out hulks of fallen trees.

"Quinn didn't last long," Nick observed.

"What's behind the bastard?" Mike tossed the question out.

"Forget it," Nick radioed. "Straight in is the only way."

"Well, straight in is suicide."

"Where the hell is Dennis?"

"I think Dennis split," Roy Craft said. "I told you I thought he would."

"So you did, Roy," Mike radioed. "So you did. Everybody just hold your position."

The words had just left Mike's mouth when Darry's rifle boomed and Roy Craft took a slug in the center of his forehead. It was a chance shot, and Darry had not expected to hit anything. But Roy raised his head just as Darry squeezed the trigger.

Mike keyed his handy-talkie. "This isn't worth a shit, boys. I'm going to give this bastard a full magazine while you two make for those woods behind you. When you get there, both of you give me cover fire.''

When the lead started howling all around him, Darry had no choice but to keep his head down, suspecting what prompted the gunfire. But when Mike's magazine was empty, Darry chanced a look and saw that the two retreating manhunters had not quite reached the timber. Darry leaped to his feet and made it across the burn area before Mike could slam home a fresh magazine.

"Son of a bitch!" he heard Mike's angry shout.

Darry went to his knees in a blow-down of tangled logs and brush, caught his breath, and sighted in on a man's head, several hundred yards away. He couldn't make out the man's features, only that it was one of the two mercs who had left the hill under cover fire. He knew the drop of the bullet at four hundred yards and held high, his finger taking up slack, and the rifle fired itself. The big bullet took Dale Williams in the left eye and splattered Nick Sharp with bits of bone, blood, and gray brains. Yelling his rage, Nick gave Darry's position a full thirty-round mag.

Mike left his cover and zigzagged across the open meadow, expecting any moment to take a round in his back. He leaped for the brush and caught his breath. "Nick?" he panted into the handy-talkie.

"Yeah. I'm all right. But Dale is dead. I'm wipin' his head off me right now."

Mike did some old-fashioned cussing for a moment. Then he lifted the transceiver. "Abort this, buddy. Meet you back at the Broncos."

"Ten-four."

Darry watched them go, waited for several minutes, and then began jogging, making a wide circle. He knew where the men had parked their vehicles, and that was a full day's hard march away.

The sky opened up, and a hard, cold rain began falling. At this rate, Darry knew from experience, it would not take long for the creeks to fill to overflowing, making many of them difficult to cross.

Mike and Nick had linked up and found a trail, leading west. "This will take us to the ranger station," Mike said. "We'll kill the man, fuck the woman before we do her, and take their vehicle."

"Sounds good to me," the Brit said, wiping the rain from his face. He grinned. "You recall that time we double-teamed that pretty little bird in Central America, fore and aft?"

Mike laughed, his eyes hard and shiny. "Yeah. She did scream some, didn't she?"

"Let's go."

An hour later, Darry cut their trail and knew where they were heading. "Shoot first and apologize later, Rick," he muttered. "You and Alberta are going up against some bad ones."

The big three networks gave the shootings in Texas and New York ninety seconds each of air time, then moved on to something much more important: the sending in of American troops to stabilize a country sixteen thousand miles away; the very important conference being held in Bora Bora on why aborigines sweat; and the annual conference in Geneva on the standardization of the screw head. The Coyote Network gave each shooting ten minutes and then offered a scathing editorial on the federal government's continuing policy of sometimes lethal overreaction against its citizens.

"I hate those goddamn people," the Pres said, during a commercial break on the Coyote Network's evening news.

"Mr. President," the AG said. "We've got to move against those people in Texas. We simply can't allow private citizens to hold federal agents at gunpoint."

The Pres gave his AG a very dark look. "Well, what

the hell do you suggest we do: saturation bombing of the town? Every time an agent makes a positive identification of one, ten citizens step up ready to swear the person was fifty miles away at the time. Those goddamn Texans confiscated and destroyed the film . . . including the film taken by IRS people. Our agents were damn lucky to get out of that town without first being tarred and feathered, or hanged or shot. Now that damn loudmouth senator from Texas is calling for straight across the board tax rates. At least, I think he is; I can't understand half of what he says. He butchers the English language worse than that loose cannon from North Carolina. And now *he's* calling for a flat tax rate. Jesus!''

"We've got to be forceful, Mr. President,'' the AG persisted. "I've prepared dozens of John Doe warrants, and I strongly urge we blanket the area with federal agents. We can use federal troops to go in and disarm the people prior to our agents moving in.''

One of the President's young aides took a hand-grenade-sized wad of bubble gum out of his mouth and said, "Boy, that would be really neat. I'd like to see that. Then we could show those ignorant redneck cowboys down there who is really running this country.''

The Pres favored him with a look that was guaranteed to melt titanium. "I was a cowboy,'' he reminded the aide. "You ditz!''

The aide sat down and concentrated on chewing his cud.

Across town, a large group of senior senators and representatives from both parties were meeting. They had already reached one unanimous and bipartisan decision: this president and his cabinet were history.

"We're going to have an armed revolt on our hands,'' Idaho said. "And it just might begin in my state.''

"Hale's far," Texas drawled. "It's done slap *begun* in my state."

"If we manage to ram through straight across the board tax rates, a lot of programs are going to be slashed to the bare bones," Massachusetts said, looking as though he might start weeping at any moment.

"That's what the middle class wants," Mississippi said. "And they're bearing the brunt of the taxes; have been for years."

Minnesota responded, "And the programs designed to help blacks will be hit the hardest."

"Some of those need to be cut," Tennessee said.

"And when we do, those of us from the South will be out of work," Georgia replied.

"We just have to prioritize where the money goes," Oregon said.

"We cannot continue to attempt to be all things to all people all the time," Maine said.

"Last year's crime bill was the biggest wad of horse-shit in recent memory," Kansas said.

"Do we have enough votes to impeach?" Arkansas asked.

"No," Michigan said.

"So where does that leave us?" Virginia asked.

"Waiting for the second revolution," Louisiana said softly.

Canada was watching the goings-on to the south with very nervous eyes. As were England and many other countries around the globe. Japan knew if the conservatives got their way in America, Japanese imports would be cut drastically. Made in America was gaining momentum with each year. Mexico knew the plug might be pulled on NAFTA and GATT and those agreements would go right down the toilet.

But Darry was not thinking about world opinion or

anything except getting to the ranger station ahead of Mike Tuttle and Nick Sharp. He was running full tilt with a sinking feeling that he was going to be too late. He could not shape-shift, for if he did that, he would lose his rifle. He was immortal, but not a magician.

The mercenaries reached the ranger station twenty minutes ahead of Darry and ten minutes before Sam Parish and his group arrived. Mike shot Rick Battle and Dennis Tipton and left them for dead in a bloody sprawl in the barn where they'd been forking hay down to the horses.

"Sorry about that, Denny old boy," Nick said, looking down at the body of the man he'd called friend for years.

The men had torn the clothing from Alberta and tied her hands to the bed posts. She was bent over at the waist, face down on the spread.

Mike was naked from the waist down and had masturbated himself into full erection. "Now, little sweet meat," he said, positioning himself behind her. "Let's hear you scream." He bulled his way into her brutally, and Alberta began shrieking.

Rick Battle, hard hit but a long way from being dead, returned to consciousness and heard the painful screaming. He looked at Dennis Tipton; the man had two holes in the center of his chest. Rick began crawling toward the station, his blood staining the mud as he laboriously made his way through the falling rain, inch by painful inch.

Johnny McBroon was finally released from jail where he had spent the past ten days after punching out an FBI agent who had been part of the teams who assaulted the people in the wilderness area. He would have been out a lot sooner, but he refused to apologize to the agent. To make matters worse, Johnny kept referring to the agent in the most uncomplimentary of invectives. A local Idaho judge, who learned of the ex-spook's incarceration, and who agreed with Johnny's verbal assessment of the Bureau, ordered him released. He was only about a mile from the ranger station when his left front tire blew. The vehicle started slewing around on the wet gravel road, and Johnny ended up in the ditch, stuck in the mud.

Johnny got out, looked at the situation briefly, cussed, pulled his hat lower and turned up his collar against the cold rain, and started walking. He had a Beretta 9mm model 92S shoved behind his belt.

Rick had managed to crawl into the station and get his pistol and a rifle from the rack when the vehicles carrying Sam Parish and his bunch arrived. Rick staggered to the bedroom, shoved open the door and without hesitation shot Mike Tuttle in the head. Nick Sharp jumped out a window, minus his shirt and boots and guns, and was rounding the corner of the house when he came face-to-face with Sam Parish. He jerked Sam's M-16 from the hands of the startled man and turned as Darry ran into the area. Nick leveled the rifle, and Darry shot him, the force of the slug lifting the man off his bare feet and slinging him backward against Sam, taking the CDL leader with him to the wet ground. The other members of the CDL, those who had them ready, leveled their weapons.

"Freeze!" Johnny spoke from behind the knot of men and women just as Rick and Alberta (wearing a robe) stepped out onto the porch, guns in their hands.

"Anybody makes any stupid moves," Darry warned, "I kill Sam Parish."

"Don't do nothin' stupid, people!" Sam hollered.

Darry cut his eyes to Rick. "You going to make it?"

"Oh, yes," the ranger said, his voice surprisingly strong.

Darry looked down at Sam Parish. "Sam, as a revolutionary, you are a total bust."

"I reckon," the man said. "I think I'll go back to cleanin' out septic tanks. Standin' in shit all day was a picnic compared to the last few weeks!"

31

By the time the sheriff and his people arrived at the ranger station, Darry had vanished into the rain and the mist of the wilderness area.

Rick and Alberta were helicoptered to a hospital, Sam Parish and his people were taken into custody, and the bodies of the dead were body-bagged and hauled away.

"I'll stay here until a ranger shows up," Johnny volunteered. "I've got to wait for a tow truck anyway."

Sheriff Paige looked at the man. "Aren't you the one who jacked the jaw of that fed a couple of weeks back?"

"That's me."

"Should have done it in my county. I could guarantee you no jail time."

"I'll remember that."

Johnny called the number Alberta had given him and spoke to the district chief. "It'll be a day or two before I can get someone in there," Tom told him.

"I'll stay," Johnny said. "If you trust me to look after things, that is."

"Oh, I trust you. Chuck says you're an all-right fellow. See you in a day or so."

Johnny stepped out onto the porch. "Come on in, Darry. It's all clear."

"Right here, Johnny." Darry spoke from the edge of the building.

Johnny turned. Darry stood there, Johnny's suitcase in one hand, the Winchester in the other.

"I got your things out of your car. I thought you might stay around for a time and you'd need them."

"Thanks. Rick's clothes ought to fit you. You sure look like you need a hot shower and a change of clothing."

The men took turns showering, and while Johnny was toweling off, Darry made coffee and turned on the satellite system. Another special report from Coyote News was on. Johnny came into the room just in time to watch it.

The reporter was verbally clawing away at the back of big government, and was pulling no punches. Darry had not heard about the killings in Texas and New York, and he was saddened by them, but not surprised by the viciousness of the government in dealing with citizens who, for whatever reasons, were unable to pay their taxes. The sight of the girl, just barely in her teen years, lying dead, half her head gone, touched him deeply.

"Pitiful. Just pitiful. The government is out of control," Johnny said, during a commercial break. "I've seen it coming for a long time. What surprises me is that they've let the Coyote Network alone for this long."

"You can bet the government is working frantically to find some way to shut them down . . . without further pissing off a large chunk of the American population." Then he told Johnny about Robert Roche.

Johnny smiled. "You're real good, Darry. You would have had a bright future in the Company."

"No, thanks," Darry said drily.

"What about the other mercenaries Roche hired?"

"They're all dead. Their bodies will never be found."

"You buried them?"

"No."

Johnny decided not to pursue that any further. "Roche has publicly committed himself to backing the Coyote

Network. He can't pull out now. He'd lose too much credibility with the American public. Mr. Big-shot has backed himself into a corner.''

''That's my thinking.''

''Are you aware that the judge who issued the order allowing citizens to use deadly force in defending themselves against mistaken entry by officers of the law was just struck down a few hours ago by a higher court?''

''No. But that doesn't surprise me. Big government at work.''

''Coyote News is planning to jump on that decision with both feet.''

''I expect so.''

''I hope Coyote understands they're going to piss off a certain breed of cop when they do.''

''Law enforcement can't afford to make mistakes. When a cop makes a mistake, someone is likely to get hurt or killed. What the courts need to do is untie cops' hands on some issues and shorten the leash on a few other issues.''

''What happens to you now, Darry?''

''I fade away, if the government will let me.''

''And you think they'll let you?''

Darry smiled. ''No government ever has.''

''What about Max Vernon?''

''He's still in Idaho. But north and east of here. I'm told that Max blames me for all his problems. Max and I will meet, sooner or later.''

''You don't sound too upset about it.''

''I'm not. I never worry about death, Johnny. Why should I?''

Due to the unrelenting pressure from the Coyote Network, all charges were dropped against Kevin Carmouche, Vince Clayderman, and Todd Noble. The Collier family's assets were freed, and they went through a very quick audit by the IRS and came out owing nothing. Charges against Paul Collier were dropped.

Beverly Stevens, the schoolteacher from Kansas, settled out of court with the government.

Rick Battle recovered from his wounds, and he and Alberta Follette were married. Together they run the ranger station.

Johnny McBroon got some truly remarkable close-up pictures of the wolf packs now living in the Idaho wilderness (thanks to a little help from Darry), and left to write the text of his book about the Wolves of Idaho.

George Eagle Dancer stayed on, working for Chuck the outfitter. Chuck said since he was getting on in years, he just might someday sell the place to George.

As of this writing, the government still hadn't decided what to do, if anything, with Sam Parish and his group. The film Ki shot of the agents attacking an unarmed group of men and women was just too damning. Sam and his CDL did kill some government people, but only after being savagely attacked and illegally detained. The President's advisors felt that since the mood of the American people was overwhelmingly antigovernment, the whole damn "incident" had best be quietly forgotten.

The President's plan to move against Darry Ransom was never put into operation. The Pres was too busy fighting for his political life to worry about one man.

Inspector Hank Wallace and Special Agent Carol Murphy remained with the FBI, as did Jack Speed and Kathy Owens.

Tom Sessions was not forced to retire, not after he went to the Coyote Network and told them his story. The government said it had all been a mistake. Welcome back, Tom.

The Coyote Network didn't do many stories about Panga-Panga, or yak drivers, or despots in Africa, but they sure as hell kept the United States government's feet to the fire . . . and never let up. Their evening news and their news specials continued to be the most watched in TV history, and never lacked for sponsors. The other networks just could not catch up to Coyote. Or would not.

The bodies of the dead mercenaries were never found.

Autumn's colors were just touching the land, and nature's paintbrush was busy and beautiful. Ki had a "little thing" going with Johnny McBroon and was with him, and Stormy was spending a few days with Darry at his cabin. At her stubborn-as-a-mule insistence, Darry had hauled in a generator and a TV satellite system and had hooked it up. When Stormy was visiting she now had electric lights and television, and hot water to bathe in that she didn't have to heat on a wood-burning stove.

"I'll bring you up to date and into the twenty-first century yet," she told Darry.

"I've already been through seven centuries," he told her. "I'm going to be rather hard to impress."

The couple was sitting on the front porch of the cabin, watching the sun go down, Pete and Repeat sleeping a few feet away.

"I think the government is finally seeing the light, Darry."

"Don't count on it."

"A lot of senators and representatives have approached Coyote, and outlined legislation they plan to introduce. It looks real good, Darry. It's a start."

"I'll believe it when I see it."

"But they've *promised,* Darry!"

"They're politicians, dear. It's like George says when he's feeling in a humorous mood: 'White man speak with forked tongue.' "

"But you'll agree it's a start?"

Darry said nothing for a moment. How to make her understand that he'd lived through centuries of seeing governments *start* to do lots of things the majority of their citizens wanted; but once momentum waned, the promises from the mouths of noblemen, knights, and kings and queens vanished like smoke in a breeze.

Darry took a sip of coffee and said, "All right, Stormy. It's a start. But you people at Coyote can't let up for an instant. Don't cut the government any slack—ever. You people have the government on the ropes now, and you've got to keep them there. Your cameras have to be there every time a citizen gets fucked over by the government. Hell, Stormy, why am I telling you your business?"

"I guess for many of us this is something new, Darry. In the eyes of the public, the majority of the press have always taken the liberal slant to most issues. We've never really gone in-depth on welfare cheaters, confronting them face-to-face and taping it. We've never taken a hard law-and-order stance. Not to my knowledge. We've always run hanky-twisting, sobbing-sisters stories about the poor, poor, underpriviledged lives of criminals. Looking back at them now, I have this urge to puke . . ."

Darry watched as Pete and Repeat both suddenly lifted their heads, staring out into the dark timber. Darry hand signaled them to stay on the porch. Stormy did not see the signal.

"What the public doesn't know is that there were some stories we *couldn't* broadcast. The network wouldn't let us."

"How many lawsuits does Coyote have against it now?"

"They were stacked up a mile high. Some people take exception to being asked why they lay up in public housing, on welfare, and continue to have babies they can't afford, while the working taxpayers have to foot the bill."

Somebody was prowling around in the timber. "You said were stacked up?"

"Most of them were thrown out of court for lack of merit; others never made it that far. But to tell you the truth, I still feel uncomfortable asking questions like that. It isn't the fault of the kids.''

"It isn't the responsibility of the working taxpayers to have to pay for someone else's careless fucking, either.''

She giggled. "I can just see me going on the air and saying that!''

Whoever or whatever it was in the timber was staying there. So far. "But it's the truth. And you know me well enough to know that color has nothing to do it.'' Darry could feel the tenseness in the hybrids. Whoever or whatever it was out in the darkness was not friendly. The hybrids were signaling danger.

"Take Pete and Repeat and go into the house, Stormy,'' Darry said softly. "Lock the doors and get the shotgun I taught you with. And be ready to use it. Don't question me, just do it. Right now.''

Without a word, Stormy rose from the chair and went into the cabin; only one lamp burned. The generator was not running. She blew that out after taking the shotgun out of the rack. At Darry's signal, the hybrids rose and went into the house. Darry sat on the porch and heard Stormy close and lock the front and back doors.

Darry silently rolled off the porch. An instant after touching the ground, his Other took shape. The huge gray wolf entered the timber as silently as stalking death . . . which in this case, it most certainly was.

Darry smelled the strong and unwashed odor of man and knew instantly that Max Vernon had made up his mind to end this stalking game of wait and see . . . one way or the other. But only Darry was certain of the outcome.

Darry picked up six distinct odors, each as different as DNA. That was something else that science had yet to learn, but they could, if only they would grow closer to the animal world and learn from them . . . and not break their promises to them.

"Why aren't those goddamn big-ass dogs barking?" a hoarse whisper cut the night air.

"Because Darry and the cunt took them inside the cabin, that's why. Darry is shoving the meat to that bitch right now. We set the cabin on fire and shoot them as they come out."

"Let's take the reporter alive, Max," another voice was added. "I want some pussy. Then we can kill her."

"Suits me. Just be sure those damned dogs are dead."

"What if it's true about Darry, Max? Maybe he is immortal."

"That's horse-shit, Marty. We've been over and over this."

Darry sprang at a dark shape. He hit him so hard and so viciously the man went down without uttering a sound, which would have been impossible anyway, since he now had no throat.

"Fred?" The one-word question was whispered.

Silence greeted the men.

"Check on him, Sonny," Max said.

Sonny eased his way through the darkness of brush and timber and was bending over the motionless body of the rogue agent when Darry leaped, long fangs glistening wet-white in the dimness. When his paws touched the ground, the fangs were crimson.

Marty Stewart saw the flash of gray and the spray of blood as the throat was ripped out of Sonny. He opened his mouth to scream, but he was so frightened no sound could push its way past fear-constricted muscles. Darry struck with blinding speed, and the man was dead seconds later.

The smell of blood was sharp in the clean, fresh air.

Pete Elkins began firing blindly all around him. Several of the rounds slammed into Richard Adams, killing him instantly. The great gray wolf leaped at Elkins and rode him down, ripping and tearing at the man's neck.

Out of the darkness Max Vernon saw a man's shape

rise from the ground. But when he lifted his M-16 and fired, the shape was no longer there.

"Ransom?" he yelled. "Goddamn you, Ransom."

"Behind you, Max."

Max spun around and blasted the night with automatic weapons fire. But he hit nothing except trees and rocks.

Darry heard the man cussing and the clank of an empty magazine striking the ground. Darry came through the darkness running all out. He leaped, and one boot struck Max in the face, knocking him backward, his nose broken, and loosening his grip on the M-16.

Max staggered to his feet and took a wild swing at Darry. Darry sidestepped and clamped powerful fingers on Max's throat. Max tried to knee him, but that was blocked. Max tried to club him with his fists, but all he could hit were thick arms and powerful shoulders.

Through a roaring in his head, Max heard Darry say, "You really should do your homework better before you assault innocent people, Max. But now it's too late, isn't it?"

Darry's fingers tightened, and Max felt his throat being crushed.

Darry released the man and let him fall. He stood over Max until he was sure the man was dead; then he turned and walked back to his cabin.

Three days later, at his home in Virginia, the director of the Federal Bureau of Investigation sat in his study and looked at the envelope on his desk.

Mail from home, he thought.

It was common knowledge that the DIR/FBI was adopted. It was common knowledge that he'd been found by a couple on their front porch one morning. Back in Idaho.

It was also common knowledge that when the DIR/FBI

became very angry, his eyes could turn a strange shade of yellow/brown, almost like an animal.

He opened the envelope and read:

Dear Cousin:

   You had six rogue agents left out here. They ain't ever gonna bother no one else again. Hope you and yours is well and happy. George Eagle Dancer is working out fine. Me and him get along. Buckskin sends his best.

                                    Chuck

ERNEST HAYCOX
IS THE KING OF THE WEST!

Over twenty-five million copies of Ernest Haycox's rip-roaring western adventures have been sold worldwide! For the very finest in straight-shooting western excitement, look for the Pinnacle brand!

RIDERS WEST   (17-123-1, $2.95)
by Ernest Haycox
Neel St. Cloud's army of professional gunslicks were fixing to turn Dan Bellew's peaceful town into an outlaw strip. With one blazing gun against a hundred, Bellew found himself fighting for his valley's life — and for his own!

MAN IN THE SADDLE   (17-124-X, $2.95)
by Ernest Haycox
The combine drove Owen Merritt from his land, branding him a coward and a killer while forcing him into hiding. But they had made one drastic, fatal mistake: they had forgotten to kill him!

SADDLE AND RIDE   (17-085-5, $2.95)
by Ernest Haycox
Clay Morgan had hated cattleman Ben Herendeen since boyhood. Now, with all of Morgan's friends either riding with Big Ben and his murderous vigilantes or running from them, Clay was fixing to put an end to the lifelong blood feud — one way or the other!

"MOVES STEADILY, RELENTLESSLY FORWARD
WITH GRIM POWER."
— THE NEW YORK TIMES

Available wherever paperbacks are sold, or order direct from the Publisher. Send cover price plus 50¢ per copy for mailing and handling to Penguin USA, P.O. Box 999, c/o Dept. 17109, Bergenfield, NJ 07621. Residents of New York and Tennessee must include sales tax. DO NOT SEND CASH.

FOR THE BEST OF THE WEST, SADDLE UP WITH
PINNACLE AND JACK CUMMINGS . . .

DEAD MAN'S MEDAL	(664-0, $3.50/$4.50)
THE DESERTER TROOP	(715-9, $3.50/$4.50)
ESCAPE FROM YUMA	(697-7, $3.50/$4.50)
ONCE A LEGEND	(650-0, $3.50/$4.50)
REBELS WEST	(525-3, $3.50/$4.50)
THE ROUGH RIDER	(481-8, $3.50/$4.50)
THE SURROGATE GUN	(607-1, $3.50/$4.50)
TIGER BUTTE	(583-0, $3.50/$4.50)

INFORMATIVE —
COMPELLING —
SCINTILLATING —
NON-FICTION FROM PINNACLE TELLS THE TRUTH!

BORN TOO SOON   (751, $4.50)
by Elizabeth Mehren
This is the poignant story of Elizabeth's daughter Emily's premature birth. As the parents of one of the 275,000 babies born prematurely each year in this country, she and her husband were plunged into the world of the Neonatal Intensive Care unit. With stunning candor, Elizabeth Mehren relates her gripping story of unshakable faith and hope — and of courage that comes in tiny little packages.

THE PROSTATE PROBLEM   (745, $4.50)
by Chet Cunningham
An essential, easy-to-use guide to the treatment and prevention of the illness that's in the headlines. This book explains in clear, practical terms all the facts. Complete with a glossary of medical terms, and a comprehensive list of health organizations and support groups, this illustrated handbook will help men combat prostate disorder and lead longer, healthier lives.

THE ACADEMY AWARDS HANDBOOK   (887, $4.50)
An interesting and easy-to-use guide for movie fans everywhere, the book features a year-to-year listing of all the Oscar nominations in every category, all the winners, an expert analysis of who wins and why, a complete index to get information quickly, and even a 99% foolproof method to pick this year's winners!

WHAT WAS HOT   (894, $4.50)
by Julian Biddle
Journey through 40 years of the trends and fads, famous and infamous figures, and momentous milestones in American history. From hoola hoops to rap music, greasers to yuppies, Elvis to Madonna — it's all here, trivia for all ages. An entertaining and evocative overview of the milestones in America from the 1950's to the 1990's!
